Catherine Cookson was born in East Jarrow and the place of her birth provides the background she so vividly creates in many of her novels. Although acclaimed as a regional writer – her novel THE ROUND TOWER won the Winifred Holtby Award for the best regional novel of 1968 – her readership spread throughout the world. Her work has been translated into twelve languages and Corgi alone has 31,000,000 copies of her novels in print, including those written under the name of Catherine Marchant.

Mrs Cookson was born the illegitimate daughter of a poverty-stricken woman, Kate, whom she believed to be her older sister. Catherine began work in service but eventually moved south to Hastings where she met and married a local grammar school master. At the age of forty she began writing with great success about the lives of the working class people of the North-East with whom she had grown up, including her intriguing autobiography, OUR KATE. Her many bestselling novels have established her as one of the most popular of contemporary women novelists.

Mrs Cookson now lives in Northumberland.

Also by Catherine Cookson

and published by Corgi Books

HAROLD
Catherine Cookson

CORGI BOOKS

HAROLD

A CORGI BOOK   0 552 12789 2

Originally published in Great Britain by William Heinemann Ltd

PRINTING HISTORY

William Heinemann edition published 1985
Corgi edition published 1986

This book is set in 10/11 point Century

Corgi Books are published by Transworld Publishers Ltd.,
61–63 Uxbridge Road, Ealing, London W5 5SA,
in Australia by Transworld Publishers (Aust.) Pty. Ltd.,
26 Harley Crescent, Condell Park, NSW 2200, and in New
Zealand by Transworld Publishers (N.Z.) Ltd, Cnr. Moselle
and Waipareira Avenues, Henderson, Auckland.

Made and printed in Great Britain by
Hunt Barnard Printing Ltd., Aylesbury, Bucks.

CONTENTS

To
BEN
In whom I saw
HAROLD

PART ONE

The Mohican

1

'Why do you want to adopt him?'

I stared at James Stoddart, the father of Harold, and I wanted to say, 'Because I love him,' but found that I couldn't use the word, not in front of this horde of the boy's uncles and aunts, and his grandmother and grandfather, not forgetting the outsider who was present. And to my dismay I heard myself sniff before I replied, 'Because I am fond of him.'

'You wouldn't like to adopt me, Mrs Leviston, now would you?' The big man grinned at me, and as the titter went round the room his mother, my dear Janet, yelled, 'You, Max Flood! I warned you now, didn't I?'

'Oh, Mum. Mrs Nardy ... I mean Mrs Leviston understands it was only a joke. Don't you, Mrs Leviston?'

'Yes.' I smiled at him. 'It was only a joke.' Then endeavouring to bring a little lightness into the proceedings, I added, 'I might have considered the proposition if you had been smaller,' only to put my foot in it through my nervousness by adding, 'But no doubt I'll be adopting some part of you because, you being his favourite uncle, Harold has picked up many of your sayings,' which brought forth from the others a chorus of protests.

'You're not his favourite uncle.'

'Who said you're his favourite uncle? I've seen to him time and time again.'

'Who took him to the Zoo last week?'

11

'*Shut up! Shut up!* the lot of you.'

All eyes now turned towards Janet, and I was amazed yet again at how this slender woman in her sixties was able to cope with this crowd of big lumbersome men and their attendant girl friends . . . so called.

Janet had become very dear to me over the past three years we had been together. I think she had resented me a little at first when I became the wife of her dear Mr Nardy. This, of course, was natural for had she not attended him since he was a baby, and later, after his mother died, become his housekeeper, although only part-time, for she still had her own growing horde to attend to. Max was the eldest, followed by Billy and Joe; the three of them, each over thirty and divorced. Then came Maggie, Harold's mother who three years ago had left her husband Jimmy Stoddart for another man, only to leave this man for yet another and go off with him to Australia. She was the only one of the family not here today. Greg, and Rodney, and Hilda had followed at yearly intervals. May, the youngest, was smart: she was well dressed. She had acquired a flat of her own, I understood, and was now a receptionist in a small hotel. To use her mother's words, she had made it, the only one of the lot of them to have done so.

But of all the family, it was Hilda and her boy friend who had held my attention mostly since I had come into the house. Janet had described them to me from time to time. Her description, however, was but a pale shadow of the reality: Hilda's hair, which hung below her shoulders, was of three distinct colours, green, blue, and yellow; she had a long thin face, her eyes seemingly enlarged with coal-black make-up, and her mouth with scarlet lipstick; her fingers were almost hidden under rings all studded with large glass stones. She was wearing a tight, very low-necked purple

12

sweater, but the cleavage of her breasts was covered by strings of beads. Her skirt was of a shiny material that reached just to her knees. She wore ankle warmers, apparently hand-knitted and of indescribable colours, and on her feet she had heavy brogues. That was Hilda, and she was well out of her teens.

Her boy friend was more easy to describe, he was simply the last of the Mohicans. No one could mistake him for anything else: not only did the ridge of his hair running across the crown of his head speak his name loud and clear, but also his whole attire was pure Mohican Indian. I had been really startled by his appearance and amazed at the lack of self-consciousness that enabled him to walk abroad looking as he did. But now I was in for another surprise.

All Janet's family talked with a cockney twang, and, with the exception of May, were no respecters of aspirates. But when the Mohican opened his mouth his voice was clear, his tone crisp and his words very much to the point: he was saying to Jimmy Stoddart, 'Why all this caffuffle about why Mrs Leviston wants to adopt Harold. It's no longer the case of *why* she would want to adopt him, it's more likely, *why* has she adopted him? The deed's done, it's all signed and sealed.' He turned towards me now and the two painted marks on his cheeks spread as he smiled and added, 'It isn't everyone that's taken for love, is it, Mrs Leviston?'

The voice was so incongruous with his get-up that I could find nothing to say at the moment; but it would have been cut off anyway for Jimmy Stoddart had risen to his feet and, with arm outstretched and finger pointing, he was crying, 'Who's askin' you to butt in, you weirdy git! This is a family affair, and what my son does is no . . .'

'That's another point, isn't it, Mr Stoddart: he's no longer your son; you signed him away this morning.'

13

The Mohican's voice was quiet and cool.

The very next moment I yelled or yelped as a small vase flew past my face, headed straight for the Mohican, and splintered against the wall just behind his head. In that instant I noticed the expression on the Mohican's face: it wasn't fear, it looked like rage as if he could have been a real Indian, and on the attack.

But now there was pandemonium in the room. Janet was shouting, 'You get out of here, Jimmy Stoddart. And the less I see of you the better.'

The men were all on their feet, except Mr Flood, who had been seated near the fire and was still seated there and still smoking, having lit one cigarette from the other, and seemingly oblivious of the commotion.

'I'll go when I'm ready.' Jimmy Stoddart was standing near the sitting-room door. He was a tall man, well built and what you might call good-looking in a flashy kind of way. His hair was dark and thick and had certainly been under the hairdresser's hands, as the waves above his ears testified. And ignoring Max, who was lumbering up to him and saying threateningly, 'I'd get goin' when the goin's good, mate,' he stepped to one side and, looking directly across the room at me, he shouted, 'I want to know when I can see 'im.'

'You never bothered seein' 'im much before.' It was the bedecked Hilda now speaking for the first time since I'd come into the room and her voice, unlike her boy friend's, had certainly no refinement in it.

I answered the man, saying, 'You know the agreement, you may see him every other Saturday and have him for a week-end once a month.'

'I know that. But which week-end? This week-end? Next week-end?'

'Let it be the last week-end in the month.'

He made no comment on this but stood still for a moment, and as he looked at me I was reminded of my first husband, Howard Stickle, who was now serving a

14

twelve years sentence for having tried to kill me by burning me to death. In the attempt he was successful only in burning my husband and so bringing him to a premature death, burning the fingers off my stepfather, and horribly disfiguring the daughter of his second wife. It came to me that there was more than one Stickle in the world.

'To hell with you! What are you anyway, the lot of you? Scum.'

There was a surge towards the figure going out, but Janet blocked the way, her voice rising above the mêlée as she cried, '*Stop it! Leave him alone.* Enough! My God! What has this house come to?' Then pushing Rodney and Billy aside, she made her way towards me and her face was crumpled in distress as she said, 'Ma'am, what can I say? The first time in my house and you meet a lot of hooligans.'

'Janet. Janet, please, don't distress yourself. They're not ... I ... I mean it's natural. Look! Give me a cup of tea, will you?'

Janet sniffed, then laughed and said, 'Oh, Mrs Leviston, ma'am, a cup of tea? Yes, of course, of course. I'll put the kettle on.'

As she hurried from the room her family awkwardly took their seats again, and as was usual on these occasions a silence enveloped us all.

It was the Mohican who broke it and surprised me yet again by turning to me and saying, 'Where do you intend to send him to school – later on I mean?'

All eyes were on me as I answered. 'I ... I don't rightly know. He should be all right where he is for a good while yet.'

'Don't ever send him to a boarding school.' His voice was flat sounding, his face looked stiff, and I replied, 'No, no; I wouldn't dream of doing that.'

'Good.'

What a strange individual. I recalled Janet telling

me a little of what she knew about him. Apparently he had been to a boarding school, spending most of his holidays there, too, with his housemaster, because his parents were travelling. When he was fifteen they were divorced. He remained at school until he was seventeen when, although he could have gone on further, he opted out. It was even rumoured he had been in the police force and was thrown out.

What a shame, I thought, because I could detect something warm and kindly about him. But yet, what was I thinking? Warm and kindly! He had been brought up two months ago for having caused actual bodily harm.

When he turned from me I looked down the room towards Max, who had been the one with most to say, and asked, 'By the way, where is the young man in question?'

'Oh, along at the Flannagans, saying goodbye to the dog I think. The dog's missed 'im, yer know.' And Max grinned at me, causing his features to take on an impish look as he ended, 'Yer see, the kid's boots ain't as big as the others.'

'Don't exaggerate, Max, nobody kicks the dog.'

'What do yer know of it, May, yer never 'ere.'

'I was brought up with their other dog, remember, and stopped you from kicking him.'

'I never kicked 'im.' Max now turned his still grinning face towards me, adding, 'I would never kick a dog.'

Looking straight at him, I replied soberly, 'I've only your word for it.' And at this there was a titter round the room and as he was saying, 'Oh, Mrs Leviston,' Janet came in with a tray on which was a teapot, a jug of milk, and four cups.

I wondered at the four cups until, glancing round the room, she said, 'If you lot want tea you know where the water an' the tea caddy is,' and proceeded to pour

16

out the tea.

Having handed me mine, she passed one on to May and one to Hilda; then, taking one herself, she sat down and, looking at her son Billy, who was sitting to the left of her, she jerked her head as she said, 'Go on, fetch him in. But I don't think you'll have to go far, he's waitin' outside the back door. I told him to stay there until he was sent for.'

Again a silence fell on the room, until there appeared in the doorway, standing by the side of his uncle, the reason for my sitting in the midst of Janet's family. My adoptive son was not yet seven years old. He wasn't tall for his age, more broad than tall, of his Uncle Max's build. He had fair hair, a round face in which were two deep brown bright eyes. His mouth was well shaped and always ready to smile.

As he wound his way through the family towards me, one and another of his uncles giving him either a dig or a wink, he said nothing until he was standing in front of me and, because he always came straight to the point, he asked, 'Are we goin' now?'

''E can't get away quick enough. What d'yer think of that? Are we goin' now?'

'That's the last we'll see of 'im; too big for his boots already.'

The laughing comments came from different quarters of the room, but the child took no notice, he just looked into my face, then made a statement, 'Mr Tommy'll be waitin'.'

'Oh, d'yer hear that, Mr Tommy'll be waitin'. 'E's got a smashin' car, not like our bangers, lads.' His Uncle Joe was nodding from one to the other in assumed indignation, and when they all took it up, my new son turned on them and bawled, 'Shut yer gobs, you lot!'

'*Harold!*' My tone was sharp; and Janet's accompanied mine but with more to say: 'We'll have none of that,' she said. 'I'm still your gran an' I've still got a

17

hand an' you've still got ears, an' they'll meet up in a minute.'

'Oh, Gag.' He turned to her. 'Well, you should stop 'em.'

'Yes' – Janet nodded at him now – 'yes, I should stop 'em, I should have stopped 'em years ago.'

I rose to my feet; the Mohican rose too, but except for Janet the others remained seated. That the oddest looking male individual should have such manners and also be considered by the rest of this family as a weirdy was odd in itself.

'Goodbye.' I looked from one to the other, and each of them nodded, but only Max and Joe answered; Mr Flood didn't even nod.

In the little hallway I straightened Harold's cap, tucked his scarf inside his coat, told him to put his gloves on, then turned to Janet, saying quietly, 'Thank you, Janet. I'll ... I'll see you on Monday then.'

For a moment she seemed overcome with emotion. She looked down on her grandson, then muttered, 'You behave yourself mind. I'll be 'earin' about it, everything you do, mind. Do you hear me?'

'Yes, Gag.' Impulsively now he put his arms up and she bent towards him, and he kissed her on the cheek. This was followed by a push that almost overbalanced him, but he laughed and gripped my hand and took me towards the front door that was being held open by the Mohican. Hilda was by his side now, and she, to my surprise, caught my arm and, after glancing at the Mohican, she said softly, 'Yer can see why I like 'im, can't yer, Mrs Leviston? 'Cos 'e's a gentleman. 'E's the only gentleman I've ever met. As the sayin' is, never judge a bull by the ring through its nose . . .'

It was her turn to be nearly knocked on her back, and the cry, 'Hilda!' certainly did sound as if it had come from the throat of an Indian Chief.

The Mohican was definitely embarrassed, but I

18

smiled at him and said, 'I don't know your name.'

'John Drake.'

'Goodbye, John,' I said now. 'It's been nice meeting you.'

I gave one last look at Janet, then walked away down the street, my son by my side. And that's how I thought of this child, my son, not adopted, he was mine. And he wanted to be mine. That was the most important thing, he wanted to be mine.

Before we reached the end of the short street I knew that the family were no longer seated in the sitting-room but that most of them were on the front pavement. And they weren't alone, because other doors were open and other people were standing on their steps. And as if Harold knew this was happening, he swung round and waved, and I, looking over my shoulder, saw a number of hands lifted in reply.

We were now in another street, in another life, both of us. I looked down at him and he looked up at me, and we smiled at each other but did not speak; my hand, though, tightened on his and he walked closer to me ...

Tommy was waiting for us in the car park. He had wanted to bring us to the house but I'd said no. The fact of him sitting outside in the flash Jaguar would certainly not have enamoured either him or me to the Flood family. He was now coming towards us. He was a tall man, six foot two, and his height always dwarfed me still further. As Gran Carter said, we looked like Mutt and Jeff, who, apparently, were two strip-cartoon figures from her childhood. He was thin and attractive, in fact quite good looking, and he was in love with me ... God alone knew why, for I wasn't even what you would call attractively plain, and I had a withered left arm. In my favour, it could be said I had a sense of humour, and I was supposed to be a good conversationalist, and I was given credit for some kind of a mind because I wrote books, weird books in the opinion of some folk, about a woman, me, talking to an imaginary horse, which horse took on a wife. That being so, I suppose some people would have agreed with the description my first husband screamed at me in the court-room less than two years ago just before he had been sentenced: 'Yes, I did it, and I'd do it again. Just give me the chance and I'll get you yet. By God! I will. I'll ... get ... you yet ... you crippled undersized, barmy sod you!'

Tommy, towering over Harold, smiled down at him as he said, 'Well now, young feller-me-lad, how does it feel to have a mother?'

'Just the same.'

'Oh, it can't be the same,' persisted Tommy; 'she's not Mrs Nardy any more, she's your mother.'

'She's still Mrs Nardy.' Harold looked up at me and ended, 'Aren't you?'

'Yes. Yes, Harold, I'm still Mrs Nardy.'

Harold now ran towards the car and, opening the door, climbed onto the back seat.

When Tommy had settled me by his side and we were driving out of the car park, he said, 'Well, Mrs Nardy,' and I was aware of the stressed title, 'What about celebrating? A slap-up tea somewhere?'

Immediately Harold's head was poked between us. 'With cream buns?'

'With cream buns, as many as you can eat.'

'Certainly not!' I said. 'All right, we'll go to tea but only one cream bun.' And I lifted my hand and tweaked Harold's nose; and he grinned at me, saying, 'In that swanky place where the men are all dolled up as if they had pokers up their ar ...?' The head was slightly withdrawn and the voice was lower as it ended, 'I mean, stiff shirts like.'

Tommy was making a strange noise in his throat. I kept my eyes straight ahead and my voice level as I replied, 'Yes, we'll go to that restaurant again.'

When Tommy remarked in an aside, 'One for effort,' I replied primly, 'Yes, yes indeed.'

It was two hours later, as we were entering the hall of my home and making our way towards the lift carrying on a conversation that had begun in the car, that we met Captain and Mrs Beckingtree-Holland. They were stepping out of the lift as Tommy said, 'You must be able to get a baby-sitter somewhere ... Oh.' He raised his hat and stood aside as the delicate-looking lady paused and divided a thin smile between us. She was wearing a well-worn fur coat, and above her china-doll face her white hair curled upwards about her ears onto a small matching fur hat. The man accompanying her had a military bearing. He wore a three-quarter length moleskin-coloured coat. He had a knotted silk scarf on his neck and a cap on his head which he raised as he passed us, at the same time extending towards me a slight bow.

They, I guessed, were the temporary occupants of the flat below ours.

The whole of this house had once belonged to my second husband, Leonard Leviston, but being too big for him he had turned it into three very spacious flats. There was a basement flat too in which the caretaker lived. He it was who kindly took my dear poodle Sandy for walks whenever possible.

We hadn't seen much of Mr and Mrs Stretton, the owners of the first floor flat as both he and she seemed to be connected with work at some ministry, and we very rarely met except in the hallway. But a fortnight ago Mr Stretton had told me he had been transferred to Germany for a year and that a distant relative of his wife was coming to look after the place until they came back. So here were Captain and Mrs Beckingtree-Holland. I didn't know their name at this time, I wasn't to know it until the next morning.

As we stepped out of the lift into our hallway, Harold confronted us both, saying flatly, 'I don't want a baby-sitter; I can look after myself.'

I glanced impatiently at Tommy. He'd no right to bring up the matter in front of the boy, but he had for some time been wanting to see *Noises Off* at the Savoy Theatre, and naturally he wanted me to go with him. He had suggested leaving the boy with Janet, but this would have meant an erosion of my efforts to improve my charge, for once Harold was back in the company of his uncles for any length of time he reverted rapidly to their ways. The boy had been living with me now for some months, in fact, ever since Nardy died, shortly before last Christmas.

I pushed Harold before me into the inner hall, saying, 'Get your things off and put your slippers on,' and turning towards where he had flung his coat on a chair, I cried, 'Hang it up! I've told you.'

Good gracious! I was acting like a mother already. And an impatient one too. And so, smiling at him, I added, 'And go and see Sandy in the kitchen; he's barking his head off. That's a good boy.' And I turned towards the drawing-room, Tommy following.

It was rarely I entered this room without feeling a sense of wonderment and pleasure. I switched on the electric fire and then sat down on the couch opposite and looked to where Tommy was now standing near the mantelpiece gazing at the artificial logs that were beginning to glow, and I said to him, 'Don't be annoyed, Tommy; you see how I'm fixed.'

Slowly he came towards me and, sitting down beside me, he took my hand and said, 'I could never be annoyed with you, Maisie, never, no matter what you said.'

'Don't be silly.' I pushed his hand away. 'I can look back and remember times when you bawled at me.'

'Oh, that was in another era, another life, when I

22

never imagined that one day I'd sit here holding your hand.' He again caught hold of my hand. 'And you know, Maisie, if you never give me any more than this I'll be satisfied.'

Of a sudden he jerked his whole body away from me, saying, 'Why am I such a damn liar? I still go on pretending. The fact is I'm not satisfied with what you give me, I want more of you – you know I do – I want the lot. What I don't want is to put my hat and coat on and say, "Good-night, Maisie".' He lowered his head, then asked quietly, 'Are you still thinking of Nardy?'

I too was looking down as I answered truthfully, 'Yes; yes, I still think of him every day. And I still miss him.'

'How long do you think you'll continue to feel like this? Oh' – he made an impatient movement by flinging out his hand – 'I don't mean that you should forget him, you know that, but life must be lived, and Nardy, above all people, knew that. He said it in his letter to me, didn't he? He knew what I was feeling. He knew why I went away last year like a sick animal searching for some dark place to die in. He sensed my hate of him, the hate that had turned from love because of you. But he didn't hold it against me, he was my friend. My God! yes, he was a friend, always had been, and I had to go and play the dirty on him by wanting to be rid of him so I could have you.' He turned and glanced at me, and there was bitterness in his voice when he added, 'Things like that shouldn't happen. I blamed you for its happening, but you were as helpless as I was. It's your nature to be kind and comforting. I think that's what I fell in love with, your nature: you were so different from anyone I'd ever come across; after years with my mother you appeared like an oasis in the desert.'

It was seldom now he mentioned his mother, a cruel, selfish, powerful, scheming woman who had kept him tied to her apron strings through supposed poverty for

23

years. He'd had to work to support her in the middle-class way she'd been accustomed to, only to find, with her death, that he had become a rich man, for she had been sitting on a fortune for years, money left to her by an aunt. Twice she had stopped him from marrying; and long before her death there had been murder in his heart towards her. After she died he became consumed with hate, then embroiled in my affairs even to the extent of his being almost burned alive in that flaming house.

I liked Tommy ... very much, but did I love him?

I look back on my life through sixteen loveless years with my mother, then twelve years of marriage to a sadist, the culmination of which led to a police cell; then divorce, followed by marriage to my editor Leonard Leviston and my meeting with his friend and publishing colleague, Tommy Balfour. Tommy had thrown up his job and gone off on a trip to Canada before Nardy, as my second husband was always known, had died; but since his return to England he had been invited to rejoin his old firm and was now a director and in effect my publisher.

Again I asked myself if I loved him.

I was saved from giving myself an answer by the opening of the door and Harold rushing in accompanied by Sandy, my beautiful big white poodle, who jumped up into my arms and licked my face. As I pushed him away, exclaiming, 'Oh Sandy! Give over,' Harold said, 'I've put the kettle on and I've washed me hands, they were sticky.' He turned them over for my inspection, then added, 'You'll have to wash me gloves, 'cos they'll be sticky an' all inside.'

'I'll see to them.'

'You goin' home now?'

The straight gaze was directed towards Tommy, and Tommy, his eyes widening, his tone full of mock indignation, said, 'Does that mean you want to be rid of me?'

'We ... ll' – the word was drawn out; Harold was nothing if not honest – 'you've been with us a long time, all 'safternoon.'

'I took you to tea, didn't I?'

'Yes.'

'Well, don't you think I should be shown some courtesy by being allowed to stay a little with my friend?'

He glanced towards me.

I fully expected my boy to speak the truth again, and he did, but in a rather diplomatic fashion: 'Well, if she wants you to,' he said, and looked directly at me.

I made no reply to this; but Tommy said, 'You make quite a good cup of tea. If you'll give me a cup, then I'll think about going.'

'Will yer?'

'Yes. Yes, I will.'

At this Harold ran from the room, and Tommy, glancing at me, said, 'You know something? I don't think he's cottoned on to me.'

'Oh yes he has, he likes you. He talks about you when you aren't here.'

'If it's in a similar vein to that of the last exchange it'll be no compliment, and if I know anything about that young gentleman, he'll make that tea, pour it straight out, and it'll be here within seconds, and just one cup, you'll see.'

'He's just a child. He's had a rough upbringing. He's learning.'

'He's a very old child.' Tommy's face was solemn now, his voice flat.

And I agreed with him in my mind: yes, Harold was an old child. Since his mother left him when he was three years old, he'd passed through the testing care of his father's girlfriends to the stern and ear-slapping guidance of my dear Janet and the colourful vocabulary of his five uncles and his Grandfather Flood, not to mention his Grandfather Stoddart with whom he had lived for a time. And so of course he was an old child. But he was a loving child and a child that needed loving, and he was my child. Yes, from now on he was really my child, and he must be my first consideration. There was no question mark in my mind about loving him.

2

It was on the Sunday morning, and we were both ready to go to church. Yes, we were going to church. I felt duty bound to see that from now on he attended church.

A month ago I'd been lucky enough to get him into a church school which was quite near. It was a small primary school. I had always thought it was a Roman Catholic school, and so no thought of sending him there had entered my head, for one stipulation of the adoption made by his father was that he would remain Church of England; not that the father followed any denomination, he had merely wanted to stress his authority and this seemed to be one of the easier ways of doing so.

But having discovered the school was C.O.E. I approached the headmaster. I told him the circumstances through which I'd come into the possession of a son and he was so understanding that I took a liking to the man straightaway. Of course, there was the unspoken agreement that Harold would become a practising Christian. So here we were ready to attend not only the main church service but also the short children's one that would follow.

It had been evident from the beginning that Harold did not take to either the main service or the children's service. He had summed up his first visit with one word, 'Tripe.' The second visit had elicited a longer comment, ''Cos I don't know what he's talkin' about.'

The third visit had resulted in a question. 'If God's everywhere why doesn't somebody see him sometime?' ... Good question. And also, if he was up in heaven why didn't we see his feet when he was walking about in the sky? Answer that one.

We were about to walk across the hall when the lift opened and out stepped Mrs Beckingtree-Holland.

'Good-morning,' she said.

'Good-morning.'

'Oh, I've come at a wrong time; I see you are about to leave.'

'No, no; I have a moment or two. Can I help you in any way?'

'Oh' – the doll-like head moved from side to side – 'it was just the remark I overhead you make, or your friend make, when we got out of the lift yesterday.'

I narrowed my eyes at her and waited.

'About a baby-sitter.' She now looked at Harold, and as he stared back at her, I gripped his hand, warning him not to speak. If he had it would have been, 'I don't want a baby-sitter, 'cos I ain't no baby.'

'Oh?'

'Would it be possible to speak to you in private?'

I was flustered for a moment, then said, 'Yes, yes. Now you stay there, Harold; I won't be a moment. Come in, Mrs ... er?'

'Beckingtree-Holland.'

'Mrs Holland.'

In the inner hall she said, 'This is a very delicate matter. You see, I ... I like to occupy my time and ... er, I ... well, where it is necessary I give lessons in deportment, and of course oblige people like your-selves by sitting with their children should they wish to go out in the evening.'

'Yes, yes, of course. I understand.'

And I did understand. This delicate, refined lady-like person wanted payment for her obliging. Well, wasn't it natural that she should? Yet, a person of her appearance and definite position ... What position? She gave it to me the next moment by saying, 'The Captain, my husband, had to leave the service because of his health. He has a small pension, added to which we had naturally our savings. But as you yourself know things have changed and what at one time afforded us a most pleasant way of living scarcely affords us existence now. It is rather humiliating, but nevertheless—' She shrugged her thin shoulders. 'Well, that is the situation.'

I wetted my lips, searched quickly for the right words, then said, 'I'd be pleased to avail myself of your services from time to time, Mrs Beckingtree-Holland.'

I sounded as correct as she.

'That is nice of you. Then I won't keep you any longer. Are you going out for a walk?'

'We are going to church.'

'Oh, to church. How civilized.'

We returned to the hall to find the lift had gone, and so had Harold. I glanced at her and she at me. The red light showed it had reached the ground floor. I pressed the button and as the lift ascended my companion said, 'I suppose he is what is known as a handful.'

'He is a boy.' My voice was stiff now.

'Yes, yes, of course. Well, I'm sure we'll enjoy looking after him. My husband will teach him to play chess. He is a very good chess player.'

'That would be nice.' The gates opened and there was Harold. I did not say, 'You should not have done that, Harold;' I just stepped in, Mrs Beckingtree-Holland followed and we descended to the next floor where Mrs Beckingtree-Holland got out, smiled, inclined her head towards me and disappeared as the lift went down to the ground floor.

'You shouldn't have done that, Harold.'

'I don't like standin' about.'

29

'You'll have to learn to stand about.'

'Why?'

'Don't start that this morning. And hold your head up and walk straight.' He did as he was bid, and we made our way to church.

The service was, as usual, dull. The parson was a nice man but nice men can be boring when let loose in a pulpit. The children's service proved to be much better and very enlightening to me, because for the first time I heard my boy sing.

'Good King Wenceslas looked out on the Feast of Stephen, Where the snow lay round about deep, and crisp, and even.'

There he was in the front row singing his head off and the sound that came from his throat was unbelievable.

'Away In a Manger' followed; then, 'Once In David's Royal City'; and Harold Leviston, as he was now, sang all the carols word perfect.

The service over, the headmaster, who was also the Sunday School teacher, came up to me and said, 'He's got a fine voice.'

'I didn't know he could sing.'

'You didn't? Well, well. I told the choirmaster about him and he would like him in the choir.'

I, too, now said, 'Well, well.'

As we walked back home Harold was unusually quiet. This often happened when he was waiting for me to put him on the spot about some misdemeanour. But this wasn't a misdemeanour.

'Why didn't you tell me you could sing?'

'You never arst.'

'Asked.'

'A . . . sked. Well, you never did.'

'But why should I have to ask you? You haven't to be given permission to sing.'

It was some seconds before he answered, ''Cos they

30

said me voice was funny, like a girl's. Me Uncle Max used to do me, make game like, an' it sounded funny, so I stopped.'

'Don't say "like" in the middle of a sentence. I've told you, like is a word that has its own meaning.'

'Like what?'

'Harold.'

He was, to use his own words, having me on. He had done so before. Oh! those uncles, especially Max, the jolly one, the one who could supposedly, by the boy's past accounts, take off all the television characters.

I said, 'It was very wrong of your Uncle Max; you've got a nice voice and you must go on singing. And you must practise; you heard what the headmaster said, you can get into the church choir.'

'*I don't want that.*' The statement was very emphatic.

'Why not?'

'They're cissies; they wear long frocks an' they sing like this:' he pulled his mouth into an elongated 'O'. Then laughing, he said, 'I did sing once in the kitchen, but Sandy started to howl an' I had to roll on the floor with him to stop him.'

Laughing at the memory, he leant his head towards me and I pressed him to my side. Then he darted off, taking leaps along the pavement and punching the air as he went. It was an expression of joy. I laughed out aloud and the sound that I made was also an expression of joy.

3

Christmas had come and gone. It had been a traumatic time; Harrods had been bombed. Only an hour before the explosion I had been shopping in the store, accompanied by Harold. I was visibly shaken when I heard the news, policemen and a policewoman dead, others terribly wounded. Good will to men.

For the remainder of the week London was on its toes but defiant: as it was said, if the blitz didn't get them down there was little chance of the IRA accomplishing it. Yet, there was no doubt about it, there was an underlying fear that no place was safe. But such is the tenacity of Londoners, the first day of the sales there they were, a little late because most of them couldn't come into the city by car, but they came by bus and train from all parts.

During the holidays Tommy and I had taken Harold to a pantomime. And twice within the last twelve days, our neighbours had baby sat for us and Tommy had taken me to see two shows. Unlike Nardy's his taste didn't run to opera.

I couldn't quite get over the fact that the baby-sitters were definitely, as Gran would have put it, of the class, but the lady, I had found, had no qualms about discussing terms: £2.50 an hour with light refreshments being left. She had suggested the necessity for the latter in a very polite way, but it was nevertheless definite.

The first evening we were out six hours. When I

handed her the two ten-pound notes, she did not say, 'You'll want some change,' but smiled sweetly, murmuring 'Thank you so much;' and the Captain had made noises in his throat, causing me to wonder for a moment if he too wanted payment. I later recalled exactly what he had said to me about Harold that first evening. 'Interesting little chap, isn't he? Certainly of the rough and tumble, cockney to the marrow and with all their wiles. I don't envy your job of chipping off the rough edges.'

I didn't care very much for the Captain, nor did I care much for his wife, yet at the same time I felt sorry for them both, that people of their standing could find themselves in such a plight. I also remembered his remarks as he was leaving after the second baby-sitting session. 'You have very good taste, Mrs Leviston.' I didn't bother to tell him that nothing in the flat was of my choosing except one or two pieces of furniture that I'd brought from my old home.

Tommy found the couple very amusing. They were, he said, of the type that sometimes visited the publishing house practically demanding that their memoirs should be published. They would often put themselves over as the only people who had travelled through the jungles of Africa, or across Russia, or lived in India during the time of the White Raj.

The couple must also have amused Harold, for after that first evening of being 'baby-sat' he, following in his Uncle Max's footsteps, 'did' the Captain and even his genteel wife. And I had great difficulty in chastizing him, for when attempting her voice he minced towards Sandy and, bending over him and patting his head, he said in a voice that was quite a good imitation of the lady's, 'And now, little boy, it's to beddie-beds,' and then prancing about and in a voice very much like that of his Uncle Max's ordinary tone, he had ended, 'Up the apples and pears!'

'That's enough of that!' I said, but I was crying with laughing, and when he flung himself against me I hugged him.

It was Friday. I didn't like Fridays: all unpleasant things seemed to happen to me on a Friday. But Friday apart I'd had an unpleasant week at least at nights, for on three occasions I had woken up with dreadful pains in my stomach and a queer ill feeling; yet in the morning the pain had gone, as had the feeling.

But this particular Friday was the last in the month and tomorrow Harold's father would be calling to take him for the week-end. It would be his fourth such visit. The more I saw of the man the less I liked him; and, strangely, this seemed to be shared by his son, for on his return from the very first outing Harold said he didn't want to go out with his father again.

The arrangement was that Harold would see his father on both the Saturday and Sunday, but that he would sleep here because his father's girl friend had always objected to him; and, anyway, Harold's two older sisters, Doris and Gloria, were now back with their father, and consequently they were short of room.

Friday too was the day I phoned Gran in Fellburn. This should have given me a great deal of pleasure: we should have laughed and joked as we used to, but since her visit following Nardy's death, when she became jealous of Janet and had caused a scene, things had changed between us. She would give me her news about the family, and I would give her mine, but we didn't laugh together any more. Even when at odd times I spoke to her son, my stepfather George, it wasn't the same: he still said, 'Hello Pet,' or 'How's my best girl?' But I was no longer his best girl, and of course I understood that, for he had, with his second marriage, adopted a family of four. The only one who remained the same over the distance of time was Mike, Doctor Kane, the man who really created Hamilton the imaginary horse that had been my friend during those lonely years. My weekly visits to Mike's surgery had been as a lifebelt to me over that long dark period, and I thank God that at least he had remained the same . . .

Mr Brown, the caretaker, had been up to take Sandy for his first walk, and after he had given me the run-down on the weather outside he asked if I would be kind enough to stop the young man, as he called Harold, from ringing his emergency bell every time he passed through the hall.

Oh, I didn't know Harold had been doing this, I said; I would certainly see to it. And I did.

'What's this I hear about your ringing Mr Brown's bell?'

'Me?'

'Stop that; you know what I mean.'

There was a shrug of the shoulders, pursing of the lips, a sidelong glance up at me before he said, 'It's only a bit of fun.'

'It's no fun having Mr Brown running up those stone steps every time you happen to pass through the hall. One of these days when there is really something wrong he won't bother to come, he'll think it's you playing up again. Now it's got to stop. Understand?'

'All right,' he said, and then sighed before making the statement: 'I don't 'ate 'im; 'e's hall right, 'e does bug me though.'

'Oh well, I'm sure he'll be glad to know you don't hate him, but he'd be more pleased if you restrained the urge to press the button.'

He now laughed up into my face and put his hand out and pushed me gently in the waist, saying, 'You know, you sound funny when you talk like that.'

I pressed my lips together, then blinked before I said,

'I had no intention of appearing funny, and you know it.'

Another sigh. 'Yes, hall right.'

'All right.'

He grinned, 'As you said, hall right.'

I drew in a long breath, 'Keep your scarf tucked in and your cap on straight and don't lose your gloves today. Now where are you going?' I said as he darted from me towards the kitchen.

'Just to say so long to Sandy.'

A minute later he was back, saying, ''E's lazy; 'e won't get out of 'is basket.'

'It's because he's tired; he's had his walk,' I said.

'I'm tired an' all.'

'Go on with you.' I pushed him into the outer hall, opened the lift doors; then bending down I kissed him, and, his arms coming round my neck, he hugged me to him for a moment. Then having to have the last word, he stepped into the lift, saying, 'Look, you've knocked me cap for six.'

'Be a good boy now, won't you?'

'Yes, all right,' he said, and as his grinning face disappeared from my view I sighed happily and turned back into the house, the while thinking, He's learning, and quickly.

This period in the morning between Harold going to school and Janet's arriving seemed the loneliest time of the day; even more so than at night after Tommy had gone, for there was never an evening passed but he called in; and although very often he stayed too long, I had to admit I was glad of his company. But he having gone, I would go straight to bed and pray that I could sleep, only of late to be woken up by this weird pain.

I thought of the pain now and did what I had promised myself to do in the middle of last night: I went to the phone and as I was a private patient I asked if I could make an appointment to see my doctor that

36

morning. When this was arranged, it being Friday morning, I phoned Gran.

I always found myself hesitating before ringing her number these days, wondering what her attitude would be. However, there was the number ringing.

'Hello, Gran.'

'Hello, there.'

'How are you?'

'Oh, not too bad.'

There was a pause, then she said, 'I've got news for you, you're in the papers again.'

'What?'

'You're in the papers again.'

'How?'

'Stickle.'

The very name caused my heart to thump against my ribs. 'What do you mean, Gran? Explain.' My voice was sharp.

'Well, there seems to have been a fight in the prison: he went for another man; the fellow's in hospital.'

'Well, what have I got to do with that?'

'Well, you were his wife, weren't you? And there it is in block letters: Husband of local author.'

'He's no longer my husband. They know that, you know that; why do you say it like that, Gran? It's as if you were enjoying it.'

'Now look here, lass, don't forget who you're talkin' to. I'm tellin' you what's in the paper. Anyway, you're out of it now, aren't you? You don't have to put up with it.'

She spoke as if she was at the receiving end of something, and then in the next moment her explanation came: 'I could hardly get through the club door last night afore there they were. "Stickle's at it again," they said, as if he was a damn relation.'

I held the phone away from my face and looked at it as if looking at her, and my mind was saying, You were glad to be classed a relation when Nardy was alive. You used to make skits about my being married to a nob and preening yourself because you were connected with me. Why did people change? What made them act as they did? It was the same emotion, I suppose, as that which made me react as I did the next instant by bringing up a topic that I knew irritated her and which I had refrained from mentioning over the past weeks.

'I didn't tell you that the adoption had gone through, did I?'

There was a short silence before she said, 'No you didn't. But all I can say in that direction is, you've made a rod for your own back.'

I felt the colour rising to my face and my irritation boiled over as I cried into the phone, 'Why don't you like him, Gran? What's the matter with you?'

'There's nothing the matter with me, lass. And you ask why I don't like him. Well, I'll tell you why, and our George thinks the same, an' Mary an' all, and it's this way, if you want to adopt a bairn it should have been somebody decent, not a raw-mouthed little cockney.'

I glared at the mouthpiece, then banged it down onto the stand, and marched away into the bedroom, slammed the door, then attempted to make the bed as if I were attacking it, throwing the clothes here and there. But all of a sudden I stopped, sat down in a chair, drooped my head and began to cry, all the time whimpering, 'Oh, Nardy. Nardy.'

If Nardy had been there he would have had an explanation of why Gran felt like this: he would have soothed my ruffled feathers; and although I thought I knew perfectly well why she felt like this, his soft voice would have put a different light on her attitude, explaining once again the tangents of our complex personalities.

But Nardy wasn't here.

After a while I got up and finished making the bed, more gently now, and when, a short time later, I left the bedroom I suddenly wished that it was evening and I could see Tommy and I could talk to him about it. Such were the vagaries of my own nature ...

Janet had hardly got in the door and said, 'Morning, Mrs Leviston, ma'am. Nippy isn't it?' before I could see she was bursting with news of some kind. She took off her hat and coat, stooped down to lift up Sandy who was barking a welcome at her before making her way to the kitchen.

I stood at one side of the kitchen table, she at the other and she nodded at me before she said, 'She's left him.'

'Who? Hilda, the Mohican, I mean John?'

Janet smiled now, saying, 'That's a good name for him; different from what some of the boys call him. Big Chief Bloody Nuisance, that's what my 'Arry calls him, 'cos he says he's never away from the door. But then that isn't true, 'cos he goes off and we never see him for days. Neither does Hilda. We don't know where he goes. But no, it wasn't him, it's the other one, Jimmy, Jimmy Stoddart the father.' She nodded to the side as if Harold were present.

My mouth widened into an 'Oh!' before I said, 'The woman's left him?'

'Flat. Apparently she was only sticking because she thought she was going to have the baby, but since the miscarriage she's acted different like. She thought young 'Arold was a nuisance, but then she found the two girls were almost as bad. It was the way she treated them: May's good; they behave themselves with her because they want to stay there. So the bold boy's on his own now, and that serves him right. But being who he is he won't be like that long if I know anything about it. From what I can gather from his piece's cousin who knows Hilda, the woman thought that

39

with Maggie coming back from Australia with that bloke and wanting to marry him and askin' for a divorce. That shook me, mind, Maggie wantin' to marry again. Anyway, Jimmy's piece thought the bloke would marry Maggie. But it seems he told her she was barking up the wrong tree. And I'll tell you this, ma'am, if Maggie hadn't had marriage in her mind again I don't think she would have agreed to the adoption; likely the bloke, whoever he is, didn't want to take on the responsibility of a ready-made family. Anyway, has the person in question' – she pulled a face here – 'been behaving himself?'

I pulled a face back at her as I said, 'Only in part. He's been ringing Mr Brown's emergency bell again.'

'Ooh! the little devil. But then that's a boy, any boy would do that. But it's his language that worries me an' what he'll get up to at that school, it being connected with the church like . . . Well, I'll make a cup of tea and then we'll get started.'

'By the way, Janet,' I said, 'I'll be popping out; I've made an appointment with Doctor Bell, he's seeing me at eleven o'clock.'

'You had that pain again?'

'Yes, a little. It's beginning to worry me.'

'Well, the best thing you can do is to see him. Put your mind at rest anyway. One thing you're certain of, it isn't your appendix this time.'

It was just over an hour later when I left the house and as I stepped out of the front door I was met by the astonishing sight of the Mohican. It was astonishing for he looked more like an Indian Chief than ever. I stammered, 'Hel . . . hello, John,' and he replied in that surprisingly well-bred tone of his, 'Good-morning, Mrs Leviston. No doubt you're surprised to see me.'

'N . . . no. No,' I stammered again; 'not at all.' He laughed gently now and leant back against the iron rail that bordered the steps to the basement and as he did so I looked past him down the street to where stood two more Indians. Well, they weren't quite Indians, and I couldn't really see from this distance whom they represented, but it certainly wasn't anyone in the British Isles.

'I just wanted to leave a message for Hilda with her mother. I've ... well, unexpectedly got to go off for a few days. I didn't know till just a little while ago, and ... and I don't want to go to the factory.' And the marks on his cheeks spread again as he added, 'She doesn't like it very much: she's with it herself, but they still kid her.'

I nodded at him, saying, 'I can understand that;' then pointedly I asked, 'Why have you to go off at a moment's notice?'

'Oh,' he said; then turned to look down the street to where his two friends had moved somewhat nearer, and I could now make out they were on the other side from the Indians, more like something left over from Custer's last stand, in fringed leather gear.

And as if remembering my question, the Mohican said slowly, 'Well, we just feel the urge, you know, to move, to get away, to do something different.' As he finished he stood up straight and, leaning slightly towards me, he said, 'I'd like to talk to you sometime, Mrs Leviston; I think you'd understand.'

For my part, at that moment I was thinking I couldn't understand the reason for his get-up, let alone his desire to do something different, when two heads appeared coming up the area steps. They were those of Mr Brown and his policeman son, and no sooner had the young policeman spotted the Mohican than defences were up on all sides.

'What do you want here?' demanded Mr Brown.

'Is he pestering you, ma'am?' This from the young policeman; and now a bark from the Mohican as he swung round, yelling, 'No! I wasn't pestering her,

41

copper.' He spat out the last name. 'I was just having a word with . . .'

'I know what you lot are just having. Now get yourself away and quick if you don't want any trouble. Now I'm . . .'

'Officer' – my voice sounded cool, icy, even to myself – 'this young man happens to be a—' I paused on the word 'friend', but I'd no sooner got it out than the Mohican put in, 'Mrs Leviston's being kind in calling me friend. I'm not a friend of hers but a friend to the daughter of her daily, and I wanted to leave a message for her. That's why I've dared to walk on the pavement in this part of town. Now what d'you make of that?'

Both Mr Brown and his son looked at me, and I said quietly now, 'He's right.' Then turning towards the young fellow, I said, 'Go on up and see her. It's the top floor.'

He made no move for a moment but glared at the policeman. Then bending to the side towards where his two companions had come within earshot, he yelled, 'I'm under surveillance,' and had just turned back to the door when it opened again and out stepped the Captain and his wife. Then an odd thing happened, and I wasn't imagining it: on the sight of them there passed over the Mohican's face a look of surprise; then he turned his head quickly away and his gaze fell on to the policeman, and I thought, Ah, someone from his past, he recognized him; but although there was little chance of he himself having been recognized, the next moment, with head down, he almost slithered past the couple and entered the hall, and the Captain, looking at Mr Brown said, 'Where's he off to?'

It was I who answered him: 'He's going up to my flat with a message, Captain,' I said.

'Well, well.' He looked from Mr Brown to the policeman, then to the two American civil war relics passing us now, and when one of them snorted like a

42

pig, he cried, 'Scum! Scum! They should be put into the army ... Perverts. I would shoot the lot of them, horsewhip them.'

What caused my silly mind to make me enquire, 'Put them in the army before or after shooting them, Captain?'

'*What?*'

And stupidly I still persisted: 'Would you horsewhip them before you shot them or after, or ...' My voice trailed off as he shifted his piercing gaze from me to his wife, then to Mr Brown, then to the policeman, and because he seemed lost for a reply I now said, 'If you'll excuse me,' and edging my way between Mr Brown and his son I walked away down the street.

When I crossed over the road towards the private gardens that fronted the terrace I knew that the four people I had just left were now deep in conversation, the while their eyes were following my progress.

Each of the tenants had a private key to the gardens and for only the third time since I'd lived here I used mine this morning and went in. The trees were bare, the shrubs and bushes heavy with hoar-frost and overall there was a silence. It was strange, as I had found before, how once you passed through the gate you were in a different world. I looked down on this garden from the drawing-room window every day, but you had to walk in it to feel its presence, and it had a presence all of its own. Now, as I passed round the shrubbery into the rose arbour where the bushes looked like bits of small dead twigs sticking out of the earth, I promised myself that I would come here more often.

Under the designed overhang of a stone wall was a wooden bench. The front of the seat still showed the frost clinging to it, but nevertheless I sat down, then drew a few deep cold breaths and looked across one of the beds to where a cherub's head protruded from a

43

wall, its mouth agape but with no water pouring from it now. The head reminded me somewhat of Harold, and I should have felt heartened by the fact, but I didn't.

It was Friday again all right. It had started with Gran as it usually did; and then this morning there was Janet with her news that Harold's father was, as one would say, a freelance now, and why this should trouble me I didn't know. Yet it did. Then that scene with the Mohican. As my mind touched on that I thought, I don't like that Captain. As for the young policeman, he was, I thought, just doing his duty as he saw it, and I had to admit that the Mohican did look very out of place in this part of town. Yet London was free and open to all. If he had just been walking up the street likely there would have been no open opposition to him; it was the fact that he stopped outside a house and he was talking to a woman, perhaps begging, even on the point of mugging her. Yes, I could see the policeman's point of view.

Oh dear me! what more today? What would that doctor say after he had examined me? Well, I must get up and on my way to find out. Yet, I was reluctant to leave this spot, although the cold was beginning to penetrate even my fur coat. I recalled other times when I had sat on a park bench, but always at these times I had had Hamilton for company. He would lean his hoofs on the back of the bench while giving me advice. As if now expecting him to appear I looked from side to side, but there was no sign of him: my mind had apparently sent him to regions beyond recall. Harold had taken his place; and Tommy too. Oh yes, Tommy too. What was I going to do about Tommy? And again the question arose: Did I love him? If I was comparing the feeling I had for him with that which I held for Nardy, no I didn't love him. Yet, were he to go out of my life now I should miss him greatly. So what

44

did I feel for him? Affection? Yes, a quite deep affection, but it wasn't love. It was more than a year now since Nardy had gone from me and the pain of his loss was still with me, not so sharp, but nevertheless there.

If you're going to the doctor's you had better get on your way.

I got abruptly to my feet: it was as if Hamilton had spoken. But then, what had Hamilton been but my inner self; I might not see him any more but his voice remained . . .

Doctor Bell had finished his ordinary surgery. He greeted me kindly. What was my trouble?

I told him.

'Ah, well, we must see what it's all about, mustn't we? Just go behind the screen and the nurse will attend to you.'

Mike had never had a nurse in attendance. What Mike had said and would still say was, 'Get your clothes off.' His manner had been rough at times, oh very rough, but he never treated me as a child.

The nurse appeared from somewhere behind the screen, smiled sweetly at me and without a word began to help me undress, making me feel very like a cross between the child suggested by the doctor and a geriatric.

Doctor Bell came in, smiled benignly, and rubbed his hands together as he said, 'It's a cold morning.' They were still cold when they touched my flesh.

After prodding and probing for a time, he said, 'You say you feel the pain mostly in the stomach?'

'Yes; mostly; but in other places too, in my chest.'

He sat me up and tapped my back; told me to say ah; told me to take a deep breath. Then he tried the reflexes of my legs; asked a few more questions, then left me to the ministrations of the nurse again.

Later, seated at one side of his desk I was again

45

reminded of Mike and my regular Monday morning visits to his surgery and his acid tones and his bristling beard, but only by comparison with this doctor who, in a very quiet voice, said, 'As far as I can ascertain, Mrs Leviston, I can find nothing wrong.' He coughed, leant back in his chair, put his fingertips together and then said, 'You are no doubt still feeling the loss of your husband, yes?'

'Oh, yes, yes, I still miss him very much.'

'Well, my dear, I think that there might lie the problem of your movable pains.'

I stiffened. 'You think I'm imagining them?'

'No, no, not at all, they're very real to you, but as far as I can gather they have no organic source: you haven't any lumps or tender spots, your chest is sound, your heart is very good. What you likely need is just a tonic, and I shall give you a prescription for that.' He leant forward now and began to write. Having finished, he got to his feet, came round the desk, handed me the slip of paper and, reverting to his fatherly manner, bent over me and said, 'Now if we don't feel any better in a week or so, drop in again and see me, eh?'

I allowed a short silence to fall between us before, looking him straight in the face, I said, 'I'll do that.'

A certain amount of indignation caused me to walk briskly home. He thought I was imagining the pain. Likely, he had read my first book, *Hamilton*, and come to the conclusion that if I could think up a horse with which I held conversations then it would be quite easy for me to create a few pains here and there.

As soon as I got in the house Janet greeted me with, 'There's been a phone call from the school. And what did you think of Big Chief Workshy having the nerve to call here? I gave him the length of me tongue. He's off again. And I ask you, Mrs Leviston, ma'am, where does he get the money? Of course, he's on the dole but

46

that doesn't pay for his flittin' 'ere and there. I said to him . . .'

'Who was it phoned from the school, Janet?'

'It was a man. I think it could have been the headmaster 'cos . . . well, he spoke nice, pleasant like.'

I almost grabbed up the phone, and when I heard the school secretary's voice at the other end I asked her to put me through to Mr Binn.

'Oh, good-morning, Mrs Leviston.'

'Good-morning . . . You wanted to speak to me?'

'Yes. I wondered, if you had the time, could you pop in sometime today?'

'What's wrong? Is anything wrong?'

'Oh no, no, no, nothing serious.'

I wanted to ask now, Is it to do with Harold? Of course it was to do with Harold. He had been up to something. Or perhaps not; perhaps it was to do with the choir. I understood the choirboys were in need of new cassocks; perhaps it was something to do with that. My voice had a light tone to it as I said, 'I could come straightaway.'

'There is no rush; whatever time suits you.'

'Very well.' I put the phone back on its stand and turned to where Janet stood near the kitchen door as she asked, 'He's in trouble?'

'No, no. As far as I can gather, no. I think it must be something to do with his going into the choir.'

She turned away laughing now, saying, 'Good Lord! Him in the choir. God help 'em!'

'He's got a lovely little voice.'

'Yes, I know that, Mrs Leviston, ma'am, but it's what 'e says with it or sings with it.'

'Oh, Janet.'

'You can say it like that, ma'am, but you'll never make an angel out of him.'

'I don't want to make an angel out of him; anything but; I like him as he is.'

47

She laughed again. 'As I said to Hilda last night when she was on about her Indian Chief, there's no accountin' for tastes.'

When I left the kitchen Sandy followed me into the study and I picked him up and when he nestled his head into my neck I walked the floor with him, rocking him gently as I would have a child. He liked this, and as I walked I talked to him: 'Funny about Janet's attitude to Harold, isn't it? She's expecting the worst. But then, so do they all. They see him as a rip, a living terror. Why is it that I see him as a little boy who needs love and gives it? I wonder what the headmaster really wants to talk about?' I looked at the clock. It was just turned twelve. They'd be at lunch now, and anyway Janet would have mine ready in a very short time.

I stopped my prancing and dropped Sandy to the floor, which he didn't take to very well, so he went and curled himself up in the corner of the couch. Then I sat down at my typewriter, telling myself that I must get down to work, back into the routine I had got out of recently for if I didn't keep on with this present book I'd lose the theme.

My good intentions lasted for only twenty minutes; then Janet called me to lunch, after which I got dressed for outdoors again, not in my fur coat and hat this time, but more soberly and ordinarily as befitted the mother of a little boy ...

Mr Binn seemed pleased to see me. 'Do take a seat, Mrs Leviston,' he said.

But he himself did not take the seat behind his desk; instead, he sat perched casually on the edge of it, seemingly to create an atmosphere that was light and easy. Yet he was reluctant to begin the conversation, so I said, 'Is it about Harold going into the choir you wish to see me?'

'No, I'm afraid not, Mrs Leviston.' His words came

out on a kind of stuttering laugh. 'Quite the reverse I would say.'

I suddenly became cold inside. Oh! dear God, don't let them tell me that Harold has been coming out with language again. He had promised me.

'Oh, don't look so concerned; it's not all that serious, it's just something that ... well, we'll have to nip in the bud, so to speak.'

'What has he done?'

'Oh, it isn't what he does, as I think you might know, it's what he says.'

'Swearing?'

'No, I wouldn't say swearing. But you know ... well, I don't need to tell you he's a bright little boy, in fact his teacher says he's amazing for his age, and he's got an imagination. Moreover he's a bit of a comic actor, besides being something of a rhymester. And this is the point in question at the moment, so if you could help us to curb his leanings in this direction things would go along more smoothly. You understand?'

'Offensive rhymes?'

'Well' – again a shaky laugh – 'not exactly offensive, more crude I would say. You know what children are.'

No, I didn't; I only knew what Harold was, and I'd heard some of his rhymes.

'You know how children get hold of a name. Look at mine for instance, Binn, my nickname's' – he leant towards me – 'Dusty, or Three-two-one. You know, the television game.'

Yes, yes, I knew the television game. But I waited, wanting to say, 'Get on with it.'

Mr Binn got on with it. 'A lot of children do this, you know, but Harold has become quite an expert at it. Candidly I was going to speak to you some time ago but I thought it would fade away, children have phases, you know, but then two things have happened this week. A little girl, she's a spoilt little thing I must admit, but she went home crying because the boys were chanting after her: it was a combined chorus of three or four of them, and our composer had gone to the trouble of printing it out so that his confederates could learn the words by heart.' He now reached back on to the desk and passed me a piece of paper, saying, 'There's more to come, I'm afraid.' The smile was still on his face.

I looked at the writing on the paper. Yes, this certainly was Harold's hand, and I read: 'Millie Stott has two bots that she sits on a lot, so she gets spots on her bot, Millie Stott, silly clot.'

What could I say? It was so silly, so childish. There was only one thing I was thankful for: he had used bot instead of bum or, even worse still, arse. I looked at the headmaster and when he said, 'Silly, isn't it?' I nodded. Then his tone altering, he said, 'Yes, it's silly to us but to a little girl being followed by three or four boys chanting that in the street, you can understand she would arrive home crying. It resulted, of course, in a visit from her mother; but I'm afraid that is not all.'

I bit my lip, and when for the moment he didn't continue to speak I felt like actually shouting, 'Well, let's have it!'

'You have met Miss Scottie?'

'Yes.'

'Well, I can tell you straight away, she is quite fond of Harold, but she has to chastize him very often. One of Miss Scottie's main endeavours is to instil good manners into her pupils, so every morning she insists that they stand up and greet her with "Good-morning, Miss Scottie." And yesterday morning she was a little late going to her class and as she approached it she heard chanting, and there was the bold Harold conducting a chant which went: "Good-morning, Miss Scottie. If you hit us again with the ruler you'll end up in the cooler".'

He laughed outright now, saying again, 'Sounds so silly, doesn't it? But as you can imagine it's very difficult to keep discipline against an opponent like Master Harold. From what I understand about the matter, she had tapped his hand with his ruler some time before when she found him eating chewing-gum.'

I drew in a deep breath. Chewing-gum. I'd forbidden him to buy chewing-gum after I'd found it stuck on the corner of his dressing-table and then between the leaves of a book.

But Mr Binn now came off the edge of the desk and faced me. 'There is something slightly more serious, innocent in a way, yet with repercussions that I am afraid could bring many parents about my ears, especially, as you know, that this is a Church School.'

I felt sick.

'As you know I had hopes of Mr Stevens taking him into the choir, and yesterday afternoon he called to see Miss Dixon. She was taking the singing class. Harold was present. As Mr Stevens wished to discuss something with Miss Dixon they walked into the corridor. I happened to come along at that moment and the three of us stood talking until we heard giggles, then smothered laughter coming from the music room. I myself glanced through the window and saw a small figure doing what I suppose would be called a turn for the rest of the class.' He paused here. 'I can still smile at his impression of Mr Frankie Vaughan doing his act. The small figure was leaning back, his legs kicking out, he was waving an imaginary straw hat and he was singing—' He stopped.

My voice was harsh now as I said, 'I'm waiting for the worst; you'd better finish.'

'Well' – he paused – 'you know his signature tune, "Give me the moonlight, give me the girl, and leave the rest to me"?'

'Yes, I know that.'

'Well—' I watched him wet his lips before he said, 'add to those lines—' Again he paused; then slowly he brought out the words, 'And I'll put a bun in your oven straight after tea.'

If Gran and George had been here they'd have howled with laughter; if Nardy had been here he would have covered his eyes and choked; but there was only me, and I certainly didn't laugh. I didn't smile. I turned my head to the side and looked through a tall window to where the children were stampeding into the schoolyard.

'You can understand my situation?'

I looked back at him and muttered, 'Yes. What ... what do you intend to do?'

'Well, really, I'm going to leave that to you. The little fellow has no idea of the implication of his rhyme.'

'It wouldn't be his rhyme,' I put in quickly; 'it's what he's heard his uncles say, at least one of them who considers himself a mimic.'

'Oh? I'm sorry this situation has arisen, but, you see, this is a Church School and ... and we have standards. Oh, I know children say naughty things, but I'm afraid our dear little Harold is a connoisseur in that direction. Anyway, do you think you can help him curb his exuberance?'

'I'll try. I have, so far, succeeded in stopping him swearing. At least I think I have.'

'Well that's good; so we'll leave the matter in abeyance for a time, shall we?'

'Thank you.'

He opened the door for me, saying kindly now, 'Try not to worry too much about the matter; we shall do our best at this end. We do know the circumstances of your taking him under your wing and I can assure you we will help to turn him into a good Christian individual.'

I did not even wish him good-bye. I walked along the corridor, passing scampering children. A good Christian individual, Harold. Anyway, where was he?

I was in the schoolyard now, and for a moment I felt like Janet: when I got hold of him I'd box his ears right and left ... No, I wouldn't; that had never done any good ... There he was, near the gate talking to two boys of his own age.

'Harold!'

He turned round towards me, 'Oh. Hello. I didn't know you were 'ere. Why'd yer come? I can go 'ome on me own ... This is me muvver.' The last statement was made to his two companions, and under other circumstances I would have felt a surge of pride for he usually had difficulty in calling me mother, except when it was preceded by Mrs Nardy.

'He's Robbie Tennant and 'im's John Rankin.' He was stabbing his finger towards each boy now. 'They're me friends.'

The boys stared at me; one sniffed, the other said, ''Allo, missis,' which made me realize just how quickly Harold's speech reverted when he was among his schoolmates; and I had been congratulating myself on the way he had seemingly responded to my correcting his speech.

'Come along,' I said. Harold now grabbed my hand and walked from his friends without more ado.

It wasn't until we had entered the house that it dawned upon him I hadn't spoken all the way from the school, and, stopping his chattering, he looked up at me, saying, 'What's the matter?'

'I'll tell you what's the matter when you get your hat and coat off and come into the study.'

Within seconds he had followed me along the corridor and into the room. When I sat down on the couch and he went to sit beside me I pulled him upwards and made him stand in front of me. And after a

53

moment of staring at him I said, 'You've done it again, haven't you?'

'What, me?'

'Yes, you.'

'I've never swored, I mean sweared ... I've never sweared at school. I never 'ave.'

'You may not have sworn but you have written silly things, and encouraged the other children to say them, and said objectionable things.'

'Object ... what object ... able things?'

'We'll come to that part in a moment.'

I reached out to my bag on the table, opened it, then handed him the piece of paper that the headmaster had given to me.

'Who wrote that?'

He looked at it, then looked at me and said, 'It was only in fun.'

'I see nothing funny about it. It is crude and rude. And what is more, you intended to hurt the little girl. I'm ashamed of you, going along the street bawling that out at a little girl.'

'She's not a little girl, an' she's daft.' He was bristling now.

'And I suppose Miss Scottie is daft too?'

'No, she's not, she's all right.'

'Then why did you make silly rhymes up about her?'

He moved from one foot to the other, pushed out his lips, looked to the side, then said, 'Well, she hit me on the knuckles with the ruler and it hurt.'

'You must have been doing something wrong for her to do that.'

'I wasn't. I was only—' He stopped, then stood staring at me, and I moved my head twice as I ended for him, 'Only sticking chewing-gum on the lid of your desk and soiling the books with it. What did I tell you about chewing-gum?'

'I never bought it.'

54

'Don't lie to me, Harold, else I'll become angry with you.'

'I'm not lyin' to yer.' There it was again; that's because he was angry. 'I don't tell lies. I don't.'

That had been true up till now; I'd never found him out in a lie.

'I didn't buy it. Millie Stott gave me a stick.'

'Oh' – I raised my eyebrows – 'Millie Stott. That's the little girl you don't like, the one you made the rhyme up about, isn't it?'

'Yes.'

'Then if you don't like her why did you take the chewing-gum from her? You shouldn't accept gifts from people you don't like.'

'I didn't take it, she pushed it into my pocket. And I don't like her, she's soppy. She wants to be me girl friend.'

'Your ... your girl ... friend?'

He wriggled self-consciously, and even as I said, 'I can't understand why a sweet little girl would want you for a boy friend,' I knew I could understand perfectly well the attraction of this tough little individual; but up till now I had dealt with the simple things, now I had to tackle the more serious bit. 'About this imitation of yours, when you were doing Frankie Vaughan.'

'I can do him as good as Uncle Max.' His face was bright.

'Maybe, but you don't sing the right words.'

'*I do.*'

'*You don't.*'

'*I do*, Mrs Nardy, *I do*: Give me the moonlight, give me the girl and leave the rest to me ...' He was standing still, but his body was moving with the words when I stopped him here, saying, 'Yes, that's what Frankie Vaughan sings, but not the next line.'

'What?' He screwed up his face. 'And I'll put a bun in your oven straight after tea. Not that line?'

'Definitely not that line.'

'*He does! Frankie Vaughan does.*'

'*He doesn't!*' My voice was a bawl now, matching his. 'Your Uncle Max made that line up and it's not nice, in fact it's very nasty.'

He put his head on one side and looked at me as if he was sorry for me because I didn't know what I was talking about. Then he said, quietly for him, 'But Gag puts buns in the oven every Sunday mornin' before she puts the meat in, and we have 'em for tea, and there's never any left, and she goes on about it.'

I closed my eyes for a moment against the transient innocence of the young. Then I said softly, 'The buns that Janet ... I mean your grandmother puts in the oven are not the same as those referred to in the line that your Uncle Max sings. Do you understand?' I asked while knowing at the same time that he didn't understand. And he shook his head before asking quietly, 'They're not Sunday buns?'

'No, they're not Sunday buns.'

'What kind of buns then?'

Oh! dear me, where did I go from here? Could I say to this small boy that the bun he was singing about referred to a baby? No, I couldn't, for his mind, being as alert as it was, would certainly go ferreting further were I to attempt to explain, so I said, 'It's just a word that refers to something else that isn't nice, nasty.'

He stared at me in perplexity for a moment. 'Like swearin'?' he said.

I paused before saying, 'Yes, yes, in a way, but more so ... nasty.'

'Than swearin'?'

'Yes, than swearing.'

'And you don't want me to say it any more?'

'I'd be happy if you didn't.'

'But I can still do Frankie Vaughan?'

'Oh yes, you may still do Frankie Vaughan.'

He smiled now. That was that for him, the chastise-ment was over, and immediately he leant towards me, his finger crooked, his head poked out. His voice had changed and he said, 'Here a minute. Here a minute; there's more. I had a letter from me mother.'

'My mother,' I said.

'*Me* mother,' he said, as he went through the motion of pulling out the imaginary letter. And it was such a good imitation of Jimmy Cricket that I burst out laughing, pulled him towards me and hugged him, and he, putting his arms around my waist, hugged me in return. Then pushing him abruptly from me, I said, 'I want you to promise me something, really promise me.'

His face was bright, his eyes were shining, he said nothing, but waited.

'I want you to promise you'll not make up any more rhymes about the children at school or the teachers. Promise?'

He nodded readily, saying, 'All right, all right, I'll promise. Stick me finger in me eye, spit and swear I hope to die.'

'What?'

'That's what we say when we promise, and if we break it we'll drop down dead.'

'Oh, I see. Well, before you decide to drop down dead I think we had better have some tea, hadn't we?'

'Yes.' He jumped away and made for the door. 'What have we got?'

'Go into the kitchen and see.'

We had just finished our meal when the bell rang and I stopped Harold from dashing into the hall by saying sharply, 'Stay put!'

When I entered the outer hall I was surprised to see Tommy stepping out of the lift.

I greeted him with, 'You're early.'

'I've been seeing an author, quite near.' He came towards me and, bending, he kissed me on the cheek.

57

As he was taking off his overcoat Harold appeared in the kitchen doorway. 'Hello,' he said. 'Want a cup of tea?'

'Oh, that would be splendid. Please.'

'O.K.' Harold disappeared, and as we walked towards the drawing-room Tommy said, 'He seems to be in good form.'

'Good form? Wait till you hear.'

As I related Harold's school performance Tommy laughed, and when I came to the Frankie Vaughan piece he lay back on the couch and bellowed until the tears ran down his cheeks.

'That boy will go far,' he said; 'but you've taken on a handful,' and after passing a handkerchief over his face he remarked nonchalantly, 'and I think you need a hand with him. What do you say?'

'Oh, Tommy.'

Quickly now his mood changed, and, gripping me by the shoulders, he pulled me round to him, saying, 'Don't say "Oh Tommy", in that way. It's over a year now since Nardy went. He understood the situation, you know he did, and he wouldn't want you to go on living alone. Oh, Maisie, apart from loving you and needing you, I want to look after you. You've had so many rough rides, I want to smooth the path ahead.'

'I didn't have a rough ride with Nardy, it was a magnificent ride. I...'

'You know what I mean. But now ... tell me truthfully now, how do you feel about me? How have you come to feel about me over the past year? Tell me.'

I looked at him; then looked away and said quietly, 'I'm very fond of you, I've grown more fond of you, but ... but, Tommy, I can't say I love you, not like I did Nardy.'

'I don't expect you to love me as you did Nardy. There are all ways of loving, all kinds of love; I'd be content with your affection, content with anything as long as I can stay near you.'

I looked back into his eyes. There must have been an amazed expression in mine that was reflected in my voice as I said, 'I can never understand it, I never will until the day I die, how men like Nardy and you could love someone like me. I sometimes think it's as if you were both under some spell that has changed your sight, and you see me as entirely different from what I am, as someone tall, slim, beautiful, gracious...'

He laughed gently now, saying, 'No, our sight was not affected, my dear; we see you as someone small, plain but petite, but with a something that neither of us could define: character is an inadequate word; you have a natural drawing power and something that created in us a tenderness...'

Again I said, 'Oh! Tommy,' interrupting his flow of words and in doing so bending slightly towards him and lifting my hand with the intention of placing it on his cheek. But the action was fatal; it had the same result as when I was dealing with Harold: Tommy's arms came round me and for the first time his mouth fell hard on mine, and to my surprise I let it remain there, and I knew that I would not have withdrawn from him but for a voice saying gruffly, 'I brought your tea.'

I pulled myself from Tommy's embrace and there, over the end of the couch, I saw Harold standing in the middle of the room, a cup and saucer in his hand. Making my voice sound ordinary, I said, 'Well, fetch it here.'

He approached slowly and the cup rattled in the saucer and the tea spilled over as he handed it to Tommy, who said quietly, 'Thank you, Harold.'

Now my boy turned and confronted me.

'He was kissin' you.'

I drew in a deep breath, saying, 'Yes, yes, he was kissing me.'

'What for?'

59

This I wasn't called upon to answer because Tommy put in quietly, 'Because I like her very much, like you do, I love her.'

'*You don't.*'

'Oh, but I do.'

'Not like me you don't. Bloody well you don't, not like me.'

'*Harold!*'

'Well, he doesn't. He's a big silly bugger all 'cos he's got a swanky car. Gag says he's a bloody mani ... nac in it. Why'd you let him?'

'*Harold!*' My voice was loud. 'That is enough. Go in the kitchen and give Sandy his tea.'

'Won't. I'm goin' 'ome.' And as he marched away I went to rise from the couch, but Tommy's hand stayed me. 'Let him go,' he said; 'it was a natural reaction, he'll get over it.'

'Will he? You don't know him. Oh dear me.' I leant back and put my hand to my brow. 'This has been the most irritating kind of day, right from early morning when I phoned Gran.' I made to rise again, and again Tommy stayed me, saying, 'Don't; he's likely packing his case.' He smiled now. 'He'll cool off, you'll see.' Then he added, 'One of the reasons I came round early was to ask you if you'd like to see *Pack of Lies* at the Lyric. Judi Dench and Michael Williams are in it.'

'Oh, I couldn't, not tonight, Tommy.'

'Yes, you could. This is the very night to do it, to leave him with the Captain and his lady. He'll miss you and likely run into your arms when you come back. And you did say he goes off with his father tomorrow, and I know that's not pleasing him. Now, is it? Well, that should show him on which side his bread's buttered. Don't worry, my dear.' Again he put his arm around me and, looking into my face, he said, 'I've kissed you, really kissed you, short but sweet' – he

60

smiled – 'but it's a beginning. What say you?'

I now did put my hand on his cheek and said quietly, 'Let it go from here then.'

'As you wish.'

'I must go and see what he's up to.'

'Go on then' – he pushed me from the couch – 'you're like a little hen with her first chick.'

A little hen with her first chick. Yes, he was right.

And he had been right too about packing the case, because there Harold was, in his bedroom, all his underwear from the top drawer of the chest thrown on the bed. He must have just pulled open the second drawer as I entered the room and was about to take out shirts.

'What are you doing?' I asked quietly.

'I'm goin' away, like I said.'

'Oh? Where are you going to?'

He swung round. 'I'm goin' back to Gag's. I told you.'

'Oh, I'm sure she'll be pleased to hear that. Well, if that's the case I'd better go and phone her and prepare her.' I had reached the door when he said, 'You don't like me any more.'

'Don't be silly.' I looked back at him over my shoulder.

'You were kissin' him.'

'Yes, of course. And I kiss you, don't I?'

'You shouldn't kiss him; he's a bloody big goof; I'll kick his shins.' Three or four shirts were sent flying across the bed.

I was immediately at his side. Gripping him by the shoulders, I shook him hard. 'Stop acting like a stupid little boy. And you know I could never let you go back to Gran's. And you know I love you more than anything in the world.'

'More than 'im?'

'In a different way.'

'What different way?'

61

'I can't explain; you'll understand when you're older. But I do love you, Harold, and I want you, and I don't want you to go back to Gran's. I'd miss you so, so much.'

His lips trembled, his eyes blinked, as I said, 'If you love me you wouldn't hurt me by saying you want to go back to Gran's.'

'I do, I do love you.' His arms were round my neck and he was gabbling unintelligibly now as the tears rained down his face, and I, stroking his hair and holding him tightly, soothed him, saying, 'There now. There now. It's all over. And you know something? Mr Tommy likes you very much. He thinks you're a very bright boy and will grow up very clever. He was talking the other day about teaching you to swim, really swim. He's a great swimmer.'

'Don't want to swim. Don't like him.'

I pressed him from me, dried his face, and said, 'Harold, you must not tell lies, you do like him. You told me you do.'

'Is he gona live here?'

'Not for a long time, not until you're older.'

'How older?'

'Oh.' I thought as I moved my head from one side to the other, then said, 'Oh, a year, perhaps two.'

This long length of time seemed to satisfy him.

'And will he sleep with you like Grandad does with Gag?'

I made myself consider for a moment before I said, 'Well, yes, perhaps.'

He gave a shake to his shoulder as he turned from me, saying, 'I'd be growed up by then in a year or two.'

'Yes, of course you will. I tell you what: I'll put your things away again if you go and tell Mr Tommy that you're sorry.'

'I can put me own things away.'

He now grabbed up some of his underwear from the

bed and as he did so I saw a pound note lying on the counterpane.

As yet I gave him only fifty pence for his pocket money at the week-end besides ten pence each day for some sweets. I asked him now, 'Where did you get that from?'

He picked up the note and, taking it to the drawer, he pushed it down the side, saying, 'Somebody gave it to me.'

'Who?'

'I'm not to tell.'

I stared at him. If his uncles had given him the money then he would have no compulsion crying aloud their generosity. It was likely his father. But why had he said not to tell? I let the matter pass, but now reverted to a little diplomacy that I found worked with him. 'Would you mind, Harold,' I asked, 'if I went out to see a show with Mr Tommy tonight?'

Never in his short but wide-awake life had he been deferred to, had anything been requested of him, or his opinion been asked. On the contrary he had been ordered to do this or that and told what would happen to him if he didn't do it. In consequence, I'd found he'd become quite amenable when deferred to. But I also saw, on this occasion, that his permission was being granted very much against his will, for after flinging some more of his underwear into the drawer, which I immediately straightened, he said, 'I don't care.'

'Thank you.' I now sat on the edge of the bed and pulled him towards me and, with my face on a level with his, I said softly, 'I love you very much, the best in the world. Always remember that.' I didn't attempt to kiss him as I didn't want any more tearful embraces, not at this moment, but, pushing him gently away, I said, 'Go on, tell Mr Tommy you're sorry you swore at him.'

Head down, he left the room, and a minute or so later

I followed him, but outside the drawing-room door, which was half open, I stopped, arrested by his voice saying, 'She says you can't sleep in her bed, not like Mr Nardy, not for two years anyway.'

'She did, did she? Not for two years?' Behind Tommy's serious tone there was a note of laughter. There followed a short silence and I was prevented from pushing the door further open by Harold's voice saying now, 'She's my muvver.'

'Yes, I know she is. You're lucky to have a mother; I haven't got a mother.'

'You're too big to have a muvver.' Oh! that word again.

'I'm not, what about all your uncles? They have a mother.'

'I didn't mean big, I mean old.'

'I'm not that old.'

'Yes, you are. Anyway, all muvvers die when you grow old, or they leave you before you're five.'

'They do?'

'Yes.'

I felt I'd better make my appearance at this stage because Tommy would not be able to work out if mothers died because they were old, or because their sons were getting old, or why they left you before you were five. That last had a deep significance: his mother had left him when he was three.

I went in brightly, saying, 'You know, Tommy, Harold and I hadn't quite finished our tea when you arrived and the cup he brought you must be cold now, so let's go into the kitchen and brew up again, eh? And Harold will give you a piece of his ginger cake. It's a very special ginger cake, it came in a tin from Fortnum and Mason's.'

Harold turned and hurried from the room, whether at the thought of having another piece of ginger cake or the fact that he was still feeling upset I didn't know, but Tommy stopped me following him by catching my arm and, bending his long length down to me, whispering, 'I understand there's been a discussion about my going into your bed.'

I slapped at him and walked off, and as he followed me he laughed, and it had a very pleasant sound, a relieved sound . . .

At seven o'clock the Captain and his lady entered the flat. As usual he was all muscle and voice, she all dignity. And tonight she was wearing a long dated evening dress and a small silk shoulder cape that had seen better days.

'Well, well, well, here we are again.'

The Captain was at his jolliest. 'And where's my protégé, the future chess champion. Oh, there you are, feller-me-lad. And already for bed. My! My!'

Harold had come from the passageway; he was dressed in his pyjamas and dressing-gown. I looked towards him, saying, 'Say good-evening to the Captain and Mrs Beckingtree-Holland.' Oh that name . . .

Harold now approached the Captain and, looking up at him, he said, 'I'm not goin' to play chess any more, I want to play rummy.'

'Rummy? Well, well. All right, sir, all right, rummy it shall be. I used to be a dab hand at rummy too. What are we going to play for tonight, pennies or pounds or liquorice allsorts?' He now put his head back and laughed and his lady wife, turning to me, said, 'It's a very wild night, you're going to be buffeted. But then, of course' – her eyes slid to Tommy – 'you have the car. How fortunate.' Her gaze rested on me again. 'About what time shall we expect you back?'

'About eleven I think. And . . . and I have left some cold salmon in the fridge and the usual accessories. There's a small gâteau, too.'

'How nice. How nice.'

I went towards Harold now and, bending down, I

kissed him on the cheek saying, 'Be a good boy and go to bed at half-past eight. You will, won't you?'

He gave a small nod of his head but said nothing. I turned from him and amid nods and good-byes we went out.

In the lift I laughed gently as I said, 'You know, I feel that I've just left some strict parents and they were allowing me out for the first time.' And Tommy, putting his arm around me, added, 'And with a man.' And for the second time he kissed me on the lips and I felt strangely happy. It was the first time I had actually felt this way since I had lost Nardy and I told myself it wasn't such a bad Friday after all. But that was only until the middle of the second half of the play when I was seized again by this awful pain in my stomach and chest and had to grip his hand tightly until it subsided.

4

Saturday morning found me tired and listless. I had gone to bed about twelve o'clock last night, only to be wakened up at half-past with the pain again. It stayed longer than usual this time and left me wide awake wondering what on earth it could be, and I decided when the weather cleared a bit, for they had been having it very rough in the north, I'd make a trip back there and see Mike and get his opinion.

So I had almost to drag myself from the bed at eight o'clock because there was only an hour before Harold's father would appear on the scene, and I wanted the child ready; I did not want that man waiting about.

Harold took a lot of rousing. 'Come on,' I said; 'that's a good boy; your father will be here shortly.'

'I don't want to go.'

'But you said he was going to take you to the pictures.'

'I don't want to go to the pictures with him.'

'Get up,' I said abruptly. 'Get washed. Do your teeth, then come and have your breakfast.'

When later he entered the kitchen and Sandy ran to him to give him his morning greeting by standing on his hind legs and licking his face, for the first time in their acquaintance he was pushed aside while his playmate said, 'Stop it! you soppy date.'

'Do you want flakes or rice crispies?'

'I don't want nothin'.'

Angrily I swung him round. 'Now look here! I'm having no more of this nonsense. You're going out with your father and you're going to behave yourself. He has a right to see you. That was the arrangement. If you try to alter those arrangements you mightn't like it. Do you understand what I mean?'

He understood all right because he sat down at the table without another word ...

By nine o'clock he was waiting in the hallway muffled up against the weather. And by five past when his father had not arrived I said, 'Go and sit in the drawing-room where it's warm.' He went, still not saying anything, and I went into the kitchen and began to wash the breakfast things.

When I next looked at the clock it was quarter past nine. Drying my hands, I now made my way to the drawing-room, but did not find Harold sitting before the fire with Sandy, who was now curled up on the hearthrug; instead, he was standing before one of the two china cabinets. The door was open and he was handling a miniature chest of drawers, pulling the drawers in and out.

'Harold! Haven't I told you about touching those pieces. You may look at them but I've told you not to take them out.'

In his haste to put the piece back on the shelf he toppled another over and I snapped at him, 'See what you've done!'

'I was only lookin'.'

'You weren't looking, you were handling them.'

As I closed the glass door of the cabinet I thought, I must clean them again.

Since coming into this house I had followed Nardy's method of twice a year polishing or washing the collection. There were over three hundred pieces in the two cabinets and not one more than six inches high. Nardy's father had been a collector of

68

miniatures, and I understood there were some priceless pieces amongst them, especially the miniature silver tea service and the silver and gold Louis suite. This little set was a delight to look at as it was upholstered in green silk tapestry. There was also the copy of an Egyptian coffee jug, two inches high and of a beautiful design in silver, with a filigree lid.

The cabinet doors were never locked; in fact, there was only one key which, the cabinets being of different designs, did not fit both locks. Whilst going through Nardy's desk after his death I had found a catalogue of the collection.

When I turned from the cabinet Harold was standing on the hearthrug, and he looked at me and cried, 'You're in a tizz, aren't you?'

'No, I'm not in a tizz, but you're in a temper ... *aren't you?*'

He now dropped onto his hunkers and began to stroke Sandy as he muttered, 'It's cold out, awful.'

'I thought you were tough,' I said quietly. When he turned his eyes up towards me and with a look almost of disdain at my stupid response, I was saved from saying anything further by the sound of the bell ringing, and I cried, 'Here he is! Come on.' And I took hold of his hand and tugged him down the room, across the inner hall and into the lift hall, just in time to see his father stepping from the cage. The man was smartly dressed if somewhat showy. He greeted us by saying, 'All ready and waitin'.' Then looking directly at me, he said, 'It isn't very nice weather for taking a day out, more fitting to sit by the fireside. What d'you say?'

What I said was, 'Harold is ready and waiting as you can see.'

'Oh, I can see that.' He put out his hand and screwed Harold's cap around, only for the child to jerk himself away and straighten his cap again.

69

'I'm a bit late but I can stick it on the other end, I suppose.'

'Yes, if you wish, but as you say the weather is rough and I don't suppose you want him to stay out longer than four o'clock.'

'Well' – he shrugged his shoulders – 'it all depends on what we decide to do, isn't it, laddie?' He now looked down on Harold who stared back at him without speaking. Then looking beyond me to the inner hall he said, 'It's bitter out. The first thing we'll do is to go and have a hot drink, I think.'

I did not take up the suggestion but said somewhat tartly, 'Well, that will fill in some of your time.'

He gave me a hard stare before swinging round towards the lift again, saying to Harold, 'Come on you!'

Harold, pausing for a moment, looked at me; and I bent down to him, saying, 'Be a good boy. I'll see you later,' and gave him a little push towards where his father was waiting, his hand now hovering over the lift button.

Looking at the child through the grid, I thought for a moment he was about to cry. I smiled at him and waved; then he was gone from my sight, and I turned and walked into the hall, where I stood looking around for a moment.

The place felt empty; in fact, it screamed emptiness. I felt I had to talk to someone and so, remembering my resolution in the night to contact Mike, I rang his number, forgetting that he would likely be in the midst of surgery at this time. Miss Price answered the phone, her polite tone enquiring who I was and what I wanted, and when I told her my name she said, 'Oh, you, Mrs Leviston. Oh, I'll tell the doctor. He's got a patient with him but I'll tell him. Just hang on. Just hang on.' It was another two minutes before I heard Mike's voice saying, 'Well, hello there.'

'Hello, Mike.'

'How are you?'

'I don't really know, in a bit of a quandary.'

'What's wrong?'

'As I said I don't really know. I ... I've been having strange pains.'

'Have you seen Doctor Bell?'

'Yes, but he seems to think I'm imagining them.'

'What makes you think that?'

'His attitude. You know I'm very good at picking up the aurae of doctors.'

'Don't be cheeky. Where's your pain?'

After I had tried to describe the pain he said, 'And you don't feel it so much in the daytime?'

'No. That's strange; I feel tired in the daytime, not well, but no pain.'

'How early does the pain start?'

'Oh, sometimes around six, or seven.'

'And it's never after two in the morning?'

'Well, as far as I can recall, no.'

'I'm afraid your Doctor Bell could be right then.'

'Oh, Mike.'

'Never mind, Oh, Mike. Now if it keeps on you go to him again and ask for a thorough examination.'

'What kind of an examination?'

'Well, how do I know unless I examined you. Get a hospital examination, there's a method now of putting a light inside, they can see everything.'

'How nice for them.'

'And for you if they find out nothing's wrong.'

'Except with my mind.'

'Could be. Could be.'

'You're very comforting, I must say. Anyway, I thought of coming up to see you.'

'I would like nothing better than to see you, but before you come you go to your own doctor and ask him for an examination. Now do you hear me?'

'All right. But I must say you haven't been much comfort.'

'I never was.'

I did not answer for a moment, then I said softly, 'You know that's not true. Anyway, how's Jane?'

'Thinking about getting a divorce as she never sees me.'

'I don't blame her.'

'Anyway, there's one thing you can be thankful for, you're not at this end of the country at the moment, there's hardly a chimney left on any of the houses, and I've had three in this morning almost decapitated with slates. The roads are blocked, there's been a blizzard raging for the last two days. But I suppose living in your sunny south you've listened to it complacently on the news.'

'Sunny South ended, it's enough to freeze you here this morning. But nevertheless, snowbound or not, I wish I was up there at this moment.'

'How's Tommy?'

'He's very well.'

'Still paying attention.'

'Yes.'

'Why don't you marry him?'

'Oh, don't start that, Mike, I've got enough on my plate at the moment.'

'What, sorry you adopted the barrow-boy?'

'No, I'm not sorry I adopted the barrow-boy. And he's no barrow-boy, he's an intelligent boy who will surprise everybody shortly.'

'Well, from what I saw of him that wouldn't surprise me. I must go now; I've got another lunatic outside ready to attack me.'

'Sorry I kept you, Mike, but I just wanted to talk to you.'

'I understand, lass. I'm always here, and the phone's handy, ring whenever you like. 'Bye now.'

'Goodbye, Mike.'

I leant my elbows on the telephone table and dropped my face onto my hands. I was fortunate to have someone like Mike, oh yes, very fortunate. And I'd do what he said about an examination and that light because I was becoming worried about the way I was feeling.

5

It was towards the end of February and I'd had the examination and I had known it. It had been preceded by a wash-out which almost knocked me out completely. Within two hours I was in the theatre, no anaesthetic, and the light certainly showed the doctor what was inside me, and I let him know it by the yell I gave. Then followed a barium test. What was left of me after that Tommy almost carried to the car; and I remained in bed the following day.

The result of the examination was there was nothing really wrong, perhaps a slight touch of diverticulitis, sort of a loose or weak bowel, so I was given to understand, which at odd times might cause pain, but nothing like the pains I described.

So Doctor Bell had sat back in his chair, put his fingertips together once more and said, 'What more can I say? You're healthy.' He had paused before adding, 'Physically, you're healthy.'

'Then I'm imagining this?' I said.

'Well, if you'd like to put it that way, Mrs Leviston ... Is there anything worrying you?'

'Not a thing.' And I could say this for Harold had seemingly reformed at school: I'd had a very good report from Mr Binn last week concerning him. No, I could say there was nothing worrying me.

'Perhaps,' he said, 'you should go away for a rest, a holiday.'

I didn't want to go away for a holiday, at least not

74

yet, and I told him so.

What I did was to go back home, look in the mirror and say, 'What's the matter with you?' Then glancing from side to side, I said, 'Hamilton, where are you? Please tell me what's the matter with me.' But Hamilton did not appear.

Then one Saturday morning about the middle of March I found something to worry about. I found another four pound notes, this time in one of Harold's drawers. I waited for him to return from taking Sandy down the road and immediately, even practically before he had his coat off, I pulled him into the bedroom, opened the drawer, took out the notes and said, 'Where did you get these other notes from?' He didn't answer for a moment, then said quietly, 'From the same place what I got the first one from.'

'Don't be cheeky, Harold; I asked you a question: who gave them to you?'

'I promised not to tell.'

'You are going to tell me. You won't go out of this house again until you do tell me, nor will you get anything to eat. You'll stay in this room until you do tell me, and I'll stay with you.'

He backed from me now and dropped down onto the edge of his bed. Then, his head down, he muttered something.

I bent over him: 'What did you say? Who?'

'The Captain.'

'*The Captain?*'

'Yes, *the Captain*. He gave them to me after we played cards, or chess, even when I didn't win, he said not to let on.'

I stared down into the boy's angry countenance. I knew that the Captain did not like Harold – all his hail fellow well met was a pose – he, I think, considered him on the same level as the Mohican, scum, and it puzzled him why I should want to adopt such a child. So why

75

should he want to give him money? Especially when they were so hard up that his wife had to baby-sit.

A few minutes later I slipped a coat on and went right down in the lift, rang the Captain's bell, then came up again onto the first floor, to be greeted by them both standing in the hallway, with a surprised look on their faces, and the lady greeted me, saying in her high-falutin' voice, 'We wondered who it was; we so seldom get visitors. But come in, my dear, come in. What can we do for you? Do you need us this evening?'

'No, no, it isn't about that I've come; I wanted to ask the Captain something.'

'Go ahead then, lady, go ahead, ask.' He was smiling.

'When you give Harold money why do you ask him not to tell me?'

I watched him turn his head and look at his wife, and she at him, before they both turned back to me when he said, 'Me, give Harold money?'

'Yes, five separate pounds.'

'Huh! Huh!'

Now he was huh-ing towards his wife: 'Did you hear that, me dear? Me giving five pounds away! Oh, Mrs Leviston' – he was addressing me again – 'would I allow my wife to go baby-sitting in order to supplement our income if I had it in my power to give away five pounds to a little boy?'

I was sick to the pit of my stomach and my voice was small as I said, 'You didn't?'

'No, of course I didn't.' He again looked at his wife who was staring at him. Then she looked at me and said, 'He said that the Captain had given him this money, really?'

'Yes.'

Her face took on a sad expression and she bit on her lip; then she asked, 'Where else do you think he might have got the money?'

Before I could make any comments the Captain said, 'What about his father? That fellow seems to be pretty warm, the little I've seen of him, the way he comes swaggering in here.'

'Yes' – I nodded – 'it could be his father.'

'Oh' – the Captain jerked his chin upwards – 'it's amazing where boys get money from: they do exchanges, sell bits of things. I shouldn't let it worry you. Then of course there's his family, you must remember that, East Enders, a rough crowd, and some of those barrow-boys have money to burn. That's likely where it came from.'

'But why would he say that you gave it to him?'

The answer came from his wife. 'I suppose the child is looking for respectability,' she said.

There was no way to answer this; it was a statement that would have to be gone in to, argued over. When I muttered, 'Thank you very much. I hope you don't mind my coming down,' they both exclaimed, 'Oh, no! not at all.' And as they accompanied me to the door the lady said, 'I will use the old phrase of making hay while the sun shines, my dear, so if you want to go out in the evenings I would take advantage of us over the next week or so; you see, my relative is returning sooner than she expected. Her husband is being transferred back. She had fully understood they would be away for a year. We'll be sorry to leave, it has been so pleasant here.'

I merely nodded, then turned from them and went towards the door, accompanied by the Captain. As he saw me into the lift he said, 'Not to worry, children get up to all kinds of tricks, especially those from the quarter from which your ward sprang. You've got to expect it.'

I actually did feel sick, so much so that I could have retched. After I had closed my door I stood gripping the knob for a moment while staring at the blankness of it.

77

I was up against something I had never considered possible. My charge had always appeared frank but now he had been proved a liar, and more, and facing up to this fact was what being a mother entailed. All the laughter, fun and games he had brought into my life sank beneath this latter vice, because stealing was a vice, acquired as the Captain had just intimated because Harold had been bred in the lowest end of the city; he had been brought up in a rough atmosphere. But enough of that! what was I talking about? There was not a more honest person on this earth than Janet, and her family might be rough-cast but each one of them, I'm sure, would have been the first to pull Harold up for lying ... or stealing by trading.

I turned from the door. What was I thinking about? I'm sure Harold wouldn't steal; he was too straight-forward, he ...

He was a liar. Hadn't he told me that the Captain had given him this money? Was that not a barefaced lie?

Indignation now carried me forward at a rush into his room. He was still on the edge of the bed, but lying on his elbow now. 'Stand up!'

He stood up, but not quickly.

'You told me the Captain had given you that money, didn't you?'

'Yes.' His head was up, he was looking straight at me.

'You were lying.'

'*What?*'

'Never mind, what, you heard what I said, you were lying.'

'*No, I bloody well wasn't!*'

'Don't you dare swear at me.'

He stepped back from me, crying loudly now. 'I bloody well wasn't lying. He did give it me, five times he give it me.'

'Harold.' It was almost a scream. 'I have just spoken to the Captain. He said he never gave you any money, and why should he when his wife and he have to baby-sit with you to earn extra money, so he can't afford to give pound notes away.'

I watched him dash round the bottom of the bed, stare at me from the other side; then, bending over, he punched his fists into the counterpane, and scream-ing now, he cried, 'Bugger! bloody hell! Hell! Hell! Hell!'

I wrenched him upwards and shook him almost fiercely. When his head stopped wagging, I said, 'Don't you dare use that language in here!'

The tears spurting from his eyes, he cried back at me, 'I will! I will! He did, he did give it me. He's a rotten bloody liar. If he says he didn't, bloody, bloody, bloody liar!'

'Stop it! Stop it this minute.'

My own heart was racing, thumping against my ribs like a hammer. I pushed him away from me and I sank onto the edge of the bed and from there I stared at him. His face was screwed up, the tears were raining down his cheeks. I could swear that he was telling the truth. But the Captain?

The bell rang, I pulled myself up from the bed, saying, 'Stay there!' only to be thrown the answer, 'Won't. Goin' to Gag's. Gag'll believe me. Goin' to Gag's.'

'You will stay there!'

Just in case he should carry out his threat I took the key from the inside of the door and locked it, and as I did so his fist battered on it and he yelled, 'I'm goin' to Gag's. I'm goin' to Gag's.'

I almost fell into Tommy's arms as he entered the hall.

'What is it? What is it, dear?'

Spluttering and almost crying myself now, I gave

79

him a brief outline of what had happened.

He did not interrupt me, and after I had finished he still remained silent for a while. Then looking along the corridor, he said, 'I'll have a word with him.'

'You'll have to turn the key; I've locked the door.'

I went into the kitchen now and sat down by the table. Why had this to happen? Why? Things would never be the same between us again, trust had been broken. And he wanted to go back to his grandmother's, not to his father I had noticed. Once outside I was sure he would make straight for.Janet's. I'd ... I'd better phone her and explain, I thought. Oh dear God! what next? I went into the hall again, got through to the corner shop and asked if they would be kind enough to ask Mrs Flood to come to the phone. I would hang on.

It was almost four minutes later when I heard Janet's voice say, 'What is it? What's wrong? what's wrong, ma'am?'

'There's a little trouble, Janet. I'll ... I'll try and be as brief as I can.'

I finished with, 'Once he's outside he'll make straight for you. I don't know what I'm going to do, Janet.'

'Mrs Leviston, ma'am, I'll say this before I see him or hear anything more, if he said that man gave him the money I'd swear on my last penny that he did. There's one thing about that child, he has every fault under the sun, but not lying; he always took a pride in standing up and facing things. I'll be round as quick as I can.'

'I'm sorry, Janet.'

I don't think she heard because the phone was banged down.

As I rose from the chair Tommy came into the hall. He took my arm and led me into the drawing-room and there he said, 'That boy's telling the truth. And I'll tell you something; I've never cared for the Captain;

80

there's something ... well, I don't know what it is, but I've met a number of his type, too much surface talk. I'll believe Harold any day before him, and I think you had better go and tell him you think the same.'

'He won't listen to me now.'

'Yes, he will. Tell him you're sorry.'

When I entered the bedroom he was standing looking out of the window. I stood behind him and put my hand on his shoulder, only to have it shrugged off.

'I'm sorry, Harold.'

He turned about. His eyes were swollen and still wet and his lips were trembling as he said, 'You seen him again and he said he did?'

'No, I haven't seen him again, but I believe you. I do really.'

'Because Mr Tommy told you to.'

'No, not because Mr Tommy told me to, but because I know now I should have believed you right from the first; you wouldn't lie to me.'

'Why ... why didn't you say that before?'

'I don't know, I'm sorry.'

'And you shook me, and 'urt me shoulders.'

'Yes, I know, and I'm sorry for that too.' I bent down until our faces were on a level and said softly, 'You don't want to go to Gag's do you? You won't leave me and go to Gag's?'

He was silent for a moment. Then his face twisted, his arms came out and round my neck, and I hugged him close to me, so thankful that I said a prayer, which was unusual for me: Thank you, God. Oh, thank you, for I knew in this moment if I had lost this child Doctor Bell would have been right in his diagnosis, for my mind would really have skipped.

I was sorry now that I had phoned Janet for she'd come scampering round and the whole thing would be gone over again. Standing up now, I said, 'Wash your face and then come and have a drink.'

I stroked his hair back from his brow, and as I made for the door, he said, 'Mr Tommy said he'd take me to a football match 'safternoon. Can I?'

'Yes, yes, of course. That'll be nice. Yes.' I smiled at him.

Tommy wasn't in the drawing-room. I found him in the kitchen making some coffee. He turned from the stove, saying, 'All right?'

'Yes, yes, I think so. Good move of yours to take him to the football match.'

'Don't worry. Come and sit down.' He pressed me on to a chair.

'I did a silly thing, I phoned Janet, she'll be round here any minute now. I was afraid he would run to her; he said he would.'

'Oh dear. Well anyway, she'll find everything back to normal.'

'I think that'll take some time.'

We both looked towards the door now as the lift bell rang and I said, 'That can't be her already. I ... I hope it isn't the Captain. What'll I do if ... ?'

'Go and see who it is.' He pressed me gently forward.

And a minute later when I opened the door into the outer hall I was amazed to see the Mohican coming towards me from the lift.

He was smiling. Today he had two marks on each cheek and they seemed to form deep ruts in his face making him look almost an old man. 'I'm deputizing,' he said. 'I've ... I've come in place of Mum.'

'Oh. Oh, come in.'

Inside the hall he stood for a moment, his glance flickering here and there as if he was appraising what he saw.

'We're in the kitchen just about to have coffee.'

He followed me, his shoes, the uppers of which had been made to appear like moccasins, padding softly.

Tommy could not altogether hide his astonishment

as he turned from the stove and saw the Indian. I had described the Mohican to him but my description did not live up to the flesh. I made the introduction fumbling somewhat: 'This is Mr ... John Drake, and this is Tommy ... Mr Balfour.' My short arm went out one way, my normal arm the other; then I said, 'Sit down. Sit down, John.'

'Thank you.' He sat down at the corner of the table, and as he did so Tommy asked him, 'Black or white?' A moment later I pushed the sugar basin towards him, saying, 'Sugar?'

'No thanks.' He smiled at me. I noticed his eyes again: they were deep brown nice eyes. Why on earth had he let himself go like this? Oh, what did it matter. Why had he come? That's what I wanted to know. And right away he gave me the answer to my unspoken question.

'If Harold said that the Captain ... so-called, gave him that money, he was telling the truth.'

'How would you know? And why do you say "so-called"?'

'Because if he's ever been a captain it would have been in the Salvation Army. But then, of course, they wouldn't have had him.' The furrows in his face deepened.

'Do you know him?' This came from Tommy.

'Oh yes, I know him.'

'How on earth do you?'

The Mohican smiled a small tight smile now as he said, 'Oh, me and my kind get around and mingle quite frequently with him and his sort.'

'He isn't what he appears to be then?'

'Not by a long chalk. Oh no, not by a long chalk, Mrs Leviston.'

I liked the way he spoke my name. 'But he sounds educated,' I said.

'Oh yes, you're right there: Public School; at least

83

until he was thrown out. And you must give him credit for trying; I don't think there's an occupation at which he hasn't tried his hand, at least not one that would befit a scion of the upper class.'

'How do you know all these things?' Tommy's voice was stiff.

'As I said, I get around.'

'I should like a different answer to that.'

There was no smile on the Mohican's face now as he replied, 'You might like but it all depends on how much I want to give.' And he stared at Tommy in evident hostility. Then looking at me he said, 'Holland is a con man. I recognized him the other morning down in the hall although I hadn't seen him for almost two years when he came out after doing a stretch for embezzlement. Beckingtree is his wife's maiden name. She's as bad as him. They muscled in to our gang up in Harrogate; they thought we'd act as go-betweens, you know, passing on bits of stolen stuff, but our lot wasn't in on that kind of thing. If we were looking for trouble we only had to have a drag or dress up like this.' He gave a slight grin now as he swept his fingers over his leather tunic, which caused the rows of spiked trinkets hanging from his neck to jangle. 'We may do lots of things that offend the public eye—' he now turned his gaze towards Tommy before looking back at me and ending, 'but nicking isn't one of them, at least—' his head went up now and he laughed deeply as he ended, 'not from friends anyway.'

'But why should he give Harold money then say he didn't?'

'That's got to be worked out, Mrs Leviston. To my mind he wants to lay something on the boy. What did he say to you when you went down to him?'

I told him practically what the Captain, so-called, had said.

'Huh! There you have got a clue in the suggestion

84

that the lad might have been doing an exchange. Have you missed anything lately around the house?'

'No, no.' I shook my head; then after a pause I said, 'Well, nothing that is evident. There are a lot of specimens in the china cabinets.' I half rose from the chair now, leant on the table and looked at Tommy and he said, 'Let's go and see.'

As we went towards the kitchen door, it opened and there stood Harold, his mouth agape, his face bright. 'Hello, Johnny,' he said.

'Hello, boyo,' said the Mohican.

'What you doin' 'ere?'

'Well, well.' The Mohican glanced at me. 'I drop in to say hello to everybody and to see you in particular and I'm asked what I'm doing here. He has no manners, Mrs Leviston.'

'He's very pleased to see you, John.'

'Well, I wish he would show it.'

Tommy pushed past us rather impatiently now, and we all followed him into the drawing-room; but there for the second time since entering the house the Mohican gazed about him. Then looking down at Harold, he said, 'You weren't wrong, were you? You're a lucky fellow. Do you want a lodger? I'll sleep under your bed.'

Harold pushed him and laughed, saying, 'You'd smell.'

'Oh boyo, no.' The Mohican's voice was serious now. 'That's one thing I don't do is smell. I have a bath every day; come hell or high water I wash. No, I don't smell.'

Tommy's voice again cut in impatiently, saying, 'Have a look here, Maisie.' He had opened the first door of one of the cabinets. 'At a glance, can you see anything missing?'

I scanned the shelves, then shook my head, saying, 'No, but all the things are catalogued.'

He walked from me down the room to the other

cabinet, and once more I was standing looking at the shelves. Then I said, 'Oh.'

'You miss something?'

'One of the chairs to the little suite.' I picked up the remaining one. 'There were two of these.'

'Have another look. What else?'

I looked again. 'The silver miniature case, it used to lie in the corner; Nardy said his grandfather had got it from a general. He used to carry it in his pocket when he went into battle; it held the picture of his wife. And ... and' – my voice was high now as I pointed to the back of the shelf – 'the beautiful Egyptian coffee jug! It was only so high.' I demonstrated with my fingers.

'Make sure it isn't on one of the other shelves.'

'It couldn't be.' I turned to Tommy. 'They've always been on the same shelf and I've never altered Nardy's arrangement, nor he his father's.'

I turned now swiftly and looked down on Harold, saying, 'Did you ever see the Captain come near the china cabinets?'

He shook his head. 'No; we just played cards or chess.'

'He'd be much too clever to let anyone see him taking an interest in the china cabinets, or anything else in the house. He's no amateur is the Captain,' said the Mohican. He now looked down on Harold, saying, 'I could do with another cup of that coffee. May he go and get me one, Mrs Leviston? Or don't you let him pour out?'

'Oh, he can pour out, and he can make tea or coffee as good as the next. Go along, Harold, and get John a cup of coffee.'

Whether Harold knew he was being dismissed or not, he didn't hesitate but left the room. And now the Mohican, looking at me, said, 'I know what you'd like to do, go down and demand that they return these things. But by this time they will have been exchanged

86

for a tenth of their value. And you'll have to be careful here because he would come back on the boy; you see you did go to him and ask if he had given the boy money. It would be only his word against the boy's. And as he said, boys are apt to do deals in exchange, and these things in here would look like little trinkets to any boy.'

'Well, you seem to have the whole business in hand, what do you suggest?' Tommy's voice sounded curt, which made me want to turn on him and say, 'You're judging him by his clothes, he's a nice boy.' Oh, what a term that is. But he was nice; I sensed it. It would not have surprised me had the Mohican taken umbrage at the tone, but he contained his immediate feelings and said, 'There are a number of shops he could have taken the stuff to, one in particular that I know of. The fellow deals with small bits like this. Could you make little drawings of the things missing?'

'Yes, yes I could, especially of the chair.'

He asked now, 'Have you a jewel-case or anything like that?'

'I haven't got a case but there are two trays fitted into the dressing-table drawer: one is fitted to hold rings, the other, brooches and suchlike, and I've got three or four little boxes with jewellery in them, pieces that my husband bought me.'

'When did you last look at them?'

'Oh, I use the ring tray practically every day; as for the others I may not have opened the boxes ... oh, perhaps for weeks.'

'Would you like to go and have a look?'

I left the room, and in the hall I passed Harold bearing the requested cup of coffee. It was white, but I made no comment; only to say, 'Mind you don't spill it.'

In my bedroom I pulled open the top drawer of the dressing-table and counted my rings. There were seven. Then I looked at the oddments on the brooch tray. As far as I could remember there was nothing missing from that. Now I picked up the first of the four boxes and in it there lay a gold-leaf spray of lily of the valley. It was a delicate thing. I recalled the day Nardy had given it to me. I closed the lid slowly on it and picked up the biggest box of the three. In it should have been a platinum and gold filigree brooch holding three small rubies and two diamonds representing the hearts and flowers in the centre of the exquisite work.

I closed my eyes tightly. My teeth were clenched together. I had the desire to rush from the room, spring into that lift, dash into that flat and accuse those two dirty thieves. Everything within me was racing. I quickly opened other boxes. One held a gold chain and pendant, the other was empty.

I entered the drawing-room, gasping now as if I had been running. I was about to burst out with my news when I saw Harold gazing at me. With an effort I held back and, looking at the Mohican, I said, 'Was your coffee all right?'

'Yes, fine.' I had noticed that the cup was empty and realized that neither the Mohican nor Tommy would ask in front of Harold what I had found. I did not realize though that I was beating my chest with the flat of my hand until Harold said, 'What you doin' that for?'

'What?'

'Hittin' yourself?'

'Oh, I have a slight pain. I think I've got a bit of cold.'

'I must be off,' the Mohican said; 'I have places to visit and things to see. I have far to go, being Thursday's child.'

Then turning to me he said, 'Could you get me that piece of paper?'

'Oh, yes, yes.' I went out and into my study and there made rough outline drawings of the things that were

88

missing, including the two brooches. When I returned to the hall both Tommy and the Mohican were standing there, and Tommy, while motioning towards the drawing-room door, said, 'I've told him to stay by the fire.'

The Mohican said, 'Well?'

'Two brooches, one very valuable.' And I handed him the paper and pointed, 'It's like that, diamonds and rubies.' Then I added, 'I can't believe it: she was so ladylike, so sweet, so friendly.'

Both Tommy and I now stared at him as, striking a pose, he said,

> 'False friend, wilt thou smile or weep
> When my life is laid asleep?
> Little cares for a smile or a tear,
> The clay-cold corpse upon the bier!
> Farewell! Heigho!
> What is this whispers low?
> There is a snake in thy smile, my dear;
> And bitter poison within thy tear.'

Tommy, who is a connoisseur of poetry, and who at one time before he became embittered against his mother, would declaim it whenever the opportunity occurred, stared at the Mohican and said, 'The Dirge of Beatrice'.

'Correct. You like Shelley?'

It was a moment before Tommy answered, 'With others, yes.'

'Don't look so surprised.' The Mohican was smiling broadly. 'Besides pot, we have our other pleasures.' And he turned to me, saying, 'Good-bye, Mrs Leviston. We'll be in touch, and shortly I hope.'

I made no reply to this but opened the door and followed him to the lift, and there I said quietly, 'Thanks, John.'

'You are very welcome, Mrs Leviston,' he said, just

as quietly.

When I returned to the hall Tommy shook his head and said, 'I can't understand him, nor that lot at all.'

'He's a nice fellow underneath.'

'Yes, perhaps, but why let himself go like that?'

'Perhaps he doesn't consider it letting himself go.'

Drawing closer to me now, he put his arm around my shoulder and asked, 'What are you going to say when they' – he thumbed towards the floor – 'phone up and ask about baby-sitting?'

'I'll say I'm not well, or some such excuse.'

'Then that will mean no more trips for us, unless you get another baby-sitter.'

I glanced up at him as I replied, 'There's always the Mohican.'

'Oh. Oh, you couldn't have him.'

I drew myself from his embrace. 'I could, you know. Definitely I could. There's much more in him than meets the eye.'

'You're right there; there would have to be.'

'They are not all alike.'

'Then why is it they all act in the same way?'

'Oh Tommy.' I visibly drooped before him. 'Don't start an argument, or even a discussion. I feel absolutely done in.'

'I'm sorry, but all this proves to me one thing: I should be here all the time, then I'd be able to take him off your hands.'

'I don't want him taken off my hands,' and I pushed him from me; 'that's the last thing I want done for me. I love him, Tommy, I need him. You'll always have to understand that.'

He stared at me hard for a moment, then said, 'Please, Maisie, don't make him into a greater opponent than Nardy; I couldn't stand it.'

6

All the week-end I was fuming inside: I wanted to get on the phone and scream down at that thieving pair below, or better still, phone the police because, as the Mohican had said, they had a record, at least he had. But, as the Mohican had also said, you have to furnish the police with more than the present suspicion concerning five pound notes and the missing pieces. And what is more, I'd had that dreadful pain in the night. I'd woken up in a sweat at about half past twelve, and my anger was intensified then by the thought of the suggestion that this excruciating pain was a figment of my imagination. And then on Sunday I hadn't had the comfort of Tommy: he had gone down to Brighton to visit Bella, a very nice oldish woman who had been a servant to his mother for years, a slave would have been a more appropriate title, and whom he had set up in a flat in a place of her choice when his mother's secret fortune had come to light.

So on this Monday morning I was glad to see Janet, at least in one way; in another, of course, I had a lot of explaining to do with regard to my frantic phone call. That she was upset was evident, and there was the same thought in her mind as to what I should have done about my neighbours, for she said, 'I told Johnny that you should have sent for the police there and then 'cos, little scamp that he is, he would never take anything that didn't belong to him. There's been a box in the kitchen for years where I leave the milk an' the paper money, an' me purse has lain about an' all, and that child has never touched a penny.'

Her indignation was evident all the morning.

It was in the afternoon that something went wrong with the tank in the roof above the bathroom: it would make a dreadful thumping noise every time taps were turned on or the cistern emptied. It was a modern cistern and easy to get at. I'd taken the top off to see if the ballcock had stuck, but that was all right.

Mr Brown's brother-in-law was a plumber and he usually saw to anything that went wrong in the flats, but because I didn't want to disturb the caretaker's teatime I left going down to see him until well after six o'clock.

Harold was sitting at the kitchen table, drawing. Sandy sat at his feet. I said to him, 'I'm just going down to see Mr Brown about that noise, I won't be a minute.'

He looked up at me, saying, 'O.K.'

He seemed to have forgotten Saturday's business, and yet not quite, because before going to school this morning, he had said, 'He's not comin' up here again is he, the Captain?' And I had replied, 'No,' then added, 'You'll remember what I asked you earlier on, won't you, not to say a word to anyone about the Captain?' and he had merely nodded.

It had been raining so I took a light mack from the hall wardrobe, then went down in the lift, and I had just opened the door into the street when to my amazement I saw Jimmy Stoddart coming towards me. He wasn't dressed as he usually was, with collar and tie, when he called on a Saturday to take Harold out, but was wearing corduroy trousers, a sweater and a loose jacket. His attire was casual, befitting his stance and manner of greeting: 'On your way out then?'

'No, I was just going down to see the caretaker.' And I motioned towards the area steps. 'Something's gone wrong in the tank, it's making a noise.' I gave a little smile.

'Oh, perhaps I can 'elp there. I can turn my 'and to anything on the job. 'Ave to at times.'

'Thank you all the same, but there is a resident plumber.' This was stretching it a bit but I didn't want this man upstairs. 'Is . . . is anything wrong?'

'No, nothing from my point of view except that tomorrow we are bein' moved down to Kent on a job an' I may not make it at the week-end, so I thought that I could take 'im out tonight.'

'Oh, it's getting on and it would mean his being out in the dark and . . .'

His chin jerked up and he laughed, saying, 'Well, I think I'd be able to protect 'im in the dark, what d'you say?' Then bending towards me he added, 'Both of you in the dark. What about you comin' along? pictures or some such.'

I pressed myself back against the stanchion of the door and all I could think to say at that moment was, '*Mr Stoddart*.'

'Oh! oh! Come off it now, you sound like somebody in one of them Victorian plays on the telly, shocked at the suitor's approach.' He let out a laugh and he seemed pleased with his description of my attitude for he went on, 'That's just how you sounded. It was funny.'

'Well, it didn't sound funny to me, and I consider it presumption on your part . . .'

'*What?*' His voice was loud. '*Presumption?* My God! you are livin' in a play, aren't you? Know your place, man, know your place.' Now his face was poking into mine as he said, 'You want to realize there's no class these days: Jack's as good as his master an' I'm as good as you any day in the week; you're only where you are by chance. Oh' – he drew his head back from me – 'you're a writer so-called. They say anybody goin'

93

round the bend could write what you've done.'

'Let me pass, Mr Stoddart.'

His hand now came out and pressed flat against the wall to the side of the door, his sleeve almost touching my face, and he said, 'I will when I'm ready. You've played the 'igh and mighty with me from the start. An' I'll tell you something now: I'm damned sorry I let the boy go. And if what I 'ear's true I could contest it on immoral grounds ... you an' the big fella. An' you know what? You've got a bloody nerve to refuse any invitation 'cos who'd pick up with you 'cept for what you've got.'

As my hand caught him a resounding slap on the face, in return I received a blow that knocked me dizzy. But the screeching of brakes penetrated the ringing in my ears. I was trying to keep my head still by holding it and my eyes were closed, but when I opened them there were two figures punching it out on the pavement, and Mr Brown yelling, 'Give over! Stop it!'

I saw Tommy's fist land on Stoddart's jaw, causing the man to reel for a moment; but then he seemed to be battering Tommy's head first one side and then the other.

I staggered forward, screaming, 'Stop it! Stop it!'

Mr Brown seemed to have disappeared, and for a moment I wondered why. Then my mind cried at me, Oh, no! No! Not the police. Not the police.

Stoddart now had Tommy bent back over the bonnet of the car. Tommy was no fighting man; he had been in an office all his life except for his trip abroad last year. I saw him now bring his knee up and Stoddart stagger back for a moment, then I put my hand tightly over my mouth as, locked together, they fell onto the roadway.

I was aware that we had a small crowd gathering, but when from out of the hall door the Captain stepped demanding, 'What's this? What's this?' I turned on him like a tigress, screaming, 'Shut up you! It's got nothing to do with you. You dare sp ... speak to ... to me.'

Later, when I had time to think, I was to realize that it was on the sound of a police car that the Captain had disappeared indoors and not because of my manner towards him.

Now I watched in horror as two policemen wrenched the combatants apart and dragged them to their feet. There was blood streaming from both their faces and it was obvious that Tommy was in a very bad way, because he could hardly stand but that Stoddart was still aggressive because he went to throw off the policeman's hold. And when the policeman said, 'We'll have none of that. Now come on. Come on,' Stoddart turned on him and there issued from his lips a spate of words that I hadn't heard since my first husband had spat them at me almost every night during the early part of our marriage.

The next minute two of the policemen were bundling Stoddart into the back of the car; and one policeman following him in, leaving the other to pull Tommy from where he was leaning against his own car and to thrust him into the front seat of the police car.

Then they were gone and the street was quiet. Nobody had spoken to me until Mr Brown, taking my arm, led me back into the hall, saying, 'What started that, Mrs Leviston?'

I stammered now as I said, 'It ... it was the boy's father. He ... he was insulting.'

Then pulling myself from his hold I said, 'I must go; they'll be at the station. I must see to Tommy ... Mr Balfour, but I must lock up. I'll take the boy with me.'

'I'll see to the boy when you bring him down; you can't take him to the station.'

'Oh, thank you, thank you, Mr Brown.' I now dashed into the lift and when, a minute later, I ran into the kitchen crying, 'Come on, get your coat on,' Harold slid from the chair saying, 'What? Where we goin'?'

'You're going down to Mr Brown's.'

'Mr Brown's? What for?'

'Look, all I can tell you at the moment' – I was bending over him now holding him by the shoulders – 'Mr Tommy has had a slight accident and he's been taken to the ... hospital. I've got to go and see him.'

'He's bashed up his car?'

'No, no; the car's all right.'

'Was he knocked down?'

'Yes. Yes.'

'Where?'

'Never mind. Never mind. Come on; get your coat on.'

'Can I take Sandy?'

'No. No, close the door.'

I now dragged him into the hall, leaving him there whilst I ran to his room for his coat; then as I thrust it onto him his questions came at me: 'Where did he have the accident? You've just gone down, how do you know?'

I pressed my lips tightly together before I said, 'It happened in the street as he was getting out of his car.' The last thing I wanted him to know was that his father was implicated.

When I reached the basement flat Mrs Brown greeted me with, 'Don't worry, he'll be all right.'

'Which hospital do you think they are likely to take him to? There's Beeside or Crunch Road.'

Hospital. The poor woman seemed stumped for a moment; but luckily, light dawning on her, she said, 'Oh, yes, yes, of course, the hospital ... Beeside, I should think.' ·

'Be a good boy.' I touched Harold's head. He looked at me intently for a moment then turned away, and I ran up the area steps.

Beeside Police Station was the nearest, five minutes walk away, four if I verged on a run.

96

I verged on a run, and didn't stop until I was outside the door of the police station. But there I stopped, my jaws locked tight: I hated police stations, I was petrified of them. I pushed the door open into a small hall, then another door into a large room. The desk ran down one side. Two policemen stood behind it, and a man in a light mackintosh was leaning rather nonchalantly on the counter. They had been talking, but they stopped and looked towards me as I approached.

'What can I do for you, miss?'

No one ever took me for a missis. 'I'm ... I'm Mrs Leviston. I ... I would like to enquire if two men, one of them my friend, were brought here a little while ago?'

'We get lots of men brought here, miss. What are their names and why were they brought in?'

I stiffened and my tone conveyed my feelings as I said, 'His name is Mr Thomas Balfour. He is a director of Rington and Houseman the publishers. He was attacked by a man named James Stoddart. Now if they have been brought in here I don't suppose they have escaped your notice and my name happens to be *Mrs Leviston.*'

The two policemen behind the counter were standing straight now, as was the man in the raincoat. The policemen exchanged glances; then the one in charge, adopting a manner similar to my own, replied, 'No, it didn't exactly escape our notice, *Mrs Leviston*, that the men in question were brought in. I can inform you that they are now in the cells awaiting attention from the doctor after being charged with causing an affray and avoiding arrest.'

'Mr Balfour did not avoid arrest, it was Stoddart, Mr Stoddart.'

'Well, ma'am, Mr Balfour will be capable of explaining for himself.'

'May I see him?'

'I'm afraid you can't, not at the moment.' He had taken pleasure in saying this and he was about to go on when the man in the raincoat moved nearer along the counter and caused me to turn on him as he said, 'Haven't I seen you before, Mrs Leviston?'

'I don't know, have you?'

His eyes travelled over me and rested for a moment on my short arm. Then his tone smooth and oily, he said, 'Aren't you Miss Miriam Carter, the writer?'

I glanced from him back to the two policemen who were now giving me their full attention, before I answered, 'Yes, I am Miriam Carter also.'

'I thought you were. I was at the trial up north when your ... your er—' He looked towards the policeman before ending, 'your first husband was sentenced.'

'You must have found it very interesting.'

I knew I was assuming the wrong attitude with these men but I couldn't help it, and I recognized too late that this man was a reporter of sorts and that I'd got his back up, as I had that of the policeman, and the fact that I was a writer would do nothing to soften their attitudes towards me. The reporter's manner had been rather deferential up till now but when he said, 'Is he your boy friend then, this Mr Balfour?' I exclaimed, 'How dare you!'

Oh my goodness, I did sound as if I was in a Victorian play. But heedlessly I went on, only now using the vernacular of the writer and making matters worse by saying, 'The connotation of boy friend that you assume in this case is wrong; Mr Balfour is my friend and he was the friend of my husband.'

'Which one?'

I looked from him to the policemen as if asking for help, for all of a sudden I felt like a pricked balloon and I knew I was about to cry: it was as if I was doing battle against three opponents and I knew I wasn't strong enough. I couldn't stop my lips from trembling or my eyes from blinking. I turned and went hastily from the room, out into the hallway, and there I stood for a moment with my hand pressed over my eyes before going into the street.

I did not run now but walked slowly and I had gone no more than a dozen steps when I heard someone coming behind me. I half turned to see the other policeman, the one who hadn't spoken, approaching. He was a tall man, over six foot, and he bent down to me and said quietly, 'Don't worry, Mrs Leviston, it's nothing serious, just a squabble. He'll be out in the morning. He will have to go before the magistrate of course, and he'll get a small fine. It's always happening.' He smiled now as he went on, 'The other one will likely get more than your friend because he had a tussle with the uniform.' He pointed to his chest.

The tears were sticking in my throat: I could bear the kindness less than I had the aggressiveness; and now they rolled down my cheeks as I muttered, 'That man, he was a reporter, wasn't he?'

'Yes. They're always around scraping up the dirt. But I shouldn't worry, he's got nothing to go on. Anyway, go home now and think no more about it. They'll both appear in court at Crunch Road round about eleven in the morning. It all depends on how many cases there are. By the way—' His long length came down even further as he ended, 'I enjoyed your book. My wife got it from the library, but the horse business tickled my fancy so I read it. And I remember thinking that the judge was right in what he said at the end about us feeling lonely at times and needing something to fill the gap and what better than an imaginary animal.'

There were nice policemen. This man was kind; yet he certainly hadn't looked it back in the station. I said, 'Thank you. Thank you so much.'

'You'll be all right.' He patted me now on the

99

shoulder as a father might but he could only have been in his mid-twenties.

'Good-bye,' I said.

'Good-bye, Mrs Leviston,' he replied.

Head down, I cried all the way back to the house. I couldn't stop myself; and I began to wish that the policeman hadn't been so kind. I went upstairs and washed my face and straightened my hair before going down to collect Harold.

'How are things?' said Mr Brown.

'All right,' I replied, forcing myself to smile because Harold's gaze was intent on me.

'Was he badly hurt?'

'No, no, not badly. He'll be coming out in the morning.'

'Oh, that's nice,' said Mrs Brown. 'And he's been a good boy,' and she chucked Harold under the chin.

After thanking them both I left without having asked Mr Brown to see to the cistern. Bangs in the roof could wait.

Once we were out of the flat and had entered the hall Harold turned to me and said, 'It was me dad, wasn't it, Uncle Tommy was fightin'?'

My mouth fell into a gape. 'Where ... where did you hear that?'

'I heard them talkin' in the other room, Mr and Mrs Brown.'

'You were listening?'

'Yes, I was listening, 'cos they were actin' funny. Why were they fightin'?'

I took off my coat and without further words led the way into the drawing-room, ignoring as I did so Sandy's barking coming from the kitchen.

When we were both seated before the fire I did not look at him but, bending forward, I joined my hands tightly together on my knee and said, 'Do you like your father, Harold?'

100

No answer came for a moment, and then he said, 'Not very much.' Then after a pause, 'No; I don't like him at all. Never 'ave. I liked me mum but she went orf. But that was a long time ago.'

Yes it was: four years and more was a long time to a child.

'Then you won't be sorry if you miss going out with him tonight?'

'Out with 'im tonight? No, no, I won't.'

'Well, that's what he came for, to take you out, because he's going away to work for a time and he wouldn't be here at the week-end. And ... and he wanted to come up and when I put him off he became—' How could I explain to him how his father had become fresh. I used the word he would understand and said, 'Nasty tempered, and he said something to me that wasn't nice and ... and I slapped him.'

'*You did?*' The tone was almost joyous. I turned and looked at him. He was grinning at me.

'Where did you 'it 'im?'

I too grinned as I said, 'Across the face.'

'An' what did he do then?'

My grin disappeared. 'He hit me back.'

'He did?' He slipped from the couch now and stood in front of me, gripping my hands. 'He hit you back, me dad?'

'Yes. I ... I suppose it was reaction.'

'When me Uncle Max knows that he'll knock his bloody head clean off.'

'Harold!' And I had begun to think he had so improved during these months he had been with me. He pulled his chin into his chest, saying now flatly, 'Well, he would. An' the others too; they don't like me dad. Gag doesn't neither; she'd swipe his ears for him if she knew he'd hit you. But did me dad push Uncle Tommy under a car?'

'No; Mr Tommy wasn't pushed under a car at all. He

101

saw what was happening as he got out of the car and that's what started the fight.'

'And now they're both in the clink?' His eyes were bright; he was enjoying this.

'Yes,' I said, 'they're both in the clink.'

'Bloody hell! Well, sorry, but ... but I'm glad Mr Tommy hit me dad, 'cos me dad hit you.' He reached out now and put his arms around my neck and as he clung to me and I held him tightly there penetrated the room Sandy's yelping bark, which caused my adoptive son to press back from me and say lightly, 'Listen to that little bugger barking his bloody head orf.'

His mouth in a wide gape, he stared at me and his nose twitched, his eyes blinked and his fingers jerked in mine before he brought out, 'Well, it's 'cos I'm excited. They always come out when I'm excited, but they'll go orf, they'll go orf. Anyway, listen to him.' And he pulled himself from my hands, backed two or three steps, then scampered from the room.

I lay back on the couch. They always come out when I'm excited. I would have to hope and pray, wouldn't I, that in future he wouldn't get excited and that they'd ... go orf. That's another thing I must see to, that *orf*.

What a night. What a week-end. And what a life.

Yes, what a life for a nondescript person such as I knew myself to be: my days should have been mundane, my life should be running smoothly, uneventfully. Even my efforts over the past months to educate had ended up with 'Listen to that little bugger barking his bloody head orf!'

7

I was in the outer hall ready to leave the flat on the Tuesday morning to go to the court when the bell rang and Tommy stepped out of the lift. His normally long lean-looking face was swollen, at least one side of it: one eye was black and puffed almost level with his nose; the lower lip seemed to be at least twice its size and it had evidently been stitched, and as he walked with a slight limp towards me I backed from him, saying, 'Oh! Tommy. Tommy. I . . . I was just on my way to . . . to the court.'

'I'm . . . just . . . on my . . . way . . . from . . . it.' His words were spaced and he spoke out of the corner of his mouth.

'I'm sorry, so sorry.' I held out my hand and took his and led him back into the flat. Janet was in the drawing-room dusting and she turned on our entry, saying, 'Oh my God! Mr Tommy. Oh my God!'

'And . . . mine too . . . and . . . mine too, Janet. But . . . please don't say . . . anything that will make me . . . want . . . to laugh.'

'Oh! Mr Tommy. Ooh! when the lads get a hold of him it won't only be his face that'll get it, I'm tellin' you . . . What did you get?'

She was asking all the questions, so I let her go on, and Tommy answered, 'Fined ten pounds and . . . and bound over to keep . . . the peace.'

'And him?'

'Fifty pounds and bound over . . . longer . . . term.'

'They should have jugged him. Who does he think he is darin' to make a pass!'

I had given Janet all the details; I couldn't have given her any reason for slapping the man otherwise.

'I knew he was up to something, dressing as he has never done before, rag-bag he used to be. But the nerve of it, him thinkin' he could get his foot in here. If I ever come across him again I'll spit in his eye.'

I tried to stop the flow: looking at Tommy, I said, 'What would you like, coffee or something stronger?'

'Stronger.'

'Will you bring the decanter, Janet, please?'

'Yes, will do.'

'And bring the sherry, too,' I called after her.

A minute or so later I had poured Tommy out a stiff measure of whisky and Janet and myself sherries. Tommy did not hold up his glass, nor did I, but Janet, raising hers, said, 'Here's hoping he falls off the scaffoldin' and breaks his blasted neck.'

'Oh! Janet. Don't.' Tommy's hand was raised in protest; then, looking at me, he said, 'I'll swear to you this moment, Maisie, that I'll never do a wrong thing in my life ... ever, nothing that will ever get me into a ... a cell again. Last night covered a whole eternity.' He drew in a sharp breath and put his hand to his ribs, then said, 'God Almighty! I don't know how they stand it. It's a ... wonder ... the prisons aren't turned into ... lunatic asylums.'

'Are your ribs paining?'

'Yes, two cracked ones. They say they can't do anything, that they heal themselves. Your son-in-law punches well ... with his feet, Janet.'

'Mr Tommy, you'll do me a favour if you'll not connect that man with me again when you're referrin' to him. He's out of our lives now and he stays out. Well, he will be when our Maggie gets her divorce, or he gets it from her, one or t'other. Oh, my goodness!' She

104

threw off the rest of her sherry, put the glass down on the tray, then said to me, 'I'll make a shepherd's pie. That'll slide down, 'cos he won't be able to chew with that mouth.'

As she left the room I sat down on the couch beside Tommy and, taking his hand, I said, 'Thank God for Janet and Harold . . . and you, my dear, for I don't know what would have happened if you hadn't come on the scene. And yet, if you hadn't you wouldn't have been in this state, nor have spent the night in a cell. Oh, *I am sorry.*'

'All in a good cause. It would be . . . gallant to say, I would do the same again, but not until . . . I get over this lot. So don't go slapping anybody else, will you . . . dear.'

'Oh, Tommy.' I gently touched his swollen face, then said, 'How are you going to business looking like that?'

'Oh, I'll be a sort of hero, don't you know. By the way, I phoned God the Father' – he was referring to Mr Houseman the head of the publishing firm – 'and the old boy came trotting along last night around ten o'clock and demanded to see me. He'd even managed to get hold of our solicitor and bring him along. It was after the doctor had been and declared I wasn't hospital . . . material. He was very concerned. He's a good old stick. He said I had done the right thing and thought it was real sporting of you to slap that fellow's face. I saw you do it, you know. I nearly ruined my brakes pulling up so . . . so quickly. Anyway, they would have got me out on bail, but the police doctor had said I was best left where I was overnight. Then I think the solicitor advised me to plead guilty this morning as that would . . . give the best chance of keeping your name out of it . . . and the way things went I reckon he – or somebody – must have got Stoddart to do the same. Maisie' – his words were coming slower now – 'do you think I could lie down for a while, I'm feeling ropy.'

'Of course, of course. Come on, get up.'

I took his arm and led him, as if he were an old man, from the room and into my bedroom. But there he stopped, saying, 'Oh, no, no; the other room where I used to kip.'

'That hasn't been aired for some time. Look; take your outer things off and get underneath the eiderdown and have a sleep; you'll feel the better for it.'

'Thanks, my dear. Thanks.'

As I left the room I thought it strange that Tommy should be lying in my bed where he had wanted to lie for such a long time, but not under these present circumstances.

When Janet left at two o'clock Tommy was still asleep. He didn't waken until four when his face seemed more swollen than ever and he had a splitting headache. I took him in a strong cup of tea and when he said, 'I must get up and away,' I replied, 'Don't be silly. And look; if you go back to the flat, who's going to see to you?'

'But I can't stay here all night, what I mean is ...'

'I know what you mean. But I've a chaperon haven't I. He's in the kitchen now demanding to come in and see you. What is more, and of which I was indirectly reminded in the police station last night, we are now living in nineteen eighty-four. So you'll stay put for tonight. By the way, could you drink some soup? I'm afraid Janet's shepherd's pie has got a little dry.'

'Nothing, thank you, dear; another cup of tea and a couple of aspirins.'

I let Harold bring the tray which, on seeing Tommy's face, he almost let fall. I took it from him, placed it on the side-table, put another pillow behind Tommy's head, then said as I handed him the cup of tea and the

106

aspirins, 'It's rather hot, be careful.' And all the while
Harold, struck into silence and mouth agape, surveyed
the result of his father's work. Then as Tommy was
about to take a sip from the cup, Harold exclaimed,
'Me dad did that to you?'

Tommy swallowed painfully before answering, 'Yes,
Harold, this is your father's handiwork.'

'Does it 'urt?'

'Yes, yes, quite a bit; he's got very hard hands, has
your father.'

'What's his face look like?'

'Well, from what I saw of him this morning, pretty
much like mine, but I didn't look closely.'

'Me Uncle Max'll sort him out. I'm glad you hit him
'cos he hit Mrs Nardy. I'm not goin' with him again on
a Saturday ... I'll tell him.'

'Come on, dear; Tommy wants to rest.' And I took
the cup from Tommy, put it onto the tray, which I then
handed to Harold, saying, 'Take it into the kitchen; I'll
be there in a minute.'

When the door had closed on him I turned to Tommy
and said, 'It looks as if there'll be trouble in that
direction. Anyway, I don't think anything more can
happen at the moment.' Then I added, 'Oh, by the way,
I've got some steak. Janet went out and got it. That's
the cure for black eyes; I'll bring it in.'

I'd said nothing more could happen. I should have
kept my mouth shut. It was about half past six when
Gran rang. Her voice was high as she almost shouted,
'That you, Maisie?'

'Yes, yes, of course, Gran. Anything wrong?'

'Nothing this end, but I see you've done it again.'

'Done what again?'

'Got yourself into the papers. My God! lass, you're
the one for notoriety.'

'What do you mean, I'm the one for ... ?'

'Well, haven't you seen the evenin' paper?'

'No, I haven't.'

'Well, you should get it. I don't know what it'll be at yon end, it's headlines here. Our name must be mud.'

I drew my head back from the phone and waited, and her voice came again, 'You there?'

'Yes, of course I'm here waiting for your bad news that you appear determined and delighted to tell me.'

'By God, lass, no, I'm not delighted to tell you this: two more men squabbling over you in the street, their faces bashed to bits, an' the heading "Local Authoress hits headlines again. Mrs Leviston, better known as Mrs Stickle, wife of the man serving twelve years for trying to burn her to death, also sports another name, Miriam Carter, under which she writes about her life with a talking horse." Then it goes on about a brawl atween the father of the boy you have adopted – I knew that would bring no good, I've said so all along – and a publisher by the name of Mr Thomas Balfour. Apparently Tommy saw you slapping the father of the child and him punching you back and so he joined in. My God! girl, what are you up to now?'

'Goodbye, Gran.' I banged the phone down and flopped into a chair near the telephone table. That was a woman who had loved me, and I had loved her. What changed people? One time she would have laughed and been proud of my name mentioned in the paper, no matter what the circumstances.

I pulled myself up from the chair, took my coat from the wardrobe, went into the kitchen and said to Harold, 'I'm just going to slip along to the paper shop.'

'I'll go for you.'

'No, no; you stay with Sandy; he misses you when you go out and he doesn't see you all day. I ... I won't be a minute or so.'

The paper shop was three streets away and just about to close. I bought two evening papers: the London one and another I'd not seen before which

108

seemed more suburban in origin. When I returned home, I went into the drawing-room and opened the first one. I scanned the pages, but could find nothing and certainly not the headlines Gran had sounded off about. Then I turned to the other, and there in a sort of gossip column feature was that reporter's handiwork.

Talk about bitchiness among women! After revealing I was better known as author Miriam Carter, the writer claimed that 'in an interview' Mrs Leviston had denied publisher Thomas Balfour was her boy friend, at least not as generally understood today, merely a close friend. How close she hadn't specified. Then he went on to say that Stoddart had stated after leaving court that he was unwarrantably attacked by Mrs Leviston's friend because the said friend thought he had struck Mrs Leviston when all he had done was try to evade a second blow from her, provoked by nothing more than his inviting her to accompany him and his son, whom she had recently adopted, out for the evening.

I put the pad of my thumb in my mouth and bit on it till I could stand the hurt no longer. Then my eyes returned to the end of the piece, and there I saw myself described as: 'a small woman, in looks and stature reminiscent of the late Edith Piaf, but not – one ventures to think – with quite the same personality. And yet, it would seem men are prepared to fight over her!'

I would see my solicitor. I knew Edith Piaf had been a wonderful singer with a strong personality, but she had died twenty years ago when I was still at school and photographs I'd seen suggested she had been oldish and a little wizened woman.

Well, wasn't I a little plain woman? I felt sick, so sick and alone I wanted someone to hang on to, to clutch at, to hold me. Life was getting me down and strangely not by catastrophes but by niggling occurrences which were sapping me both physically and mentally, the former definitely through that pain in my stomach ...

I did not tell Tommy of the newspaper report for he, too, I knew, was very low: his ribs were paining, his head was throbbing, his mouth seemed more swollen than ever. When I had insisted he must stay the night he hadn't protested over much. He had said it was the first time since his schooldays that he had been in a scrap and he was definitely out of practice.

It was just after eight o'clock when the phone rang again and I welcomed the sound of Mike's voice. 'How are you?' he said.

'Pretty ropy at the moment,' I answered.

'Gran was in the surgery tonight.'

'Oh yes?' I knew what was coming.

'Don't worry your head about that report; you've got to get used to that kind of thing.'

'What, have two men fighting over me?'

'Oh, Maisie, the things that happen to you. Elizabeth Taylor will soon have to look to her laurels with this kind of competition.'

'Mike, don't joke about this.'

'You've got to joke about it, you've got to laugh about it, girl. Anyway, I haven't phoned up about that. I'm attending a conference in Brighton at the weekend, Friday till Monday, and it was my intention to look in. Besides wanting to see your funny face again, I'd thought we'd have a talk about this strange disease of yours. I'm not happy about the sound of it; it's gone on too long. You still getting the pain?'

'Yes, I am, and it was bad last night.'

'Aggravated by worry, I suppose.'

'It needs no aggravation, Mike. When I'm feeling perfectly all right it hits me, and it's getting me down. I'm ... I'm so glad you're coming, Mike. When I said I was coming up to see you I fully expected to, but now

110

... well, I don't think I could stand the journey; I feel so weak at times. Oh, I'll be glad to see you, Mike. I wish you were here at this moment; I want a shoulder to cry on.'

'Where's Tommy?'

'In my bed, *Doctor Kane*, at this moment.'

'You don't say!'

'I do say. I also say that the poor fellow's in a bit of a mess.'

'My! my! Anyway, I must be off now, I've got some calls to make because I'm the only doctor in Fellburn, or in the whole of the county for that matter.'

'You are?'

'Yes, I'm positive of it, because during my nights on call the phone never stops ringing.'

'You've got two partners, what about them?'

'Oh, they're no good. I tell you, I'm the only real doctor about, so I must away.' Then his jocular tone changing, he said, 'Good-bye, dear. Keep your pecker up, and when things get bad just remember that people are sinking all around you but you are on a raft.'

People sinking all around you but you are on a raft.

That was telling me there were many worse off than myself. At one time Hamilton would have put in an appearance and I would have nodded at him and said, 'Remember that and be thankful, you're on a raft.' But there was no Hamilton now. I might be on a raft, but it was a straw one.

111

8

It had been an eventful week. I had to call the doctor in to see to Tommy.

Doctor Bell had apparently read the evening paper, so he did not raise his eyebrows at finding in my bed a man whom he had never seen before when visiting the house. Anyway, he said Tommy should stay where he was for the next two or three days as he was running a slight temperature.

Following this I scampered about: I went to Tommy's flat and brought him back some night clothes, besides another suit and accessories.

It was a weird feeling to see that big fellow lying in my bed. Nardy had been of medium height and slim, my own height hadn't been dwarfed by his, but Tommy's six foot two made me feel like a pygmy at times, especially when we were outside and must appear like father and child, at least from the back.

So busy had I been looking after Tommy that the affair concerning our neighbours sank a little into the background, though never for a moment actually forgotten, for whenever I heard the phone ring, or the lift bell, I was ready for battle, thinking it might be the Captain being barefaced enough to call. And at times I would feel irritable at the thought that I'd let the Mohican persuade me to hold my hand.

By the Thursday I was glad that Tommy was out of bed dressed and sitting in the drawing-room because I myself was feeling far from well. Strangely, I did not feel this odd pain during the day, but every night now it either stopped me from going to sleep or woke me up, and its effects were staying with me now long after it was gone.

One thing I was pleased about: since the fight, the child's attitude towards Tommy had changed. It seemed that he was pleased Tommy had hit his father, when it should have been the other way round. Perhaps I felt that Tommy too was seeing the boy in a different light for he had smiled as he said, 'He's a taking little imp, isn't he? And there's no doubt that he's been brought up among a bunch of men.'

It was on the Friday evening when Tommy was almost ready to go – Mr Brown had brought his car round from the garage – when the lift bell rang, and, bracing myself once again to meet the Captain, I went into the outer hall. But it was the Mohican who appeared. He was looking slightly different for the marks on his cheeks were vertical now and there was a sort of star on his brow.

'Good-evening, Mrs Leviston.'

'Good-evening . . . John.'

His gaze left me and looked towards Tommy who was standing at the inner door. 'Good-evening, Mr Balfour.'

'Hello there,' said Tommy quietly.

I still could not associate the Mohican's voice with his get-up and I had no doubt he could change it to fit the company.

'Feeling better?' he asked Tommy as he passed him, and to this Tommy answered, 'Somewhat.'

'It must have been a good fight. How many rounds did you last?'

I saw that Tommy wasn't amused and so I broke in, saying, 'Have you any news?'

'Yes. Yes, I have news, unless I find it isn't news to you that your neighbours have flitted.'

113

'Flitted? Gone?'

'Flitted, gone, yes.'

'When?'

'Oh, as far back as Tuesday. They must have seen the red light.'

I let out a long irritated breath as I said, 'I should have got the police straightaway; they couldn't have implicated the child.' And as Tommy, looking at the Mohican, said, 'That's that then; we've seen the last of them and their hoard.'

'Not necessarily; I know where they are and are likely to stay put for a time. As for the hoard, well, it's likely been spread around and, as often is the case unless it's sold abroad right away, it will be kept dark for a time and brought out later. They even have the nerve to bring the stuff back into the country and sell it. And it's legal. Funny business.'

'You know where they are, I mean those two?'

'Yes, Mrs Leviston; they've returned to the bed-sit that they lived in before they got the chance to take up residence here.'

His use of words somehow indicated the educated man behind that dreadful gear. Why? Why? There were drop-outs of all kinds, but the Mohican's kind was particularly sad to me.

'How did you find out?'

'Oh, I get about. And I'm not alone.' He grinned at me now. 'We're a kind of club, you know, we Cowboys and Indians. Oh yes, we have a lot of Cowboys among us; in fact, there's a place down in Kent where they play at riding the range.'

'You're referring to a different set of men.' Tommy's tone was cold, but the Mohican's was even more icy as he retorted, 'Don't you believe it! Because they come back on a Monday and take up a job they're deemed respectable, but they're the same as us under the skin.'

'At least, as you say, they take up a job, but how do

your kind exist? Where do you get the money from for your' – he paused and flapped his hand up and down – 'rig-outs and pot and . . . ?'

'*Tommy! Please.*'

'Oh, it's all right, Mrs Leviston, don't you worry.' The Mohican was wagging his finger at me. 'It was a natural follow-up question. Well, sir' – he had turned to Tommy again – 'some of us exist on the dole alone, and that is the word, exist; others amongst us get a little extra aid from the establishment; and further there are those like myself who run messages.'

Tommy's eyes narrowed, and I gaped a little at the Mohican while he inclined his head from one to the other of us as he smiled and said, 'Yes, run messages. It's amazing what you learn running messages and who you run messages for. It's amazing how some people are interested in what other people are up to.'

'Private detective?'

His head went back and he laughed. 'Oh, Mrs Leviston, don't get romantic. Me a private detective?' Then still smiling he said, 'No, I'm not a private detective, I'm a real Indian: I'm always on the alert; the only thing I don't use is smoke signals.' He turned now and looked at Tommy, saying, 'There's other work in the world besides sitting on a stool, and although those like me dress a bit way-out, we're not all thugs and druggers. Well' – he shrugged now – 'not on the hard stuff anyway.'

Oh, Mohican, why? Why? Not on the hard stuff. I felt so sad for him.

'Anyway' – he was addressing me again – 'I thought I'd better let you know in case you hadn't already found out. Another thing is, it's a good job that the single gentleman in the bottom flat has been away in Barbados these last few months or he might have been rifled too. But they wouldn't break in; that isn't their style.'

115

Not a little surprised, I said, 'You seem to know more about the goings on in this house than I do myself, John.'

'Oh, I only had that information a few minutes ago. Mr Brown spoke to me in the hall ... and *civilly*. Fancy that.' He grimaced which made the lines on his face seemingly become alive, like worms wriggling up to his eyebrows. 'Now I must away to run some more messages.' He glanced at Tommy, and to my surprise Tommy said, 'Can I drive you anywhere?'

The Mohican stared at him for a full thirty seconds before he said quietly, 'Thank you very much for the offer; there's nothing better I would enjoy than to get into your car. I've always liked Jags. But it would be slightly incongruous, don't you think, me in this gear and you looking the city gent, at least by your rig at the moment. Why, we would get our name up.'

Tommy was forced to smile, then said, 'Well, I made the offer.'

'And it was very kind of you and I'm grateful, but if any of the gang saw me spinning along in that I'd be under suspicion of leading a double life.'

'Well, aren't you?'

Again the Mohican paused before he answered, 'Yes, I suppose so in a way. Yes; none of us are what we seem, there's always the inner man trying to get out. And—' Turning to me and smiling widely, he said, 'And mine has certainly got out, hasn't it, Mrs Leviston?'

'Oh, John.'

'Mrs Leviston, when you say, Oh, John, like that, I could dash downstairs – in the lift of course – rush to the nearest second-hand shop and swap this lot for a suit.'

'Go along with you!'

'That's a point: one of us has got to go first; we can't both go out in that street together, can we? Can we, Mr Balfour?'

116

'I don't mind.'

'I do, so I won't embarrass you. Goodbye. But by the way, where's Harold?'

'In his room. He can't have heard you, or else he'd have been out.'

'Well, goodbye,' he said and turned away.

We stood watching him cross the hall and enter the lift, and as this disappeared from view Tommy said, 'Waste, utter waste of a life.'

'Yes, I suppose so.'

'Well now, here I go.'

When the green light appeared he pressed the button; then turning to me, he said, 'Except for the pain in my eye, my lip, and my ribs, this has been the happiest four days of my life.'

'Oh Tommy,' my voice was small.

Seeming to bend over me now, he said and in just as low a voice as mine, 'I never thought I could love you more than I did, but having lived with you for four days ... not nights' – he pulled a little face – 'you're even more dear to me.'

When he kissed me hard on the mouth I did not draw back.

'Take care,' he said. 'See you tomorrow.' And as he stepped into the lift he said softly, 'You'll have some explaining to do; we're being watched.'

'What! Oh, dear!'

When a moment later I turned towards the hall door, there he was, his face tight, and before I had a chance to close the door he had reached up, his handkerchief in his hand, and rubbed it across my lips.

I stood back from him, saying, 'What was that for?'

''Cos you always do that after Sandy kisses you.'

'Yes, but Sandy is a dog and, as I've told you, you shouldn't let him kiss you on the mouth.'

'You let him kiss you on the mouth.'

'I let you kiss me.'

117

'That's 'cos you love me.'

I evaded taking up the inference and said wearily, 'I thought we'd been over all this and that you liked Mr Tommy.'

He shrugged his shoulders and half turned away, saying, 'He's all right, but he shouldn't kiss you like that. Anyway, he's too big, he fills up the house. I like the Indian. He's been. I like him.'

My expression must have shown my surprise. 'If you knew the Mohican was here why didn't you come and see him?' I said.

''Cos I was makin' something with gum and it was sticky. It's for a present.' He glanced sideways at me. 'It's a secret.'

'Oh.'

'One day I'm gona have a rig like the Indian 'cos I like him.'

He now ran from me making war-cry noises with his hand across his mouth, and as I stood for a moment watching him I thought, Over my dead body you will. And yet I liked the Indian too. There was something about him, something beneath that weird rig-out that got to you. It had got to me anyway.

But why should the fact disturb me?

9

I waited with impatience for the sight of Mike on Monday morning and when I eventually saw him I fell unrestrainedly into his arms and cried before I said a word.

'Well! well! This is a welcome, isn't it, being drowned before I get to the door.'

'Oh, Mike, I'm so pleased to see you.'

He held me from him, then said, 'Well, I'm not so pleased to see you, not by the look of you. You hadn't much flesh on you a while ago but you're just skin and bone. Where's it gone to?'

'You tell me.'

'Hello there, Janet.' He turned from me as Janet came out of the kitchen carrying the coffee tray. 'Hello, Doctor,' she replied. 'You're just in time; you must have smelt it.'

'Not as it is, Janet; it's got to have a stiffener in it before it gets up my nose.'

A moment or so later I said to Janet, 'Fetch the brandy, will you, please, and a glass? I'm going to measure it.'

'Don't you bother with the glass, Janet.'

And so the chaffing went on until, left alone, we sat looking at each other on the couch before, leaning back, he spread his arms along it saying, 'Well, come on now, start at the beginning, at least of that pain.'

Strangely, when I tried to trace the pain back to when I first had it I couldn't actually pin-point the time, except to say, 'I think I had a twinge when Nardy was still in hospital back home' – I still referred to Fellburn as home – 'but whenever I had such a pain we put it down to Gran's cooking, all fries and plenty of fat. I think I first felt it as a real pain when Nardy was home here and I saw him fading away. I thought then it was the result of worry, and I didn't take much notice of it. Then after he died and it seemed to increase I naturally put it down to my missing him, and at that time if it hadn't been for Harold I would certainly, I feel sure, have snapped. But lately it seems to have intensified.'

'Describe it,' he said.

'I can't really, except to say it starts like a sharp stab, then turns into a grinding cramp.'

'Whereabouts?'

'That's another thing, it's nearly always in my middle, first to one side then the other.'

When he sighed I felt apprehensive and said quickly, 'I'm not imagining this, Mike. Don't do a Doctor Bell on me, please.'

'I'm not doing a Doctor Bell or anybody else on you, girl. You have a pain and there's evidence of it in that the flesh is dropping off you, because even after Nardy went you weren't like this. You say it's always at night that you feel it?'

'Yes, yes; but I seem to have a reaction to it during the day, more so of late, I feel so tired. Oh, Mike' – I caught at his hand and, my voice breaking now, I whimpered something that I had promised myself not to say, 'There are times in the night when I feel I'm going to die.'

He made no reply to this but sat looking at me; then he rubbed his hand round the thick grey bush of his face before he said, 'You're not my patient now, but who's to know? Get your things off and I'll give you the once over.'

It was like being back in the surgery again on a Monday morning, but I didn't smile as I rose from the couch. I went quickly down the room and into the bedroom.

I was lying waiting when he came in ...

What did I expect from his examination? I don't know, but I thought, He's doing the same things as Doctor Bell did. But then he examined my throat and ears, and when he had finished he sat on the side of the bed and said, 'From the outside, as far as I can see, there's nothing wrong; and you've had barium tests and the inside examined; and quite candidly, Maisie, apart from splitting you open I can't see what more can be done, at least to your body.'

'*Oh! Mike. Oh! Mike*, don't tell me I'm going barmy.'

'I'm not telling you you're going barmy, dear, but what I will tell you is, there may be something deep in your mind that is worrying you, and I think Doctor Bell was right when he suggested you might do worse than see a psychiatrist.'

I turned my head away from him and covered my eyes, saying, 'Mike, there's nothing in my mind that hasn't been cleared out.'

'That's what you think. Remember Hamilton. Where is he, by the way?'

'Gone.'

'Ah! Ah!'

I pulled myself up in the bed now, hugging the sheet around me. 'Mike, for God's sake don't suggest that because I've lost Hamilton and Nardy I've replaced them with one hell of a pain.'

His laughter shook the bed. 'You know who you sounded like there? Your charge. You only needed to add, What the bloody hell do you mean by suggesting ... et cetera, et cetera! Learning goes both ways. But listen to me.' He reached and gripped my wrists and shook them. 'Something's causing this pain,

121

something's causing you to look all skin and bone and eyes. Even at your worst, on your weekly visits I never remember you with great dark shadows under your eyes. Whatever's troubling you, and I fear' – he nodded at me now – 'yes, I fear, there's something in your mind that is troubling you, I say now, and firmly, do as Doctor Bell advised, go and see a brain char and have it swept out. He'll be the best one to advise you on that point. And don't be afraid; these fellows are just ordinary blokes who get paid for keeping their mouths shut and listening.' He smiled now as he punched my cheek gently, adding, 'Come on, come on. I'm sure there's nothing wrong with you that can't be sorted out. But that's the thing, it's got to be sorted out. Come on, get dressed, and I'll take you out to lunch in one of your fancy restaurants. That's if I can rise to it.'

'Expensive week-end?'

'No, no, that was all free, compliments of a drug company. My! my! the liquor that some people get through. I'm not averse to moistening my gums, but at these do's I can see the reason for some doctors' early demise. Still, we have one life and we can do what we like with it, and who am I to criticize. I was so sozzled myself last night, my last thought when I was in bed was, I hope I'm not on call . . . Go on, jump to it!'

I didn't exactly jump to it, but a half an hour later we left the house. We took a taxi into the centre of London and to Brown's Hotel, because Nardy used to like Brown's. He had been not an infrequent visitor there because certain American publishers made it their headquarters while in London.

It was over lunch that I regaled Mike with the story of my neighbours and the description of the Mohican. But it was when I came to describe Harold's progress at school and in a quiet voice recited: 'Give me the moonlight, give me the girl, and leave the rest to me, and I'll put a bun in your oven straight after tea,' that he choked. His mouth was full of ice-cream sundae one minute, the next, this was sprayed across the table, to the indignant looks of our near neighbour. And when I wiped a narrow streak of ice-cream from my coat he muttered, 'Oh, Maisie, Maisie, I'm sorry, but—' The tears were running out of his eyes now, and he dabbed at them with his handkerchief. Then taking his napkin he also dabbed at his glass and the table-cloth and the condiment set, and as he was doing so a waiter came up to us and, smiling broadly, he said, 'Don't worry, sir, don't worry. As I always say, a good laugh saves a visit to a doctor.'

At this Mike's head went back again and there issued from his beard a deep rumbling sound, while I, in my turn, almost spluttered now, as looking up at the waiter, I said, 'He is a doctor.'

'Oh my! Oh my!' The waiter too was laughing now.

Altogether it was a most enjoyable lunch and we lingered over it with coffee and liqueurs and the hovering attention of the nice waiter.

Mike's train was due out at six o'clock, and since he had expressed a wish to meet up again with my 'stick for her own back', Gran's description of Harold apparently, we took a taxi back home, and it was as I led the way to the house door that it opened and out stepped the Mohican.

Although I had already and fairly fully described him to Mike, his reactions were nevertheless similar to those of Tommy on first viewing the young fellow. His make-up was slightly different today: the white streaks were running from his cheek-bones to his ears; there were strange marks on his brow, and his lower lip looked scarlet.

'Hello, Mrs Leviston. I'm glad I caught you.'

'Hello, John. By the way, this is my friend, Doctor Kane.'

'How do you do, sir.'

123

Mike made no response to the greeting, he just stared; and even when the Mohican added, 'I've heard Mrs Flood speak of you,' Mike did not make any reply.

Turning to me, the Mohican said, 'I've been tipped off about one of the missing pieces, at least I'm pretty sure it must be from your description, it's the little coffee jug. But if I'm right, and as I told you last week, it'll be kept under wraps for a while yet. I know it's not the usual shop, and I'll have to keep nosing around – with a little help from my friends! – until a certain individual risks putting it out on sale. That's when I can arrange to take you along, or' – his face stretched, and the lines with it – 'direct you where to identify it. Trust me, and I promise to let you know the moment I've got something definite. Now I must be off again. Goodbye, Mrs Leviston.' He now turned to Mike, adding, 'Goodbye, Doctor. And don't worry about the numbness my appearance has caused, it will wear off: it falls into the same category as shock; a strong cup of tea helps.'

I saw Mike stiffen, and I put my hand out quickly and caught his arm, saying, 'Come on, come on.'

It wasn't until we were in the drawing-room again that, turning to me and his voice serious, he said, 'I may have been worried about that odd pain you have when I came in before, but now I'm much more worried about your acquaintance with that individual. Now Maisie ... Be quiet!' He wagged his finger at me. 'Let me have my say. About these stolen things. It's the police you've got to go to, not the likes of that ... because that lot are twisted, their minds are warped, and more so his kind because, going by his voice, he's had a decent upbringing, and apparently he's got a mind that works if his tongue's anything to go by. But it's working, like all of his kin, in the wrong direction, sustained by drugs.'

'Mike, Mike, I don't think ...' If I could have gone on

124

and said, I don't think he's connected with drugs, it wouldn't have been absolutely true, but Mike's finger was still stabbing at me as he said, 'And don't you say, you don't think he's on drugs, that get-up is the first indication of it.'

Now I did put in, 'Oh, Mike, no, don't go by his clothes, please. There are lots of youngsters dressed like that and they are not on drugs. I'm sure of it.'

'You can be sure of nothing with that lot, Maisie; you've had no experience of them. You want to see some of the poor creatures who are inveigled into that life fighting withdrawal symptoms, screaming like tortured wild animals, willing that you should cut off their hand if only you give them some of the poison. And that fellow, he's got brains and has the makings of a pusher. Oh, they're very suave fellows the pushers. And he's right in the middle of his own set, I suppose, if in fact, not leading it. I tell you, Maisie, break off all connections with him. Cut your losses with regards to the silver and your miniatures, it will be worth it in the end.'

'Mike' – my voice was loud now – 'are you suggesting he'll get me on drugs?'

'No, I'm not suggesting it, but as you've mentioned it, it could be a possibility.'

'*Oh, Mike.*'

'Never mind, *oh Mike*, in that tone of voice; you know nothing about what goes on in his kind of life. I wish I could take you down to the police cells one night, that would open your eyes. And tell me this, has he got a job, at least one that you know of?'

No, he hadn't, not as far as I knew, and he made those odd trips away. Oh, I hoped Mike wasn't right because ... yes, as I had admitted to myself before, I liked the Mohican; there was something about him ... Yes, there was something about him, and likely this is what got other people. Perhaps Mike was right after all.

I swept the thought away by saying, 'He's Janet's daughter's boy friend. As far as I know he's on the dole.' Then my attitude and voice softening, I said, 'Oh, Mike, I know you're concerned and I'll take heed of what you say, I'll be careful and I'll try to find out more about him.'

'Don't do any such thing, Maisie, just drop him.'

'But, Mike, it's very rarely I see him. I haven't met up with him more than four times altogether.'

'Well, all I can say is his manner seemed very familiar for four times, even his Mrs Leviston had a touch of familiarity about it.'

I laughed now, saying, 'Come on; sit down, and draw in those bristles from your beard, you look like a porcupine. Anyway, I've always wanted to ask you, how does Jane put up with that forest on your face?'

His jocular manner returning, he said, 'She likes it: she buries herself in it at night, it keeps her warm.'

I was about to leave him to go and make the tea when the lift bell rang. Turning, I said, 'That'll be the boyo.'

A minute later Harold came barging into the hall, crying, 'I gorra star.'

'You've *got* a star. Is that what you said?'

'Yes, yes, I gorra star for writin'.'

'You *got* a star.'

'Oh, you, I ... got ... a ... star.'

'That's better. We've got a visitor.'

'Who?'

'Come and see.' I took his hand, and when we entered the drawing-room and he saw Mike sitting on the couch he smiled and walked slowly towards him.

'Well, say hello to Doctor Kane.'

My charge did not say, Hello, or, Hello Doctor Kane, but, his smile turning into a grin and casting a sidelong glance up at me, a mischievous wicked look that always preceded some cheeky remark he was about to make, he said, 'Flannagan's dog!'

126

For the second time that afternoon Mike let out a bellow. I too laughed because during the conversation that had ensued after their first meeting Harold had likened Mike to Flannagan's dog.

When the laughter died down, Mike said, 'I've had my beard trimmed this week, let me tell you, sir.'

'It still looks raggy.'

Mike now looked at me, saying, 'Apparently the education of this young man hasn't reached the social graces yet. Anyway' – he held out his hand towards Harold – 'come and sit down here and tell me what you've been up to at that school of yours. And in the meantime, Mrs Leviston, you can go out and make that cup of tea.'

I left the room smiling; but as I prepared the tea my thoughts kept dwelling on the Mohican. I knew Mike was right in most of what he said, and I wondered why I should be so concerned that the Mohican should not be involved in the drug racket. Surely, if he had been, I told myself, the men in Janet's family would have found out something about him before now. And as for Janet herself, she would not have let her daughter bring him into the house. Yet, what had Janet said to me a while ago? They make their own friends these days and if you say anything against them you don't see them or their friends. That's the pass families have come to in this day and age.

As I entered the room Mike was saying, 'Oh, I know a funnier rhyme than that. I used to say it when I was a boy. It went like this:

There was a bloomin' spuggy
Went up a bloomin' spout,
And then the bloomin' rain came down
And washed that bloomin' spuggy out.
Up came the bloomin' sun and dried up the bloomin'
    rain,

And then that bloomin' spuggy
Went up the bloomin' spout again.'

It was years since I'd heard that one, and as Mike
finished the last line in a rush as it was meant to be
said, Harold lay back on the couch, drew up his knees
and rocked himself while laughing hilariously.

Suddenly stopping, he said, 'What's a spuggy?'

'A sparrow.'

'A sparrow. Cor! we call sparrows spadgers. And I
know a funny one, me Uncle Max sings it.'

'Harold!' There was a reprimand in my tone, and he
looked up at me, saying, 'It's all right, there's no
swearin' in it.'

'I'm not worried so much about the swearing ... at
least, I am and everything else your Uncle Max sings.'

'Me Uncle Max's funny.'

'It all depends on what you call funny.'

'Come on, come on,' said Mike, 'let's hear it, what
your Uncle Max says.'

'Now Mike!'

'Oh, woman, be quiet! We are boys together. Come
on, Harold, let's hear your Uncle Max's funny one.'

'Can I?' His face was bright, his eyes shining as he
appealed to me.

'If there's no swearing in it.'

'No, there's no swearin' in it.'

'You're sure?'

'Yes, it goes to "Rule Britannia".'

I started to pour the tea before I said, 'All right, go
on.'

So he began in that surprising, beautifully clear
voice. Now he sang:

> 'Rule Britannia,
> Eat kippers when they're ripe,
> Fish ... ish never, never, nev ... ver
> shall be tripe.'

128

I saw Mike's stomach wobbling; then before I had time to make any comment on the silliness of the words, Harold went into the next part. The tune changing, he sang:

'Alway ... ays, wear ... ear your bikini in the sun,
And pa ... a ... a ... a ... anties too ... oo ... oo ... oo ... oo!
And be a goo ... ood girl, now come, come, co ... ome, come,
Else you'll get bli ... i ... i ... isters on your bum!'

Mike had turned his face away from the vocalist, but I hadn't.

'I don't think that's funny, Harold; it's silly.'

''Tisn't. There's a lot more, an' Uncle Max says ...'

'I don't want to hear any more of what your Uncle Max says.'

His eyes blinking, Mike now turned to Harold, saying, 'You've got a fine voice there, young fellow.'

'I know, an' I'm goin' in the choir with it.'

'God help the choir.' Mike's words were muffled in laughter, and Harold said, 'What did you say?'

'I said, Good for the choir ... Is your Uncle Max in the choir?'

Now it was Harold's turn to throw himself into a paroxysm of laughter, and when it was over and looking at Mike, he said, 'No, silly, me Uncle Max sings in the pub.'

'Yes, of course he would. Of course he would. As you said, it's silly of me.'

When I handed Mike a cup of tea he said, 'I envy you, you know; he's doing the same for you as you did for me on those far gone Monday mornings.'

'You think so?' My voice was flat.

'Sure of it.'

Harold was quick to take the conversation up,

asking Mike now, 'What did yer do for her on Monday mornin's?'

'Oh, I gave her a dose of castor oil and watered her horse.'

When Harold now punched him in the arm, saying, 'You're funnin',' I cried at him, 'Don't do that! Harold.'

'Well, he's funnin'.'

'So are you.'

'I know another ...'

'We don't want to hear any more, Harold, at least none of your Uncle Max's compositions. Now sit up straight and have your tea unless you want to have it in the kitchen.'

'No, I don't want to have it in the kitchen, but can I bring Sandy in? I haven't seen him.'

'No you may not bring Sandy in.'

'Aw!' This protest came from Mike, and I drew in a long deep breath, and when he said, 'I wouldn't mind going into the kitchen and having my tea with Sandy,' I said harshly, 'Doctor Kane!'

'Yes, Mrs Leviston?'

Harold looked from one to the other, and when I said, 'Go on ... fetch him in,' he sprang from the couch and ran down the room.

I looked sternly at Mike. 'I wouldn't want to attempt to bring up that boy if you were in the house all the time.'

'You know something, Maisie? As long as you've got him I'm not really going to worry about you, with your mysterious pains in the stomach and your questionable Indians.'

From the moment Harold came bouncing back into the room accompanied by the equally bouncing Sandy our conversation became general. And when at half past five Mike left to catch his train his last words to me were, 'See Doctor Bell as soon as you can about that other business, eh?'

'As you say, Doctor. As you say.'

On the Tuesday morning I saw Doctor Bell. He was pleased at my decision. He rang up immediately and tried to make an early appointment for me, but the earliest I could get, apparently, was a week come Wednesday, eight days time.

And it should happen that I didn't go to see the psychiatrist.

10

It was on the Thursday night about eleven o'clock, only a short while before I'd said goodbye to Tommy and he had put his arms around me and said, 'Maisie, I'm worried about you. Look, until you make up your mind to marry me ... And you will, you will one of these days, I know you will. You must. I couldn't feel about you the way I do without a little of it rubbing off on you, and then coming back to me. So, until then, what about me coming and staying here? Just to be near you. It's '84; nobody cares a damn what people do. And the time is going on; the older one gets the quicker it goes, and a day not spent near you is a day lost. What do you say?'

What I had said was, and gently, that I couldn't and that he was to give me a little more time. And I had added, 'Let me get this pain business cleared up first; I don't want to take you as a night nurse.' I had laughed but he hadn't.

After locking up I had looked in on Harold who had been asleep these past two hours. He was lying curled up in a ball and looked almost angelic. But he was no cherub, was Harold. I then went to bed, but I did not go straight to sleep, I lay awake waiting for the pain to start, but it didn't, and I was about to fall off to sleep when I experienced the most strange sensation: I was choking; it was as if I was dreaming I was choking. I turned from side to side and tried to throw something off, I didn't know what, I knew only that I was choking.

I tried to cry out but no sound came, like in a dream when you are calling for help, when your voice is but a squeak...

I remembered no more, until I woke up hours later. I looked at the clock. It was twenty-past six. I'd had a good night's rest, an unbroken night.

I rose slowly from the bed, but feeling somewhat strange. I had no way of explaining the feeling, only that I wasn't worrying that this was Friday and tomorrow was the day when Jimmy Stoddart would call for his son. I would meet that obstacle when it arose, I told myself.

I had made a pot of tea and taken it into the drawing-room, switched on the electric fire, sat down and finished a second cup of tea. Only then did I question how I felt. And I could give myself no explanation why the night past was the only night for months that I hadn't been racked more or less with that pain...

The day passed pleasantly, and when Tommy called late afternoon and said I looked better – did I feel better? – and I said, yes, strangely I did, he stayed only a short while because he had been invited out to dinner at the Housemans and, as he said, you couldn't refuse an invitation to be present at the table of God.

Alone, only one thing was worrying me: Gran hadn't phoned, nor when I had phoned her had there been any reply, and I had tried several times during the day.

When about seven o'clock the phone rang, there she was, and her first words to me were, 'Have you seen the papers then?'

'No, I haven't seen the papers, Gran.'

'You're in them again.'

I held the mouthpiece back from me as if I were staring at her and in doing so missed something that she was saying. Then her voice came loud and clear – she always shouted on the phone – 'I've just got in. I've been on a trip to Seahouses with the club, and there it

133

was staring me in the face.'

I waited, then said, 'What was?'

'Stickle.'

'*Stickle?*'

'Yes. You remember him ... Stickle.'

'Don't be funny, Gran, please.'

'I'm not being funny but you said it as if his name was new to you. Well, he won't trouble you any more, he's committed suicide.'

If I'd heard the news of someone I'd dearly loved I could have understood my groping for a chair and sitting down and gasping as if for breath as I'd done in the early hours of this morning.

'What did you say, Gran?' My voice was small.

'It's in the papers, he's committed suicide.'

Stickle would never commit suicide; he thought too much of himself. 'You must have got it wrong, Gran.'

Her words were lost in the shout she gave. Again I held the phone away from me, and when once more I could distinguish her words she was saying, 'Headlines two inches deep and there underneath: Former husband of local writer, serving twelve years, et cetera, et cetera.'

'All right, Gran, all right. But,' I asked quietly now, 'how could he hang himself in prison?'

'Don't ask me, it just says he was found hanged in a wash-place?'

'In a wash-place?'

'That's what it says.'

'Well, in a wash-place there would be bound to be somebody about.'

'What's the matter with you, lass? Does it matter where he did it as long as he's gone? That's what I say, 'cos the way that fellow was made, twelve years would have been nothing to him, he would have had you in the end, of that I'm certain, and you know it inside yourself ... I've got to go now; I promised to go down to

134

Mary's. It's John's birthday, if you remembered.'

When I was silent the voice came at me, 'No, of course you wouldn't, you've got other interests now.'

'Oh, Gran, why can't you let up?'

'Good-night, lass.'

The phone went dead and I sank back into the chair. Yes, I'd forgotten John's birthday. But what did that matter against this other news? Suddenly I shivered violently, then shook my head again, remembering that strange choking feeling last night ... It couldn't be possible, it couldn't. I didn't believe in things like that.

I hastily pulled myself up from the chair. The phone rang again.

'Maisie.'

'Oh, hello, Mike.'

'I have news for you.'

'I think I've just heard it; Gran's been on the phone.'

'Oh, yes she would. Now listen, dear. I've ... I've got something to tell you, but I can't go into it over the phone. It's private, so I'm popping down tomorrow. It's my week-end off, I'll get the early train. I'll see you somewhere around twelve ... Are you there?'

'Yes, Mike, I'm here. I'm bewildered.'

'You'll be more so, dear, when you've heard my news. No more now; we're going to a show in Newcastle and Jane is waiting. See you tomorrow then, dear. Good-night.'

Again the phone was put down abruptly.

I must have been walking like someone drunk across the hall because Harold, coming from his room with an exercise book in his hand, said, 'You feelin' dizzy? You got a headache?'

I looked down at him but didn't seem to see him for a moment; then I blinked, saying, 'Yes, a bad one.'

'Will I make you a cup of tea?'

'Would you, dear?'

135

'Yes. But look' – he handed me the exercise book – 'I've got to do that sum an' I've done it twice an' I've got different answers, an' I've done it on the computer. Will you look at it?'

'Yes, dear, yes.' I took the book from him and he ran into the kitchen.

Sandy had been by his side, but now he didn't turn and go with him but followed me into the drawing-room. And when I sat on the couch he jumped into my arms and cuddled his head into my neck and I sat rocking him, and with each movement my mind jerked at the thought: It couldn't be. It couldn't be. Hate wasn't that strong.

Once again I was roused by the phone ringing. Slowly I rose and put Sandy on the floor. What now? Reporters?

When I lifted the phone I was relieved to hear Janet's voice saying, 'That you, Mrs Leviston, eh?'

I wondered whom she expected, and I managed to say lightly, 'Yes, Janet; who would you think it would be?'

She laughed, saying, 'Well, your voice sounded different somehow.'

Yes, it would sound different.

'Anything the matter, Janet?'

'No; I only thought I'd better tell you, you won't be seein' his nibs tomorrow, Stoddart. You'll never believe it, but he's gone down to have a talk with Maggie; he's goin' to try and stop the divorce. He wants to get back with her, so I hear. Oh, I hope she gives him his answer. But you never know, not with Maggie. And I understand her belly's full ... well, she's pregnant again, so I wonder what he'll do when he sees that? Hie back I suppose as if the devil was after him, for he was never a one to stand his own responsibilities, let alone some other bloke's. Anyway, I thought I would tell you you're let off the hook tomorrow.'

136

'Thank goodness for that, Janet.'

'You all right?'

'Yes, yes, I'm all right, Janet.'

'How's his nibs?'

'Splendid, acting like an angel.'

'Huh!' I heard her laugh; 'that'll be the day. Well, see you on Monday.'

'Yes, Janet, see you on Monday. Good-night.'

I'd had a peaceful night and had woken with a light feeling as if something had been drained from me. What, I didn't know, but I eagerly looked forward to Mike's arrival.

When he did come he didn't greet me with any jocular comment, but after being greeted by Harold and Sandy he said in an aside, 'Can you get rid of the terror for the next ten minutes or so?' And this I did by going into the kitchen and setting the percolator going and telling Harold to watch it and in the meantime to set a tray properly, and asking if he was capable of doing me a slice of toast as I'd had no breakfast.

In the drawing-room, Mike was sitting near the window that overlooked the gardens, and when I was seated he nodded towards them, saying, 'Nice view,' and I said, 'Yes; it's a lovely garden, it's a pity it's not used more.' Then looking at him, I asked, 'What is it, Mike?' And in answer he asked a question, 'How do you feel?'

I paused for a while before I replied, 'You know, I can't really tell you: it's as if I was getting over an illness.'

'Did you have any pain last night?'

'No; no, I didn't, nor the night before, Thursday night, although I had a most weird feeling around midnight. Why do you ask?'

'Well' – he let out a sigh – 'what I'm going to tell you

137

is off the cuff. It won't appear in the papers, I feel sure of that. Some things are better kept quiet, because both the papers and the television are accountable, in my opinion, for half the trouble that the young get up to. You only grow from babyhood to youth and then to man by copying. You see something on the telly tonight or read it in the papers, and you bet your life somebody takes it as a pattern tomorrow. Not that what I'm going to tell you is really new in that way, because there are groups at it here and there, but very much underground.'

'What are you saying, Mike?'

'I'm saying this: you've been the victim over the past year, at least since Stickle started his time, if not before, but definitely since he started his time, of deep, deep hate thought.'

I shuddered, and he said, 'Yes, the result in your case was your pain.'

'No.' I could hardly hear the word myself, but he nodded as he repeated, 'Yes. Definitely, yes. You see, it's this way. I happened to be working on a case with the prison doctor. I was called in as the second opinion. It was the morning after Stickle was found and I don't think ... This is really off the cuff, mind, and you must never mention it to anyone, nor the rest of what I'm going to say. Now I don't think he hanged himself, not he, he wasn't that kind of fellow, he was hanged by some other inmates, not yet known. Never will be, I should imagine. Apparently he could never have done it himself; he was attached to the pipe above the cistern and his feet were only a few inches from the ground. I don't think he was quite dead when the warder found him, but he died all right. It seems he was hated by his fellow prisoners, especially by the friends of the man he'd had a fight with earlier on. Anyway, he had a hobby. It was modelling. He worked with clay and, I understand, turned out some quite good birds and animals. Two men he had shared a cell with said he could even work in the dark, but what he modelled in the dark wasn't animals or birds, it was a figure of you. When his things were examined there was part of a torso that hadn't been squashed up into a ball – he had likely been interrupted – and it was studded with matchsticks.'

His hands were on my shoulders and he was saying now, 'It's all right, it's all right, it's over, finished, ended. He'll hurt you no more. So come on, come on.' He patted my cheeks quite hard. He waited; then he sat back on the chair and said, 'This kind of thing isn't unknown, but I've never known it be so effective before, except we do know now of witch doctors willing men of their tribes to die, and they die. I've not much use for the God put over by the church, or the devil either, but what I do know is, there is evil in the world and in so many cases it proves to be stronger than good; as it has in your case, because I'm sure if it had gone on it would have affected your mind, even if it hadn't finished your body off first. You know, you are not all that robust and the human frame can stand up to only so much battering.'

I laid my head back against the chair and said quietly now, 'He must have got inside me because I know this, the moment he died I was choking. I didn't have any pain in my stomach or anywhere else but I knew I was choking. And then I went to sleep, and on Thursday morning when I woke up I had a strange feeling. Looking back now it was as if I had been released from something.'

'You've been released all right. But now I must insist again, that you must not pass this on, not to Tommy or anyone else, because this part of the business hasn't been made public for reasons I've already made plain to you. Doctor Harper only told me because we're old friends and medically connected. Of course, through time it might leak out if there's talk, but by that time, should the papers get hold of anything, they will see that the recipient of Stickle's hate is alive and well and thriving.'

'Shall we have a drink?' I asked quietly; 'I feel I need it.'

'Why not? And why not lunch somewhere? But not at Brown's again; two posh lunches in a week is beyond me.'

'I'd love to, Mike, but I have my charge.'

'Well, we'll take him along.'

'Would you?'

'Why not? We'll make it his day an' all.'

'You wouldn't like to go and see the new James Bond film, would you? Apparently that's where his father was going to take him today but he had other business.'

'Why not? Why not? I've never been to the pictures for years.' He rose from the chair and pulled me upwards, saying, 'It's all in the past. Remember that. It's a new life ahead of you; nothing worse can ever happen to you.'

Not being God, Mike did not know my fate and what lay before me.

11

During the following weeks I felt myself a new woman.
I seemed to walk on air; a great weight had been lifted
from my mind. The pain had vanished with Stickle's
death, I'd cancelled my appointment with the psychiatrist, and Doctor Bell had confessed himself
amazed by the sudden and sustained change in me.
With each new week I couldn't get into my study
quickly enough to start writing. And when Janet
heard me singing about the flat, she said, 'You won the
pools, Mrs Leviston, ma'am?'

'Kind of,' I said; and the reply puzzled her.

Now, incredibly it seemed, we were in August.
Harold had broken up for the school holidays, and I
had let him go off to spend a few days with one of his
new friends. The Mohican had been largely silent,
apart from occasional rather cryptic messages to the
effect that he was still keeping watch; and then later
on this Thursday afternoon he phoned me, his voice
sounding very adult as he said, 'Mrs Leviston, this is
the Indian Chief.'

'Oh, hello John.' My voice was light, though tinged
with surprise.

'I'm sorry this has all taken so long, but do you think
you could meet me tomorrow morning? At last I can
take you to the shop where the coffee jug is; now on
offer, I may say as a solid silver antique with filigree lid
and inner container. Did you know it had an inner
container?'

'No, no, I didn't.'

'Well, at that size, it's a work of art to have an inner container. Priced at one hundred and twenty-five pounds. Cheap at that, I should say, because at Sotheby's it would likely go for two or three times that price.'

'Really?'

'Yes. Yes.'

Why was I thinking that the person on the other end of the phone was dressed as an ordinary human being to match his voice?

'Can you manage it?'

'Yes. But where shall I meet you?'

'I'll be outside Liverpool Street station, the main entrance. I won't ask you to come and speak to me because I don't think you'd feel comfortable walking with me, would you?'

I stammered as I replied, 'I ... I wouldn't mind, John, knowing that under that make-up you're no Indian.'

'Thank you once again, Mrs Leviston. Anyway, if you'll just follow me, I think it'll be better. It's about five minutes walk from there. I'll stand outside the shop and you can go in. Pretend you're looking for something. Don't remark on the jug or anything else you might see that's yours. Just take note. When you come out of the shop, there's a turning about twenty yards further down. It's a quiet part. Go up there. I'll be waiting ... And, Mrs Leviston.'

'Yes, John?'

'There's something else. In case there are people about and I can't have a word with you: I've ... I've got to go off for a few days, you know on a jaunt again, itchy feet; I wonder if you'd tell Mum to tell Hilda ...'

'Why can't you tell her yourself, John?'

'Well, I won't be back tonight, and as I said, I don't like going to the factory. If you would tell Mum in the morning ...'

'Won't Hilda worry?'

'Oh, I don't think Hilda worries very much, Mrs Leviston, she takes life as it comes. Anyway, will I see you in the morning because it's the only chance I'll have of showing you the shop?'

My voice was curt now as I said, 'Couldn't you just tell me the name of it?'

There was a long pause before he said, 'Yes, yes I could, but I ... I wanted to have a word with you, as Mum would say, private like, if that's at all possible. You see I ... Well, how can I put it? I feel you're on my side and I thought if ... well, if I could explain something ...'

I cut off his hesitant words by saying, 'I'll be there.'

'Fine, fine. Good-night, Mrs Leviston.'

I didn't reply but put the phone down.

Why didn't I tell Tommy that I was going to meet the Mohican in the morning? I spent almost four hours with him later on, so why didn't I tell him? Because I knew that he would do everything in his power to stop me, or make it his business to come along with me, and somehow I knew that the Mohican wouldn't like that ...

Next morning, when I gave Janet the message for her daughter, she put her hands on her hips and wagged her head as she said, 'That's just like him, isn't it? He never turned up last night. Our Hilda came round about ten. I was gettin' ready for bed. Had anybody seen him? she asked. Nobody had. Joe was there and he went for her and said she was a blood ... bloomin' fool and she wanted her head looked at; he was just playin' fast and loose with her. And what did he get up to on his jaunts? And when Joe said that he was likely on drugs, she went for him and said he wasn't. But to my mind she protested too quickly an' too loudly. Then I went for her, and I told her if I thought for half a minute she was on the stuff she

143

wouldn't dare put her face in that door again ever. And you know what, Mrs Leviston, ma'am? She did what I've never seen her do in me life, she started to cry. She said she loved him; no matter what he was, she loved him. Ooh! I tell you there was a scene, and at that time at night. And of course after she left, an' when one after the other of them came in, Joe had to give them the whole tale over again. And there they were, the lot of them, havin' a committee meetin' about it, and they ended up all being of one mind, there was something fishy about the Indian. And as their dad went up to bed he said to Greg, "You're chatty with that young market bobby, aren't you? Tell him what you think; it can do no harm and it'll put us in the clear if anything does come out about him."'

Self-preservation, I thought. But they were right to try to find out what took the Mohican away on these trips of his.

A short while later I said to Janet, 'I've got to go out to see my solicitor. I should be back before you leave.'

'I'll keep something hot for you,' she said.

'Thanks, Janet.'

I had put on a grey costume and wore a head scarf as there was a high wind blowing. I took the bus to Liverpool Street station, and walked over to the main entrance; and from there I saw, in the distance, the Mohican. He was standing on the kerb looking as if he was waiting for an opening in the traffic to cross the road. He looked first one way then the other. Then it appeared as if he had decided not to cross over but to walk straight on: he turned away and sauntered along the road; and I followed.

A short time later I followed him across a road; and whilst he was waiting to cross a second, I came up almost behind him. But when I reached the other side I let him get ahead. I had never been in this part of town before. It wasn't a business district, and it certainly

144

wasn't spruce.

I was now following him down a street that had a number of shops on one side only; on the opposite side the buildings looked like warehouses. I saw the Mohican stop in front of a shop window, then move on. By the time I reached the shop he had turned the corner he had spoken about.

I stood looking into the shop window. In the front were displayed two old guns in cases, behind them two naval swords, while round about was a conglomeration of brass and pewter and copper articles, urns and jugs and vases. There was a whole set of green plates, perhaps thirty pieces in all. To the side of the window there were three plates on stands. Two were Coalport, similar to those of my dinner service, and they were priced at thirty-five pounds each. Next to them was a smaller plate, the tag said Dresden. It had a tiny crack in the top but it was marked forty-five pounds. But standing between that and the Coalport was the miniature silver coffee jug. And yes there it was priced at one hundred and twenty-five pounds. And further along the shelf lay the portrait locket that the General had carried in the breast pocket of his uniform. It was open, and pinned to the faded blue velvet interior was a tag, which read: Solid silver nineteenth century miniature locket. £140.

I didn't go into the shop; I felt I shouldn't be able to act as an ordinary customer. As I turned away from the window a big black car drew up at the kerb and the driver looked towards the window, as did one of the two men in the back. At least that's what I thought at the time. I walked quickly down the street to a turning which brought me into a broad thoroughfare at the far end of which was another street parallel to the one I had just walked down, and about half-way along it stood the Mohican talking to another man as oddly dressed as himself.

As I approached them I realized they were arguing, and I had almost reached them when I saw the man grab the Mohican by the throat, but seemingly in an instant the Mohican twisted free and at the same time he yelled something at me. What it was, I couldn't make out, but I must have taken it as a cry for help, for I screamed at the man, 'Leave him alone!' And at this, the man swung round and made a grab at me.

What followed happened so quickly that even now I cannot explain it except that there was the black car again and three men pouring out of it, two of them going to the assistance of the Mohican's assailant and trying now to drag John into the car, whilst the third one, a huge individual with a nose that seemed spread right across his face, grabbed me and held me tightly against him with his hand across my mouth to stop my screaming. And all the time my dominant feeling was one of amazement that the Mohican could continue to kick and twist and punch at his assailants. But then the man who was dressed similarly to the Mohican stuck the knife into him.

When I saw the Mohican slide to the ground with the blood spurting from his neck my heart seemed to bleed too as my mind yelled, 'Oh, no. No!' and one of the men cried, 'You blasted fool!' and the man throwing the knife down whined back, 'He would have grassed anyway.'

'Not until he talked, you bloody idiot!' the man growled. Then turning to his companion, he said, 'Come on! Let's get goin', and pronto!'

'What about this 'un, she's in on it?' my assailant yelled.

'Throw her in the back.'

And that's what he did, he literally picked me up as if I were a feather and threw me onto the floor of the car, where I lay stunned for a moment until I felt his feet on me, and then I let out a high piercing scream which

146

was half smothered by the grinding brakes of the car.

A voice above me said, 'Shut her up!'

The next moment a hand came on my face and grabbed my nose. I opened my mouth naturally to yell again, and something was stuffed into it, almost choking me.

The voice above me said something again which I couldn't make out, but I soon knew when I was roughly turned over onto my face with the ease of someone lifting a shopping basket. And when my arms were wrenched behind my back my whole being screamed out, but silently, with the agony. When my ankles, too, were tied I was lying in such a position that I felt I couldn't bear it and prayed to lose consciousness. I didn't; I was kept awake through fear, petrifying fear. Tommy was right, they'd all been right, the Mohican had not been what he seemed, and now he had paid for it. Oh, the poor Mohican.

And me, what would they do to me? I had no doubt in my mind that these were dreadful men and that because I had seen their faces they would never let me go. And there was Harold. Oh Harold, Harold. Oh my dear Harold. And Tommy. Strange, but Tommy was fated not to have me. Dear God, why did these things happen to me. Why had I to get mixed up with such men, me of all people?

I must have lost consciousness for I didn't remember being carried from the car or arriving in this room or wherever I was for I was lying on a bed or a couch. It was soft and for a moment I didn't feel any pain; but just for a moment, for when I tried to move I experienced the feeling through my flesh and bones that I could only put down to being crucified. The last thing I could recall was being kicked. I had wriggled on the floor of the car and the boot had come into my side.

I was aware of the people talking. They were quite

near. I kept my eyes closed. It was a woman's voice that got through to me first. She was arguing, shouting. Or was she pleading? She was calling someone Bunty. I couldn't imagine any of those men being called such a silly name as Bunty, but she was saying, 'Now you won't do anything here with her, Bunty, will you? Promise me?'

'Be quiet! Be quiet!'

'I'll not be quiet. This is my place and so far I've been with you all along the line. But not that. And even if you did, you've still got to get rid of her. And what then? I tell you, Bunty, I'm havin' no Benson affair here, not above me shop. I couldn't stand it. I couldn't live here after.'

'Will you shut up, Liz!'

'No, I won't shut up, I won't.'

'I don't want to have to make you.'

'Now don't you start with that on me, Bunty. I'm warnin' you, I'm no green kid, you should know that.'

'It could be done quietly, Liz, with the needle.'

That was a different voice, and now the woman's voice came again, louder now. 'You shut up, Trucker,' she said, 'else you'll find that nose spread to your ears, I'm tellin' you. Give her the needle, you say, and then what? Little parcels goin' out of the door? You're a bastard. You always have been, always will be. If I had my way ...'

A third voice entered into the conversation now, a soft voice. It said, 'Couldn't you get her to promise to keep her mouth shut? Put her on the stuff ... keep her for a time ...' noculate her like?'

There was dead silence. I strained my ears, thinking they had closed the door or gone. I moved my head to the side. Then the first man's voice said quite quietly, 'Danny, when this load goes through I'm goin' to see to it that you go to a shrinker; he'll open up that bloody head of yours and insert a new brain, a monkey's will

148

do because it'll be better than the one you've got.'

'You're funny, Bunty.' There was the high voice again; it was almost like a woman's. 'I was only thinkin'.'

'Well, don't!' It was a bawl from the man now. Then the woman's voice came in, saying, 'And about this lot? When are you goin' to get it out of the store-room?'

'All in good time, Liz.'

'Never mind about good time. I spew every time I see a copper pass the window.'

'Well, you'll have to go on spewin' because I can't let it go all at once; I don't know what that bloody Indian was up to.'

'He and Patsy took the last lot to Liverpool, didn't they?'

'Yes, they did. But why was Patsy picked up at the customs later? He's made that trip to Ireland fifty times before. Could he have been a police nark, the Indian?'

'No, Danny, no' – it was the first man talking now – 'I've had him watched. Anyway, he's disposed of too many lots himself. No, he was featherin' his nest, startin' the game on his own, thinkin' he was a big boy because he had a bit of education. They always come a cropper that lot. And now he won't need his education any more.'

'I'm not interested in what's happened to the Indian' – it was the woman again – 'I'm only wantin' to know what you're goin' to do about her. But whatever it is you're not doin' it here.'

'Why don't you give her the needle and walk her over the cliff?'

'Just like that: give her the needle and walk her over the cliff.' It was the voice of the big man now, the one that had held me, the one with the flat nose.

Again there was a silence, longer this time; then the man I had come to think of as the ringleader, the one

149

who was associated with the girl called Liz and whom she called Bunty, said, 'I take it back, Danny, about havin' your head seen to. Why don't we give her the needle and walk her over the cliff? Now, now, now, that's a very ... good ... idea.'

The last words brought Harold vividly to mind for they were mimicking Max Bygraves, and again my mind leapt away from my present situation and cried, Oh, Harold. Harold. Then, Tommy, Tommy. And I felt I was choking and I wanted to be sick.

I was brought back to the voices again by the man Trucker saying, 'Beachy Head, Eastbourne.'

Then the thin voice, 'No, not Beachy Head; that bloody sloping green gives me the jitters. Hastings, that's it. You can take the car a good way along towards the cliff top there, up Fairlight way you know. Then what would be wrong to see a young girl ... well, if you don't look at her face, her build gives you that idea, walking along with her mother and father, say.'

'No, you don't! You bloody well don't get me on anything like that. Oh, no! Have another think, Bunty. Mother and father indeed! If you're doin' that kind of dirty work you're doin' it without me.'

The man's voice held no offence as he said, 'Well, she could be walkin' along with two friends, her father and her brother, me or Trucker or Danny there.'

'Not me, Bunty, I'll be sittin' in the car waitin'. You know.'

'Yes, yes, I know, Danny, you've got a weak stomach. Something will have to be done about it, and soon.'

'Well, that's settled then. She has the needle and she thinks she's out for a trip to the seaside.'

The woman's voice came to me again, asking now, 'What has she to do with this business anyway?'

'Quite a bit I should say,' came the reply, 'on the sideline with the Indian. She lives in a posh house, and

150

he's been there visitin'. We got the tip off The Tiger who used to go round with him. He said the Indian's girl friend's ma worked for the dame. She was supposed to be a writer, but it was a cover up. She's a bit of a hard case by all accounts: tried to do her first man in with a bottle or two on his head, but she got off; then he tries to murder her, supposedly, and he was doing twelve years for it when not long ago he hanged himself in stir; at least, that's what they said. And on top of that, about the same time I reckon, she had two blokes fightin' over her; she's adopted a boy and the kid's old man went for her boy friend. Oh, I don't think we need cry over her demise. Anyway, that's settled, so come on there, Liz, I need a drink.'

'You can get it yourself. I've got a shop to see to and Jessie's got as much brain as Danny there when she's left to herself. By the way, you're sure nobody saw you comin' in the back way?'

'Does anybody ever see us comin' in the back way?'

'Yes, they do. I had to explain to old Nosey Wheatley across the lane last week when the car blocked her doorway that you were a rep, and that you'd got a ticket for parkin' too long in the front.'

'Well, she would see nothin' today. We used some black polythene to carry the lady inside. If Ma Wheatley remarks on it, it's a dressmaker's dummy.'

I was going to be sick; I was choking; I heaved and with the reaction my knees came up, and I opened my eyes. The next minute I was hoicked into a sitting position which racked my bones and brought from me a shuddering muffled groan.

I did not at first take in my surroundings, only the face hanging above mine. It was thin, as was the hair above it, and its owner said, 'We're awake then, are we?' and he straightened up as the woman spoke again, saying, 'If you want her to do any walkin' you'd better untie her else you'll really have to carry her like the dressmaker's dummy.'

The man moved back from me now, saying, 'Take her coat off, Trucker.'

I looked towards the man with the flat nose. He too was stepping back, saying, 'Not me; that short arm of hers gives me the creeps. Had a job to pull them together. There's things I don't mind 'andlin', but not that.'

'God Almighty! Did you ever hear anything like it, coming from that mouth? I'll have two Dannys on my hands shortly.'

The man called Danny, the youngest of the three I now noted, said brightly, 'I'll do it. I don't mind strippin'.'

'There's no strippin', just untie her and get her coat off.'

'What about the gag?'

'Leave that; we don't want her screamin'.' It was the woman's voice now.

'What if she takes it out?'

'Don't worry. It'll be some minutes before she can use her arms. By that time she won't want to.'

He was quite right about the time it would take me to use my arms. I screamed aloud inside when the rope was taken off my wrists and I tried to bring my limbs forward.

The man with the thin face came towards me. He wrenched my good arm forward, pushed up the sleeve of my blouse, and when I saw what he was going to do I suddenly became convulsed and managed to half rise from the couch before he knocked me back.

When the needle was rammed into my flesh I remembered thinking, Oh, dear God, let me die now. And when a voice said, 'Hold her still, you fool!' the man called Danny sat with a plop on my lap, winding me for a moment, and when my head hit the back of the wooden rim of the couch I went limp and dizzy. Then, as if I was going into sleep with my eyes open, everything inside me settled into a quiet acceptance, and when the gag was taken from my mouth I can remember saying, 'Water.'

The figures had moved away from me. I was looking down a room which was part sitting-room and part kitchen-cum-diner. There was a trellis-work some way along the room with a plant entwined in it. I saw the back of the woman and I heard a tap being turned on; then I saw her hand a glass to one of the men, but she herself didn't turn round. From the back she looked smart: she was wearing a blue summer dress, and her hair was a light blonde and dressed high on top of her head. I heard her say, 'I'm goin' down now; keep it quiet.' Then she disappeared from my view.

When I saw the glass of water being held before my face I went to lift my hand to take it, but, as in a slow motion picture, it didn't reach it. The man put the glass to my lips and I gulped on the water and choked, and gulped again and choked; and it dribbled down my chin and onto my neck, but I did nothing about it.

I sat on that couch a long, long time and it was an equally long, long time before I could make myself utter the word, 'Lava ... tory.'

When the flat-nosed man pointed to a door, a voice barked him down, saying, 'Bloody fool! There's a window in there.'

'Well, what can she do now?'

'You never know.'

I watched the man now walk over to a phone attached to the wall and speak into it, and after a few minutes the woman entered the room. She came straight towards me. Her eyes were downcast, almost completely hidden by her false eyelashes; she was heavily made-up and I could see that she wasn't young

... well, she was older than me, around forty I would have said. She took hold of my hand and when I was on my feet I swayed and would have fallen had she not steadied me.

Whilst walking to the far door I seemed to be picking my feet quite high from the floor; and yes, there was the window. I recall that all the time I was in the bathroom the woman leant her back against the door while continuing to look at me, and every now and again she would move her head from side to side. I can't remember her leading me out nor what happened afterwards, except that someone gave me a cup of tea and offered me a biscuit from a plate, and that as I looked at the plate I thought of Harold, not with any regret but just with a sadness because I knew I would never see him again. Yet, all the while there was a great unrest in me: I was dimly aware that some part of me was fighting to get out, it was wanting to scream, but I knew that I couldn't supply the energy.

One after another the men went out, but the one that seemed to penetrate my lethargy and reach that tearing part of me in which was fear, was the man called Danny, the young one. Once he sat close beside me on the couch and the fear almost got control when he started to fondle me, until a voice seemed to come from nowhere, yelling at him, 'Out of that, you!' And I was surprised it was the woman's voice because it was so loud and angry-sounding. She went on talking rapidly at the man who was now saying, 'Oh, Liz. Oh, Liz, it was only a bit of fun.' And then she said, 'If it's the last thing I do I'll see that Bunty kicks your arse out of here. It's in the loony-bin you should be, you perverted little bastard.'

Yet all the while she was upbraiding him he kept smiling at her. I recall she did not leave the room until her boy friend came back, and then she spat words at him, too, and he seemed to be trying to placate her. But

154

when she had gone he said nothing by way of a reprimand to the man Danny.

As time went on the lethargic feeling seemed to weaken and that part of me that was screaming got stronger. Once, it forced me to my feet and I was stumbling towards a window when there was a shout and I was hurled bodily back to the couch.

'That wasn't stiff enough, boss.'

'We want her to walk, don't we?'

Although I struggled with them I knew I had as much chance as a fly had against a swatter. The needle stabbed me again and once more my inward yelling gradually receded.

It seemed that I'd sat on that couch for a lifetime watching the comings and goings before the woman helped me into my coat. When she had buttoned it I saw her bow her head and mutter, 'Christ Almighty!' And then she turned on the men, her voice a hiss now and hardly audible: 'This is the last,' she said; 'I'm finished, through. And as for you two, don't put your faces in here again or else you'll find yourselves takin' a long jump, and it'll be quicker than any you dish out for I'll shoot you both, I'll promise you that. And you, *big boss*, can have the job of disposing of the bodies. You're good at that. Now get her out of here before I do something I'll be sorry for an' so will you.'

When they drew me down the room I walked slowly but steadily with them; then on down the stairs, and as we reached the bottom it was the flat-nosed man who said, 'She's another one that'll have to be seen to if you ask me anything.'

'You shut your trap. You lay a hand on her and by God! I'll finish you off meself. An' that goes for you too.' He turned to the younger man. 'Now I'm warnin' you. I'm also warnin' you she meant what she said, so it's up to me to save your skins and get somebody else to come back and do the loading.'

155

They now sat me in the back seat of the car, my body crushed tightly between them; and then the car was backed out of the yard and we were away.

It seemed a long time before we reached the country, at least before I glimpsed green fields and hedges.

When the flat-nosed man, for the second time, took a drink from a bottle the man Bunty said, 'Cold feet, Trucker?' and Trucker, looking across at me laughed and said, 'You know me, Bunty. I always wear woollen socks.'

The shaking of his body penetrated mine and seemed to force a crack within my mind that held the fear, and when I wriggled the Trucker man said, 'She's laughin' at it,' and the other answered, 'I wouldn't reckon on it.' Then he leant towards the driver asking now, 'Will we get there before it wears off, Danny?'

'Yes, plenty of time, and it'll be on dark,' the young man answered.

'It'll be a good two hours before it's dark.'

'But we're not half-way there yet, are we? And anyway' – the young man laughed now – 'we can sit and look at the view. That's what people do in their cars along the seafront there, they sit and look at the view, 'cept when they go to sleep.' His head came back and he laughed again, and his boss said harshly, 'We're not bloody well goin' into Hastings.'

'No, you're right there, you're right there. Fairlight it is now. But you won't have to leave it too late else you won't find your own way back; the top of that cliff has as many scallops as a cockleshell.'

The big man now laughed while the other said, 'Thanks for the warnin'. Very kind of you.'

'You're welcome. You're welcome, boss.'

The note of jollity in the car seemed underlined with threats. My mind, although still muzzy, suggested I wasn't the only one in danger: any one of these men could do for the other what they were about to do for

156

me, and without compunction. It came to me dimly that they were together simply because of the need of each other for whatever work they did, and my mind began to grope as to why I was here: what brought me here? Who brought me here? And the dim answer was, the Mohican. If I hadn't met the Mohican I wouldn't be in this situation. But then, as minds do, mine took me back to how and when I'd met the Mohican. It was because I was sitting in Janet's living-room meeting her family for the first time. And why was I sitting there? I had adopted her grandson. So if I hadn't adopted her grandson I wouldn't have met the Mohican. But the mind then took another leap. I wouldn't have adopted Harold if it hadn't been that I was acquainted with Janet, and Janet, in desperation, had brought the boy to work with her. Yet that hadn't made me adopt him. No; Janet had worked for Nardy and his parents for years. Back further: If I hadn't written a story called *Hamilton* and had it accepted by a publishing house called Rington and Houseman of which Mr Leviston was an editor, I would never have met Janet. Then back further still: Why had I written a book about a horse that had become my companion during the lonely years married to a sadistic man called Howard Stickle? And why had I married him? Why? Because I'd thought he'd be the only man ever to want to marry me. But he hadn't wanted to marry me, he had wanted to marry my house and the bit of money I had.

Where did things begin and how did they end? They ended here sitting in a car bowling towards some cliffs over which I was to be thrown. Death was the end. All life was planned. This was the end of my plan. But I'd be with Nardy. Yes, I'd be with Nardy. Yet, why was it I didn't want to go to Nardy? Not yet anyway, not yet.

'We'll have to stop for petrol.'

'God Almighty! I thought you had filled up.'

'I had, but that was yesterday. Trottin' round the town eats it, you know that.'

The car stopped. The driver got out. He was now talking to two men on the forecourt; I could see them through the windscreen. A while later one of the men came to the half-open window and, looking in, said, 'Lovely evening, sir.'

'Yes, very nice. A bit too warm for me though.'

'Oh, it won't last long. It never does, not in England.'

The man was looking at me. I tried to lift my hand towards him. It was a slow movement, but it only got a few inches away from my knee when the big man took it and patted it.

The face was withdrawn from the window, and the voice said, 'Good-evening, sir,' as the driver got back into the car, and the flat-nosed man said, 'Did you see that, Bunty? She lifted her hand. She should have another jab.'

'Don't be a fool; she's got to walk, hasn't she? You don't want to support a drunken woman along the cliffs, do you?' ...

When they eventually helped me out of the car I drew in a long breath. There was the smell of the sea. The last time I'd smelt it was the Saturday Tommy had run us down to Hastings and we had walked from one end of the long promenade to the other, ending up in the old town where we'd watched Harold enjoying himself in the small funfair. Afterwards we'd all played clock-golf, then stood at a stall and ate a plate of whelks. It had been a lovely day. But that had happened in another life.

When they began to walk me away from the car I glanced back. There were lights appearing in houses inland from the cliff and quite near was the sound of waves lashing against the rocks. A wind had come up and my hair was blowing into my eyes.

When a dog came bounding towards us I filled my throat with a cry, but it was muted. I wanted to call, 'Sandy!' but it was a labrador and it did not even pause but went straight on past us. Then its owner appeared and when he said, 'Good-evening,' my whole body jerked from the arms linked with mine and my mouth opened and my head went back, but my hair was again in my eyes. I lifted my hand towards the man but it was grabbed and shaken playfully while one of them answered the man's greeting. Then they both laughed quite loudly as if we were enjoying a joke.

We walked on, until suddenly I was pulled behind some gorse bushes and thrust onto the ground.

The door to full consciousness was gradually opening: I could hear the thunder of the waves more clearly now as they battered the rocks; there was a great rushing feeling inside me.

One voice said to the other, 'Go and saunter to the edge.'

'What?'

'You heard. Have a decko right an' left.'

'But you can hardly see now.'

'Oh, God above!'

I knew one of them had stepped from the gorse and I began to pray and I knew in this moment that no matter who we are or what we have previously thought about there being a God or no God, in the knowledge of approaching eternity we turn to whatever is there and speak in the only way we know. And I said, 'Our Father, who art in heaven, hallowed be Thy name, Thy Kingdom come, Thy will be done on earth as it is in heaven.'

My mind stopped the prayer at this point for there, standing before me, was Nardy and with him was Hamilton, and it was Hamilton who said, It's all right. It's all right; it just takes a second.

And it only took a second because, having been led

forward to the edge of the cliff, I flew into the air and it swept through my body as if pumped by a fire hose. There was a great roaring. It was the voice of God and it deafened me. Then all was still.

PART TWO

Tommy

1

How many times can one die? Dozens of times. Hundreds of times. Dying was good, it was peaceful; it was when you were brought back to life, that's when the pain started. Life wasn't good. Life was this dreadful feeling of being dragged up from great black depths, up, up, through mud and water, up, up, past screaming voices, until you could stand no more, and you died again.

Every time I was dragged back to life I prayed to die, and I died.

It became more painful when there were longer intervals between the dying. I had once read that some people had been dead for so many seconds and when questioned about what they had experienced they had said, 'Nothing, it was a mere blank;' and I knew this to be true, because when I died again and again there was nothing.

There was one period of living that I hated more than the others when this voice would come at me asking me questions, until God stopped it. And God had the voice of a woman. But this time the voice said, 'I've got to ask; it's important. And look; she's opened her eyes.'

Were my eyes open? I didn't know; everything was misty and I couldn't think of anything but the torture that they were applying to my body. That must be the man with the needle. He kept sticking it in me, and even up my nose and down my throat. But the voice kept on. It was saying, 'Mrs Leviston. Mrs Leviston.'

I thought dimly that it sounded like the Mohican's voice, but the Mohican was dead. I knew that; I had seen him just before I died; he was dead.

'Mrs Leviston. Mrs Leviston. Can you remember where they took you, dear?'

'Look, sister' – the voice had changed now – 'I've got to get this information out of her, it's imperative. It's weeks now.'

'It may be, but she's not fit yet, she's not fully round. Oh, you lot!'

'Yes, I know, us lot.'

'Mrs Leviston. Mrs Leviston. Can you remember where they took you?'

Could I remember where they took me? Who took me? I'm going to die. I want to die. I can't stand any more. There's nothing that will make me stand any more.

'Mrs Leviston. Mrs Leviston.'

Then another voice: 'This is Tommy, Maisie darling. Can you hear me?'

'Tommy.'

'She said Tommy, so she's round. Mrs Leviston. Mrs Leviston.'

Why was Tommy calling me Mrs Leviston?

'Can you give us an idea where they took you in that black car?'

In the black car? Yes, I had been in a black car. And I went to Liz. Yes, Liz, in the dress shop, boutique.

'Liz?'

'Yes. Yes, Liz. Go on. Go on. Oh, please, Mrs Leviston.'

'Boutique ... dresses, Liz, stiff hair ... boutique ...'

'My God! Yes, yes, that little dress shop. It's called, Liz's. Yes, yes, Bainsworthy Place. Oh, Mrs Leviston, you're wonderful. I always knew you were wonderful, and brave and kind ... I'll be back shortly, Tommy.'

164

'Can you manage? Will you be all right? Are you fit enough?'

'Fit enough for this.'

How nice of the man to say, 'Mrs Leviston I always knew you were wonderful.' I'd never been wonderful. Yet Nardy had thought so, and Tommy thought so. But I want to die; I'm so tired of all this I just want to die. And my head, my head, my head.

As I sank into the blackness again a woman's voice said, 'Let her be. Let her be; it'll be longer next time.'

2

How many times can one die? Why did I still keep asking myself that question? One time when I had been returned to life I knew I was being wheeled into a room full of glaring lights, and I died again.

I was in great pain after I became alive that time, but from then I never died fully again. And the day I realized there'd be no more dying, at least not yet anyway, I really woke up and for a moment thought I was back in the drawing-room because this place, where I was, was full of yellow light. And then I saw two white-robed figures, one on each side of me. Their hands were around me and both together they said, 'One, two, three, up we come!' and I groaned aloud and cried, 'Oh. Oh. Oh.'

But they took no notice of my moans and said, 'There you are; there's a bonny girl for you.'

I looked from one to the other. Their faces were bright.

'Good-morning, Mrs Leviston.'

My mind said good-morning, but I didn't voice it. 'What's happened?' I said. Was that my voice? I could hardly hear it, it was only a squeak.

They laughed now and one of them, striking a pose, said, 'One of these days ... *I'll tell you a story.*'

A streak of fear ran through me. That was Max Bygraves again, and a man had said those words. But ... but I was alive, I wasn't dead. I spoke again, 'I'm alive.'

'Of course you're alive.'

'Where am I?'

'Now where do you think? You're in hospital.'

'Where?'

'In London, of course.'

'But ... but how?'

'Now don't ask so many questions all at once, save your breath to meet all these visitors that you'll be having. To tell you the truth' – a smiling face came down to mine – 'I'm sick of them tramping in and out of my ward.'

'What's that?' I said, but as I motioned with my head to this thing sticking up at the bottom of the bed the pain ran down the back of my neck, causing me to close my eyes, and the nurse said, 'That's your leg, Mrs Leviston. And what caused that pain was jerking your head. Now what you've got to do is to lie still and be a good girl or else we'll have to say no to your visitors.'

'But my leg?'

'It was broken. And your arm too.'

Slowly I looked down at my arm. It was my good arm, and it was lying straight out and bandaged up to the shoulder. Slowly I realized that my head too was bandaged. Then I became aware of a tightness around my ribs. The only parts of my body that seemed to belong to me were my short arm and my left leg.

'Now no more talking. Just lie quiet and we'll make you pretty.' A hand came out and gently patted my cheek; the voice was gentle too as it said, 'You're a very, very lucky woman, Mrs Leviston, a very lucky woman.'

A quirk in my mind that was still there said: Apparently a broken leg, a broken arm and an acute pain inside my stomach. Yes, I was a very lucky woman ...

They washed me; they put my short arm into a clean bed jacket, the other arm of which was draped over my shoulder.

167

'There now, there now,' one said.

Then they brought my breakfast. But they wouldn't let me feed myself, although I assured them I could use my short arm. But no, they fed me.

They were treating me like a baby.

'The doctor will be round shortly; he will be so pleased with you.'

'Why?'

They looked from one to the other; then one laughed and said, 'Because he thinks he's a clever so-and-so putting your skull to rights.'

'My skull?' I put my hand up and touched my head. It seemed that I had a stiff cap on it.

'What was wrong with it?'

'You ask him, my dear, he'll tell you.'

When, a short while later, a small dark-skinned man came into the room I had no need to ask, for he started straightaway: 'Well, well! Merry and bright. That's more like it. How do you feel?'

When my answer wasn't immediately forthcoming he went on, 'Perhaps not so merry and bright, eh? But how's the head? Aching a bit? Well, that's to be expected. Give it a few more days and you won't know you've got one, a head.' More laughter, accompanied this time by murmurs from the sister and the nurse in attendance.

'Lucky little woman. Do you know that? That's what you are, a lucky little woman.' His dark face was beaming. 'Related to the cat family, nine lives ... How's the rest going?' He had turned to the sister now, and she answered, 'Very well, Doctor. Very well.'

'Good, good. And the sooner we get the therapist on the left leg the better. But not yet, not yet.' He was smiling at me again, and again I felt a child as he said, 'We want no more trouble from you, you understand? You've got a whole arm and a leg' – he had called my deformed arm a whole arm – 'and look after them,

168

because I don't want to see you in that theatre any more.'

'What day is it?'

He seemed surprised at my question. 'Saturday,' he said.

'What Saturday?'

He glanced at the sister, then laughed again, 'This is Saturday, the twenty-second of September, nineteen eighty-*four*. God be praised.'

The sudden effort to sit up straight brought a shudder through my strapped and stiffened limbs and the sister quickly to my bedside, 'There now, there now,' she said. 'Don't jump out of bed all at once.'

'Can't be September.'

'Can't be September, she says, sister. Are we wrong?'

Sister smiled broadly as if the doctor had just uttered some great witticism, and she answered, 'I don't think so, doctor.'

'It was August when you were brought here from Hastings, the second week, wasn't it, sister?'

'Yes, doctor, the second week.'

His face was near mine now. 'You've overstayed your welcome, do you know that? And we'll have you on our hands for some time yet, so behave yourself.'

I made no reply. My lids were blinking as I tried to reckon up how long it was since that Friday morning when I went to meet the Mohican ... *Oh, the poor Mohican.* I'd forgotten about the Mohican.

'Has he been buried?'

'What?'

'Has the Mohican been buried?'

The three occupants of the room now exchanged glances, and the smile went from the doctor's face. He looked perturbed.

'That's ... that's what I called him, the Mohican. He dressed like an Indian, and they stabbed him.' My mind, I found, was rapidly sorting things out.

169

'Oh, *that* Indian.' The doctor was nodding now, the smile back on his face. 'No, he hasn't been buried, not yet.'

'It's a long time since August.'

'Oh, now, now, you mustn't cry. I can't stand women who cry because then I cry too. I must away. Be a good girl now. Be a good girl.'

The doctor turned and, accompanied by the sister, went from the room. But the nurse stayed, and she wiped my eyes, saying, 'You don't want red lamps when you've got a gentleman waiting to see you.'

'Oh. Tommy?' I said.

'No, not Tommy, but doubtless he'll be here any minute. How is it you have so many men after you? And mostly big ones. There's that one from the north, Georgie, and . . .'

'Georgie? Gran's Georgie?'

'Well, I suppose he's somebody's Georgie. And there's the other one from the North with a complete shrubbery around his face.'

'Mike.'

'Is that what they call him? We know him as Doctor Kane.'

'They've been here?'

'I'll say, and some more, and here's me can't even keep a boy friend. Now, behave yourself.' She patted my cheek, laid my short arm on the coverlet, then went from the room. And the door had hardly closed on her when it opened again and a man entered.

He was a stranger; I had never seen him before. His neck was bandaged and he had one arm in a sling. He walked stiffly towards me; then pulling a chair up to the bedside he smiled at me. I looked at him: his hair was black, parted down the centre and flattened to each side of his head, yet it didn't reach his ears and cover the bald patches there. His face was pale-skinned. He had a straight nose and wide mouth and

170

deep-set eyes of a dark brown colour.

He said, 'Hello, Mrs Leviston.'

That voice. I knew that voice. I looked downwards to his clothes. He was wearing a light grey suit and an open-necked shirt. His hand came out and lay on top of mine. I wouldn't believe what I was thinking, not even when he said, 'John Drake, at your service, ma'am.'

'The Mohican.'

His smile widened and he nodded, 'Yes, the Mohican.'

'I . . . I thought.'

'That they had done for me? I thought so too, and I wasn't the only one.'

'You've . . . you've changed.'

'No, this is me, or will be when my hair grows again.'

When my face screwed up in disbelief the effect was painful for my skin seemed to crack and my voice was a mere whisper as I said, 'You weren't really one of them?'

'No; only pretending. But it was a long pretence, over two years. In the end I . . . well, I really felt that I had become . . . the Mohican.'

'You're a . . . ?'

'Policeman.'

'Never!'

'Yes. Don't I look like one?'

'No, not at all.'

'Well, I am. Detective Sergeant James Bainbridge, at your service.'

'Not John Drake?'

'No, James Bainbridge.'

'What happened to you, I mean after? It seemed to go in your neck, the knife.'

'Well, it did somewhat, but just above the shoulder blade, and luckily missed the jugular. But it would have been Goodbye Mr Chips if it hadn't been for my connection. He had learned they were on to me, and he

171

was about to get in contact when he saw me walk away from the shop. There was a signal he would have given me as he passed, but then he recognized you. I don't suppose you'll remember an American tourist with a slouched hat when you crossed the road? Anyway, he expected you to go into the shop and was about to pass you when you changed your mind and walked on. It was then he became aware of the car; he recognized the driver and immediately contacted a squad car. They arrived just too late to rescue you and pick the others up but soon enough to get me to the hospital. So there you have it, the story of my life.'

'What was it all about . . . drugs?'

'Yes, drugs. And in a big way.'

While he spoke I found myself sitting on the couch in that room and my head swam as I jerked and said excitedly, 'I . . . I know where they are stored. In a dress shop, she's called Liz, a sort of boutique.'

He squeezed my hand between both of his now, saying, 'Yes, I know, my dear.' He called me my dear so naturally. 'I got the information out of you some time ago, and because of it the sister nearly finished me off; the effort had been too much for you and you sank back into yourself for two or three days. They wouldn't let me in after that.'

'And you went there?'

'Yes, but in a bunch.'

'Did you get those men?'

'Oh, they'd been picked up sometime before. Trucker and the psycho, and the ringleader of that little mob who went under the name of Bunty, they were clear for almost a week after they dumped you. And I don't suppose you'll remember a man and his dog walking along the cliff path that night?'

I started to grope in my mind, and then I saw a bounding labrador and I said, 'Yes, yes, I do. Yes, I remember, especially the dog.'

172

'Well, that man was a bit curious when later, and almost dark, he saw those two men that he had passed earlier on get into a car, but there was no sign of the girl they'd had in tow. There are some houses close by and he thought they might have been taking the girl home. That was until it came out in the papers that you were missing; and I was sufficiently round by then to give a description of the black car and the three that were in it. It all linked up, and the search for you began along the foot of the cliffs. Without much hope at first; they thought you would have been swept out to sea because the tides were high about that time and a bit rough. But you hadn't even reached the shore; there you were on a narrow jutting piece of rock and being held in place by some shrub. You hadn't fallen half-way down the cliffs. But when you landed you did yourself a great deal of damage, and they never expected you to pull through. You know, you're a miracle: there wasn't a part of your body that wasn't bruised or battered or broken, even your left leg, they tell me, is lacerated. Strange, that this' – he wagged my short arm – 'should escape.'

I had that frightened feeling on me again.

'What did you find in the shop?' I asked.

'What we expected, a good hoard. It would have brought in about two million pounds on the street. And not only that. She was petrified, Miss Liz, and to save her skin she blurted out quite a bit of very helpful information, something that we had been trying to piece together for the last four or five years. It was a connection with a yacht that was lying along the river and owned by a very respectable citizen and an old tub based in Hull that did trips across the channel and linked up with a foreign craft.'

He drew in a long breath and slumped back in his chair before he said, 'I'm glad it's over. I was sickened at times. And you know, it's the easiest thing in the

173

world to take to that stuff, and I must admit it was difficult at times not to, especially being a ... Mohican.' He now pressed my hand and added softly, 'I liked the sound of the Mohican and I liked you from the day we sat at Mum's table when I faced up to Stoddart. I felt we had a lot in common then; and we have shared quite a bit since, haven't we?'

I don't know if there was any colour in my face but it felt hot. To dampen down on my emotion I asked, 'Didn't anyone know the truth about you?'

'No; that would have been fatal. I was sent from another area, and I was soon on the black list of the fellows in two of the stations. The only connection I had was the American tourist, Dave Radlett; we were in the same squad. Of course, he wasn't an American tourist all the time' – he laughed now – 'he was a barrow boy one time until some of the real ones threatened to do him in. The same happened when he took up a paper stand. Oh, we were very versatile, we blokes. And by the way, it was Dave who collared our gentleman friend and his lady wife, Mrs Beckingtree-Holland. He's doing eighteen months now, and she's on probation. Oh yes; to say the least we are very versatile ... and frightened out of our wits half the time.'

'Oh, John.'

'Do you think you could call me Jim?'

'No, I don't. I'll never be able to think of you as anyone other than John or the Mohican.'

'That's a pity.'

The look in his eyes brought the colour to my face again, and I asked, 'How did Hilda not guess?'

'Oh, Hilda. Hilda never questions.'

'Was she always like that? I mean, did she always dress like that?'

'No, no. Give her her due, she was almost a replica of May when I met her, but of course with only half of

174

May's intelligence. But she's easily influenced is Hilda.'

I said somewhat stiffly now, 'She's a very nice girl really, I think.'

'Yes, she is, she is, and she was much too good for a ... Mohican or anyone of his breed. But as things are now ... well.'

I let my head fall back into the pillows. He had used Hilda. That wasn't like the Mohican. And he was being patronizing towards her, and that wasn't like the Mohican, at least not like the Mohican I thought I knew.

'What does the family think of what has happened?'

'Oh, they are very chuffed. You can imagine it. Funny how people's opinions can be altered by the clothes you wear.'

'Well, you can't blame them for that.'

'No, I suppose not. But you know, the reason some of the kids dress up in this gear or dye their hair six different colours is mostly through boredom. You know, we're all imitators and gregarious: we live in mobs and we know that if we aspire to be different we're ostracized.'

In the ensuing silence the door opened again and in came Tommy, and on the sight of me sitting up, my eyes open, he let out a long drawn, 'Oh ... h!', placed a great bunch of flowers on the side table, then came round the bed and, bending over me, he took my hand, which I'd taken from my visitor's, and holding it tightly pressed it against his chest, and he said, 'Oh! my dear. How wonderful. You're looking grand.'

'Don't be silly, Tommy.' I closed my eyes. 'I'm plaster from head to foot; how can I be looking grand?'

'Don't talk back to me, woman; when I say you're looking grand, you're looking grand.' He bent and kissed me on the lips, and when he straightened up he looked across the bed to where the Mohican was

175

standing now, and he said, 'Isn't she marvellous?'

'Yes, she's marvellous, and I've just been telling her so.'

'Good. Good. Oh.' He bent over me again and, taking my face in his hands, he squeezed it, and again my skin seemed to crackle. 'We'll soon have you out of that. And I've got news for you.'

'I'll have to be going now.'

We both looked to where the young man was standing very straight in spite of the fact that his neck and arm were bandaged, and Tommy said, 'Be seeing you then.'

'Yes, be seeing you. Goodbye, Mrs Leviston.'

'Goodbye . . . John.'

The Mohican smiled, then turned about and went out.

'Nice fellow that, brave as they come. My goodness me! To think what he's been doing all this time. I take it all back what I said about him. Anyway –' Tommy now pulled a chair up to the bedside, then went on, 'I was right in a way, he wasn't what he appeared to be. And like you, he's lucky to be alive. Oh, darling.' He now hitched the chair nearer to the head of the bed and, stroking my cheek, he said, 'You've got no idea what I've been through all these weeks.'

It was still in me to laugh. My head shook, my arm and my leg shook; I daren't let my stomach or my ribs shake, they were too painful.

And now he was laughing out loud, saying, 'That was funny, wasn't it, saying that to you. But you know what I mean: I've been in agony every day, and they've had to throw me out; I've become a perfect nuisance.'

My face was wet. Then after a moment, as I sat looking at him, I suddenly thought of Harold and asked myself why I hadn't thought of him before.

'How's Harold?' I said sharply. 'Where is he? Who's had him?'

'Harold's fine. He's with Janet, and she's going to bring him this afternoon. But he's been here a dozen times already. And you know, I don't think you need worry any more about the fight for priority in our affection for you, we've come to a sort of truce. And strangely, he seems to think your living or dying depended solely on me, and he promised he would do anything in the future if only I would see that you would be all right. Strangely, too, he's gone off the Mohican since he knows he's a policeman; in fact, he blamed him very verbally for getting you into all this trouble. And you know, he was right. And I blamed him too. I wanted to murder him at first, that was when you disappeared; policeman or no policeman, it made no difference. By the way, did he tell you that the Captain and his lady had been picked up?'

'Yes. Yes, he did.'

'But it didn't come about through what they had taken from you; the Captain, at his original game, had been getting things on approval including a nice little bit of jewellery, and, of course, giving a wrong address. And you'll be pleased to know that you've got your miniatures back, but not your rings.'

'It doesn't matter.'

'You tired, my dear?'

'No, no. I was just thinking what a lot of stock we put on possessions, and yet they are only ours for a very short time. All that collection in the china cabinet: they all belonged to somebody else, going back down the years; they're no use to them now as they'll be no use to me some day.'

'Come on, come on, stop thinking in that way. As I said, I've some news. How would you like to go to sea?'

'I wouldn't; I'm not struck on the sea, I'm seasick.'

'Well, you'll have to get over being seasick, I'm buying a boat. Oh no, I mustn't just call it a boat, it's a yacht.'

'You're not.'

'I am, and with you in mind. You'll love it.'

'You'll never get me on a thing that depends on sails ...'

'This doesn't depend on sails, it's got twin screws and Volvo engines. And they're dependable enough. Oh my dear, wait till you see it. It's a peach; I've never seen anything like it. He's sorry to part with it himself ... Mr Percy Liddle.'

'Then why is he parting with it? It's likely got a leak somewhere.'

Tommy laughed loudly now, saying, '*Spring Fever* wouldn't deign to have a leak. No; he's selling her because he's going back to Switzerland. He's got a business there. He had one here but like many another it's losing money, and it's an expensive business keeping a boat in harbour if you're only going to use it at holiday time.'

'What about the expenses to you, or whoever buys it?'

'I can afford it.'

'How much is it? I mean how much is it costing?'

'Well, I'm getting him down a bit. He wanted thirty-five thousand for it.'

I nearly lifted from the bed, then pulled my hand from his and held it to my head.

'Oh, I'm sorry, dear. Does it hurt?'

'Yes, it hurts. And that sum hurts too. You must be mad.'

'No, I'm not mad. That boat today would cost between sixty and seventy thousand and be cheap at that. If things weren't tight all round I wouldn't stand a chance of getting it for the price I am willing to pay.'

'It'll take all your money.'

'Don't be silly. During the last two years, dear Mama's little fortune has made more capital and I don't use it, I'm a working man earning a salary. And anyway, if I lost every penny I've still got that property in the West End. I could sell it for a fortune now and would do so only the damn tax man would grab so much of it. And I'm not really used to that yet. Don't worry.'

'How big is it?'

'About thirty-five feet. And it has a beautiful saloon upholstered in green and gold, carpets right through. It sleeps six, and has a real double bedroom with bathroom and shower. And that room has everything, wardrobes, dressing-table, lounge couch, you wouldn't believe what they can get into thirty-five feet. There're two smaller cabins, single bunks, and then there's another two singles which I understand were used by the crew.'

'It needs a crew?' My squeak hurt my throat.

'Well, he had an ex-merchant navy officer as captain and another fellow who cooked and did general cleaning duties . . . oh, the galley. You'd be amazed. It's a kitchen, and has a real washing machine.'

'Never!' There was a deep sarcastic note in my voice, and I closed my eyes. Apart from being tired by Tommy's enthusiasm and the thought that his boat would be wasted on me for he'd never get me on it no matter if it turned out to be a luxury liner – the cruise I'd spent with Nardy had proved that neither of us were sailors – I wasn't feeling well.

'I've tired you. I'm sorry, dear. I'm thoughtless. But . . . well, I imagined it would cheer you up. Anyway, if we never put out to sea in it, it would be nice just to go and sit in it at weekends. People . . . do you know, they have boats that have never gone under London Bridge or moved up river. Look, I'll be quiet; you go to sleep.'

I did not protest and say, No, I'm all right; I kept my eyes closed and my mouth shut. I was tired and I was in pain. Although very little of my body seemed to belong

179

to me, it nevertheless registered aches and strange pains, especially the lower part of my stomach. I must ask about that. I wished Tommy would go. I wished everybody would go, especially the Mohican. Why had I said that? He had gone. I had a great desire to sink into that peaceful nothingness again. But not to die, except if I was going to do it properly, for I didn't want to go through the experience of being dragged back into life.

I knew the nurse had entered the room and I knew that she was standing at the other side of the bed looking down at me. Then her whispered words came to me: 'She's very tired. I'd let her rest.'

Tommy was asking her a question. I didn't know what it was until I heard the answer and the nurse saying, 'Oh, some long time yet, weeks, weeks. It's very early days.'

I don't know how long I slept this time but when I awoke I was conscious of a small hand holding mine, and I lay for a while savouring the feeling before I opened my eyes; and there, standing close to the bedside, was Harold.

'Harold.'

He did not answer me. Then I heard Janet's voice come from the other side of the bed, saying, 'Well, say hello to Mrs Nardy. You've been talkin' enough about what you're goin' to tell her.'

Still he didn't speak; but his eyes became wide and damp like my own, and when he bent and laid his head on top of the hand that was holding mine the tears flowed gently down my face. And Janet's voice was stringent, yet with a break in it: 'There you are now,' she said, 'see what you've done. The nurse'll turf you out. I told you.'

'Oh, Janet.' I turned my head towards her.

'How are you, dear?'

She had never before called me dear.

'Better, Janet. Fine.'

'Oh, yes, you're fine.' Janet's head was nodding vigorously now in denial.

'I've got three stars.'

It was as if he knew what would please me most, and I said, 'Never!'

He nodded, sniffed, and when his grandmother said, 'Use your hanky. What have you got one for?' he dived into his pocket, took out a clean square and blew his nose; then looking at me with the look of the old Harold, he said, 'She always keeps on ... Gag. Me Uncle Max says that's what they're goin' to get her for Christmas, a big one, a gag.' He hunched his shoulders as he looked across the bed at the frowning Janet, and I looked from one to the other and felt back home.

'What did you get the stars for?'

'Singin' and writin' and ... an' behavin'.' His lips were nipped in; his eyes were sparkling, laughing at himself.

'Wonderful.'

Now bringing his face nearer to mine and his voice taking on that rapid, non-stop, chatter that I loved so much, he said, 'And they're all suckin' up, wantin' to be me friend, all 'cos of you an' the Indian, an' the racket. And Millie Stott's mother asked me to go to tea, she did. She was waitin' outside the railin's and she asked me. But I'm not goin' ...'

'You are.' Again I looked from one to the other. They were exchanging glances, and now Harold said, 'She's soppy, Gag.'

'She's a nice little girl, what I've seen of her. You should thank your lucky stars someone like that takes an interest in you, clodhopper that you are.'

Oh, I definitely was back home, and it was lovely.

'Ah, Gag.'

Janet was looking at me now, her eyes twinkling. I

181

said to her, 'Has he been a good boy?' And she pursed
her lips and wrinkled her nose, but then, her face
straightening, she said softly, 'Yes, ma'am, yes, he's
been a very good boy. And so upset. Like all of us. Oh,
ma'am' – she reached across and caught my hand –
'what you've gone through. And all through the Indian
an' meetin' him in my house. I felt sort of responsible,
we all did, all the lads. They were so bothered. You
know, our Rodney and Max, they took a day off an'
went down to help them search after that man came
forward an' said where he had seen you. And they had
just found you when they got down to Hastings.
Nobody thought you would live, you know.' She
paused, then said, 'Oh! ma'am, you were in a dreadful
state.'

I forced myself to smile now to prevent myself from
crying again, and, nodding towards my leg, I said, 'I
still am, Janet. They've got to feed me, wash me ... the
lot.'

She sniffed now, then straightened up. 'We haven't
got to tire you else that nurse'll be on us again,' she
said.

Indicating Harold, I asked quietly, 'Has his father
been around again?'

'Oh.' Janet raised her eyes to the ceiling, saying,
'There's a tale there. You won't believe it. I can't
believe it, I just can't. I'll tell you some other time.'

'Me mum's comin' back.'

'You shut your mouth, young 'Arold.'

'His mother's comin' back?' There was apprehen-
sion in my voice, and Janet said, 'It's a long story, but
it's got nothin' to do with him.' She jerked her head
towards Harold. 'You're all right; so's he; an' if I could
laugh about the whole affair I would, especially at
Stoddart, but I can't. Oh! our Maggie.'

My hand was tugged, and I looked at Harold as he
asked quietly, 'When you comin' home, Mrs Nardy?'

'I'm not quite sure, Harold. Next week...'

'You'll be lucky.' We both looked at Janet. Then again I turned my attention to Harold, saying, 'Soon. As soon as possible because I miss you.'

When his arms jerked upwards and around my neck I almost screamed as the pain shot down my spine, but I closed my eyes and with my short arm I held him to me. His nose was pressed into the only part of me that didn't seem to be bandaged up, a space above my short arm and below my chin. And when it became wet I said, 'Now, now, you'll have me crying and then the nurses will go for me.'

His words were smothered but I heard them, and when I answered, 'I love you too, darling,' Janet got to her feet and made her way to a table near the window on which was a huge flower arrangement in a basket. After a moment she turned and said, 'I ... I think you've had enough, ma'am. I think you've had enough. Come on you. Come on.'

I pressed my son from me, because that's what he was, he was my son and the love I had for him was of a quality I'd never before experienced. I could have given him birth so close was the feeling I had for this child, and he for me. Oh yes, and he for me.

He was standing now with his head bowed, rubbing his nose on the side of his first finger, and I endeavoured to bring things back to everyday normality by saying, 'Harold Leviston, what have I told you about that finger and your nose?'

'Oh, you!' He was groping for his handkerchief again and when he put it to his face he made great play of blowing into it while his eyes blinked at me.

When we kissed goodbye, he said, 'See you tomorrow.'

'You'll not.'

I looked at Janet.

'Well, you're not fit yet, ma'am.'

183

'Of course I am ... please.'

'All right then. Well, I'll let one of the others bring him because they're all mad to come. Oh, I must tell you.' She came and bent over me and her mouth moved from one side to the other before she said, 'My 'Arry sent you a message, ma'am. "Give her my best respects," he said. Did you ever! Give her my best respects. I said to him, "That sayin' went out with your granny."'

'That was very nice of him, Janet.'

She sighed. 'Yes,' she said, 'I suppose it was, because he never gives a damn, I mean a thought to anybody but himself. Yes.' She laughed now. 'Huh! Yes, I suppose it was when you come to think of it ... Come on, you!' She held out her hand; then looking at me tenderly, she said, 'Take care. The house isn't the same. It won't be until you get inside again.' And at this, she grabbed her grandson and without further ado made for the door; and when from there he shouted his last goodbye I lay back and closed my eyes, and smiled.

I had been asleep again. I was always wanting to sleep; I was so tired. I remember they woke me up for dinner, which I insisted on managing myself after they had cut up everything to size. Yet when the nurse came to take the tray away she said, 'You've hardly touched a thing.'

'I'm not hungry, nurse.'

'You've got to eat.'

Yes, I had to eat, but what I wanted more was just to sleep, peacefully sleep, because when I slept now I dreamt. I dreamt that all my limbs were moving: I was walking; I was running; I was sitting; I was standing; I was chasing Harold and Sandy across the heath ... Sandy. I never asked where Sandy was. Oh no, he couldn't be left on his own from Janet leaving in the

184

early afternoon until she returned the next morning. My worry must have shown on my face for the nurse asked, 'Now what's the matter?'

'My dog. I don't know what's happened to my dog.'

'Oh, your dog. The white poodle?'

'Yes, the white poodle.'

'Oh, I understand your caretaker's looking after him. He and his wife brought him the other day. They kept him in the forecourt; the husband thought you might be able to see him out of the window; he didn't know you hadn't come round. I wouldn't worry about him. If you were as well as him you would do, my dear. What you've got to worry about is yourself, and eating.'

I wondered as she fussed over me how she and all her like managed to keep this caring attitude for one and another of those that passed through their hands. I was sure I couldn't do it. They were a special breed; but all different. Some were a bit stiff and proper, never thinking of calling you, my dear, but giving you your full title while doing everything that was required of them.

Later that night, as I dropped off to sleep, I knew there was someone else who was caring for me, and very deeply, for Tommy was still sitting there, just as, I understood, he had done most nights since I was first brought into hospital.

I had been transferred to a private ward and visitors were allowed in any time. However, they didn't usually put in an appearance until after the doctor's round which I had come to know was usually over by eleven o'clock. But on this Sunday morning the breakfast tray had hardly been taken away when a head appeared round the door. The bush around the face seemed to get greyer every time I saw it, and on this appearance I again caused a pain to shoot down my spine as I tried to turn on my side as I cried, 'Mike! Oh, Mike! Where've you sprung from?' I was muttering the words into his beard as he kissed me.

'A quite comfortable hotel, madam. I came down last night late on, couldn't get away earlier. Jane had arranged to come with me when at the last moment her dear mother arrived. You've never met my mother-in-law, have you?'

'No. No, Mike.' I was smiling widely.

'Well, she's the original stand-up comic's target.'

'Oh, Mike.'

As he pulled a chair up towards the bed, he said, 'She's not really; but she comes on the hop, no phone message, nothing, just lands on the doorstep and expects her only daughter to wait on her as she did before we were married ... How are you feeling, dear?' His voice had dropped.

'Which part are you enquiring about, Mike?'

He chuckled. 'Oh, you're reviving,' he said; 'I think my journey's been unnecessary. Well, we'll start with the head. That got the most bashing.'

'It aches.'

'It's bound to. But he did a good job on you, he's a clever fellow. They don't come any better, so I understand. Your leg and your arm. Oh, that's ordinary, just compound fractures, they're nothing.' He pulled a face. 'How's the middle?'

'I don't know, Mike. What did they do to the middle?'

'Oh, I think they untangled your guts. Put a couple of rivets or so in your pelvis and sorted it out generally.'

'Oh, is that all?'

'As far as I know.' He caught my hand now, saying, 'You're the luckiest girl alive. My God! You should have died with that sub-dural haematoma.'

'What's that?'

'Well, to put it simply, it's a blood clot between the bone of the skull and the brain. That's why you were fluctuating in and out of consciousness.'

'Really?'

'Yes, really. It was a tricky business. He had to drill a burr hole in your skull and aspirate the blood clot. It was touch and go with you for a time. I hope those three get their just deserts, the same as Stickle got his. Odd that you had to get rid of that pain only to have a worse one taking its place. Anyway, attempted murder will take care of them for some time, I'm sure of that. But by! you do pick 'em, don't you, the men in your life?'

'Yes, I seem to, don't I? But don't forget there was Nardy, and before him George, and now Tommy, and all the while, right from the beginning, you.'

The whole bush of hair round his face moved as he muttered, 'Stop your soft-soaping.' Then he added, 'But it's good to see you looking ... well, different. I hadn't much hope the first time I glimpsed you.'

'You've been before?'

'What do you think? I've been twice. You spoke to me the second time, and you know what you said?'

'No?'

'Hamilton.'

'I didn't.'

'You did. Had he come back?'

I tried to think, then said, 'Yes, yes, I think he did.'

'You are going to marry Tommy?'

'Oh.' I thought a moment, then said, 'Yes. Yes, I suppose so, sometime.'

'Don't make it sometime, make it soon. He's a good fellow. He's another Nardy, only twice the size.'

'There could never be another Nardy, Mike.'

'They say there's never a good but there's a better, but in this case I'll say he's as good as.'

'Have you met the Mohican?' Why should I talk

187

about the Mohican when we were talking about Tommy? 'I mean since he stopped being the Indian.'

'Yes; I've met him once since he reverted to himself and I take back all I said about him. He's a brave man. They've got to be, doing that kind of job. Over two years he played that game, so I understand; it's a wonder he didn't become an addict himself. I said he was, didn't I?'

'Yes, you did. He's a nice person, Mike, very nice.'

'I've no doubt of it, none whatever.' He put his head to one side, then asked, 'How old is he, do you think?'

'Twenty-seven, twenty-eight.'

'Oh, I wouldn't have thought he was that; a bit younger I would have said, twenty-four.'

'I thought they had to be a certain age before they got into the C.I.D.'

'Oh yes, yes, perhaps. Well now' – his tone became brisk – 'this is a short visit, my dear, because I promised Jane I'd be home shortly after two, so I'll have to catch that eleven o'clock, and before I leave I want to have a word with your man. Sister tells me he should be around about this time, being Sunday.'

As he looked at his watch I said, 'It was good of you to come, Mike. I'm ... I'm so grateful. It's been almost as good as my Monday visit to the surgery.'

He now rose and bent over me, saying, 'Nothing will ever be as good or as amusing or aggravating as those Monday morning visits. Do you exclaim "wh ... at" to the doctor when he comes round?'

'Yes, every time.'

He laughed. 'That was a funny habit you had, wasn't it? I've never heard anybody exclaim what! like you did.'

'There weren't many patients like me, Mike.'

'No, you're right there. By, you're right there. Well, my dear ...' Again he kissed me, and I put my hand onto his thick hair as I said, 'Give my love to Jane, and thank her for sparing you. She's a very understanding woman. Goodbye, love.'

He patted my cheek, walked two or three steps backwards, saluted, then turned and hurried out.

I loved that man. Yes, yes, I did, I loved him, and I wasn't going to differentiate between a father and a brother or a husband or a lover, I just loved him.

I knew that Tommy wouldn't be in until later in the afternoon because he had run down to Brighton to see Bella, who too was ill.

It being Sunday, however, I knew there would probably be visitors after lunch; but the only one I was looking forward to seeing was Harold.

I had just settled myself for yet another nap when the door opened and the nurse called, 'You have some visitors, Mrs Leviston.' And there, as large as life, were Gran and George.

'Hello, pet.'

'Hello, love.'

They were bending over me.

'How you feelin'? Eeh! what a mess-up.' That was Gran. 'My God! lass, where've you gone to? You were little afore, but look at you!'

I hadn't been able to say a word. They were now seated close together at the side of the bed and my voice was thick as I said, 'How lovely to see you.'

'Not half as lovely as seein' you, lass.'

I smiled at George. He was looking older: his hair was quite grey, in fact it was as if I hadn't seen him for years. Gran looked the same. She was ageless. And the next moment she proved that her tongue too had not altered, for she said, 'Eeh by! you're the one for notoriety, aren't you? Gettin' yourself into the papers. My God! for two days you hit the front pages, all mixed up with Indians and gangsters and drug runners. We couldn't believe it, could we, Georgie?'

189

At this point, leaning towards me, Georgie picked up my hand and said, 'But she was a hero ... female-like, heroine.'

'Well, it's all how you look at it; she might have been a dead heroine. You don't look half alive yet.' And she put out her fingers and patted my face.

'*Oh, Gran.*'

'What d'you say it like that for, lass? You could have been dead, all through gettin' mixed up with those funny people. You should never have left home; they're a queer lot up this end. I've said it afore, and I'll say it again. And when Georgie here came back and told me how you looked, eeh! I couldn't believe it. I couldn't come 'cos Mary was down with a summer cold. It hung on, and I had to see to the bairns.' Gran was nodding as if to emphasize her words.

Mary and the bairns were her first concern now. How things changed; how people changed. But then, in this case, that's how it should be.

Gran leant towards me as she said, 'Kitty sends her love.'

The fact that Gran was telling me that Kitty had sent her love was in the form of a reproach. Whether intended or not, that's how I saw it, and that it all stemmed from my interest in Harold. And this seemed to be verified by her very next words: 'It's goin' to be a long time afore you're yourself again, lass, and able to see to that youngster.'

'Oh, it won't be all that long.' I tried to keep my tone level. 'And anyway, he's staying with Janet. She's seeing to him.'

'Best place for him, among his own kind.'

'Mam!' George's voice was loud. 'I told you, didn't I, keep off it.'

'Yes, I know what you told me. But I know what I think, and all this trouble started with him.'

'Gran.'

'Aye, lass.' Her voice had softened.

'It isn't fair; you're hitting me when I'm down, because I'm not up to a fight.'

'Who wants to fight? Not me. But you know me, I have to say what I think.'

Yes, yes, I knew Gran: she had to say what she thought. But years ago her thoughts had been softer, more tender. That was when I had needed her.

It was George who now asked, 'You in much pain, lass?'

'Not too much,' I answered, 'nothing that I can't manage. A bit of a headache all the time.'

'My! they were a lot of dirty buggers weren't they?'

'Yes, Gran; they were a lot of dirty buggers.'

My head, as I'd said, ached all the time, but now it thumped with her next words.

'It said in the papers the other day that they can't bring them to trial yet until you're well enough to give evidence. That'll be another big splash in the papers.'

I closed my eyes and drew in a long breath. A court case. I'd never thought about that. Of course, I'd never thought about much since I'd come round. Things had to be triggered off in my mind, and Gran's remarks certainly triggered off my fear of being in a court. Even thinking about my past experience filled me with a sick dread, let along the thought of facing those men again.

I was aware that George was whispering something to Gran, and for answer she dug him with her elbow; then bending to the side, she picked up her carrier bag and from it brought out a fancy wrapped box which she laid on the bed saying, 'That's from Mary. It's chocolates. And this' – she now handed me a large envelope – 'is letters from the bairns.' Then dipping into her bag again, she brought out another small parcel, saying, 'That's from me, it's scent.'

'Oh, thanks, Gran.'

191

'It's not cheap stuff mind, it's a good make.'

'Of course I know you wouldn't buy anything but a good make.' I now said, 'You must have had to leave early.'

'Aye,' George nodded, 'just after seven. But we were up from half-past five or thereabouts.' He jerked his head towards his mother. 'If she'd had her own way we wouldn't have gone to bed in case we missed the train. And don't those trains move! And now that we're here I thought it would be a good idea to take her round London.' He again jerked his head towards his mother. 'She might get to like it.' And as he laughed she put in, 'Never on your life.'

'There are some beautiful parts, Gran,' I said quietly, 'and so much to see.'

'There might be, lass, but it isn't places I'm concerned with, it's people. To my mind you get no response from big houses and palaces, it's the people that matter.'

'Well,' I felt forced to say, 'there are some nice people live in the big houses and palaces. There's the Queen for instance.'

'Aye, there is,' George said with a grin. 'Now that's something, Mam, we might look in on her 'safternoon, an' she might give us a cuppa, save us having to spend out.'

Surprisingly Gran answered, 'She might an' all. I wouldn't put it past her, for she seems to be the only canny body in this neck of the woods.'

Although it caused me pain in my chest and in my rearranged guts, as Mike had called them, I joined my laugh to George's.

But the next minute there was almost an explosion when he said, 'If you want a lesson in bigotry you come to the north-east, especially from types like this 'un.' He now dug his elbow towards Gran. 'I've travelled the country in me time, as you know, lass, and what I

192

found was, if you look for the bad 'uns you'll find 'em. And she needn't look any further than her own street, silly old jenny.'

'What did you call me?'

'A jenny.'

'That isn't me name. What you up to?'

'I know it isn't your name, Mam, it's another name for an ass.'

I didn't listen to Gran's explosion, but I looked at George. He didn't change; he held no animosity: he had lost three fingers in the fire, burnt off to the bone, but he held no bitterness towards me. He didn't say, as his wife had done, if it hadn't been for my letting them have the house to live in they wouldn't have suffered as they did in the fire, and her youngest daughter wouldn't have been scarred for life...

As I had done once before, after they left, in order, as Gran said, to have a meal before they got on the train, 'cos they weren't paying train prices, I criticized myself for feeling relieved of their presence, at least of Gran's; no, not of George's, never George's.

I must have been very tired following their visit for I went to sleep and I remember little of what followed that day except Tommy saying 'Sleep, dear.' And that's what I did for the next three days: I ate and I slept and my mind stopped working. I think this must have been the outcome of the numerous pills they had given me to swallow...

Towards the end of the week, however, I was feeling different, brighter, more alert. I no longer had a headache and, too, on the Friday morning the bandage was taken from my head, and although this had revealed that I was bald above one ear, I quite readily agreed with the doctor that all I had to do was to alter my parting.

It was on the Friday afternoon that I had another

visit from the Mohican. I could never think of him by
any other name; not that there was any resemblance to
him in the very smart young man who took his seat
beside my bed, saying, 'What a difference! You look
marvellous.'

Why did people always say I looked marvellous? I'd
never looked marvellous in my life. And so the answer
I gave was, 'Not even the term exaggeration could fit
that remark,' to which he replied, 'And the remark
proves that you are yourself again.' Then a little
hesitantly he went on, 'I thought I'd call in to say
goodbye, at least for the present. I'm being sent home
to my old station, but as soon as the case comes up I'll
be back. It's amazing what's been unearthed: one
thing's led to another.'

'Are they going to make you Chief Constable?'

There was a touch of sarcasm in my tone, and he
answered it, 'Not yet. No, not yet.' He pulled a face at
himself. 'Undercover men are just undercover men.
There are a number of us.'

'Are you taking Hilda with you?' I asked.

I saw the expression on his face change and his lips
purse before he answered, 'I shouldn't think so.'

'Why not?'

'Well' – he shrugged his shoulder now – 'Hilda
belongs to a chapter that is past, or is passing.'

'Just like that.'

'Oh, Mrs Leviston, you know Hilda, you've seen her,
you've heard her. Anyway, she understands. Even
as ... the Mohican, she realized there was nothing
permanent in our association, there never is with the
Mohican types.'

'Or other types, I should imagine.'

'You're condemning me?'

'I ... I think Hilda's very fond of you and you used
her.'

'No, I didn't. Well, not in the way you mean; she

194

picked me out. And anyway, look at us as we are now, chalk and very much cheese. Now if she had a mind like yours. We, for instance, recognized each other, didn't we, even when I was the Mohican?' His head had come forward; he was looking at me in an odd penetrating way. 'How old are you?' he asked. And I just prevented myself from saying, 'What?' but answered, 'Thirty-five, hitting thirty-six. How old are you?'

'Twenty-seven hitting twenty-eight. There's not much difference between us age-wise, or any other way that I can see, and I recognized it the first time we met.'

I pressed myself back into the pillows. What was this? Yet I knew what it was, and I knew he was right. Yes, I had felt something in him the first time we met. It was in his voice. I had felt my heartbeat quicken as it didn't do when Tommy was near me. Oh my God! this was silly, stupid really, ridiculous. I forced myself to turn my face to him and say in a heavy tone, 'I have one adopted son, I don't want another.'

'Oh ... oh, don't be silly, my dear ... Mrs ... Leviston ... Maisie.'

'*Please.*'

'Please what?'

'Don't you be silly.'

'Are you going to marry Tommy Balfour?'

'That's ... that's my business.'

'Then you are not sure?'

'Yes, I am sure of what I mean to do, but again I say that's my business. And ... and now I'm very tired.'

He stood up and looked down at me, saying, 'End of act two, that's a good line to finish on, but the play has some way to go yet. Goodbye, my dear.' Then quickly and before I could prevent him, he kissed me. And now he was smiling as he said, 'And we've got that in common, too: we've both got bald patches behind our ears.'

195

I did not look at him leaving the room. My heart was beating against my still painful ribs. What, in the name of God, was the matter with me! What was it that people saw in me so much that they could hate me to death, or love me? Nardy, Tommy, and now this attractive young being. There was something weird about me, there must be. It had come out with the horse. But this latest business: no; no, never. Pull yourself together. Yes, yes, I must, and when Tommy comes tonight I'll tell him . . . I'll tell him that I'll marry him. Definitely I'll tell him.

Tommy came as I knew he would, but I didn't tell him I would marry him.

3

In whatever way my emotions were affected by the Mohican they were definitely put in their place the following day when I had a surprise visit from Hilda. The first part of the surprise was that she was no longer wearing her extraordinary get-up that had matched the Mohican's but was dressed in a green skirt and a three-quarter length coat to match. The white blouse had a bow at the neck and the whole outfit looked so simple, and so unlike Hilda that at first glance I did not recognize her; even her hair style was different, soft, hanging down onto her shoulders.

'Hello, Mrs Leviston.'

'Hello, Hilda. Oh, how nice to see you.'

'I hope you don't mind me comin' in?'

'Of course not. Of course not. Sit down.'

As she sat down to the side of the bed she said, 'I haven't brought you anything. Well, you see, I didn't think I would come in, have the nerve like.'

'Why not? Don't be silly; why shouldn't you come in and see me?'

'Because of me mum. Not that I said I was comin'. She stopped May and Max. He wanted to bring Harold. And you know Max, or at least you don't, Mrs Leviston, but he'd make a cat laugh at times and Mum said it pains you to laugh.'

'Oh, not any more; and it's good to laugh.'

I was smiling widely now but Hilda wasn't, she was looking down at her hands and the two fingers that were seemingly picking another hole in the white honeycombed bed cover.

I waited for a moment or so before I asked, 'Is anything wrong, Hilda?'

She lifted her head. Her eyes were blinking, and she looked away to the far window as she said, 'I shouldn't have come, an' he'd go for me right, left'n centre, if he knew, for ... for he likes you. He ... he thinks you're very clever and understandin', and I thought –' she swallowed deeply before she brought her eyes to mine and ended, 'you might have a word with him and persuade him like. I know we are different and I'm not up to his standards, I'm dim, like, I know I am. I know I am.'

'*You're not*, Hilda.'

Her eyes were blinking more rapidly now and her voice was slow and definite as she said, 'Oh, yes I am, Mrs Leviston. Now if I'd been like May, things would've been different. But he's ... he's a gentleman. He is you know, you know he is, Mrs Leviston. You saw the difference straightaway. He always said you could see below the skin.'

She was again looking down at her fingers which were plucking more quickly now at the bedspread and her voice was a mere whisper as she said, 'I love him. I'd die for him. I'd do anything for him. I'd keep in the background. I told him I would as long as he would let me be there near him. I said I would try to learn to speak proper an' all that, and how to act and ...'

My short arm came out and almost dragged her fingers from their plucking and my voice was harsh as I said, 'Don't denigrate yourself like that, Hilda! you're as good as he is any day.'

'Oh no, Mrs Leviston.' Her head was shaking.

'I mean it, Hilda. There's more things in life than being able to talk properly, as you say, and act as if you were somebody you're not. You've got what many people would envy, capacity to love, and that's a great thing, Hilda.'

'You think so, Mrs Leviston?'

'I don't just think so, I'm sure of it. Now you get it into your head that you are worth loving, and you tell him so. Don't crawl, Hilda. Don't crawl.'

'Oh, Mrs Leviston, I'll always crawl where he's concerned; he's just got to open his mouth. And ... and Max is always singin' "Less than the dust 'neath thy chariot wheels". He sings it funnily, but ... but I've often thought that's how I feel with regards to John. I can never think of him by any other name but John. And things would have been different if he'd let me keep the baby ...'

She finished this sentence with her mouth agape; then, her hands linking together, she shook them as she said, 'Mum warned me, I've only to open me mouth and I'd get somebody hung.'

'You have a baby?' I'd pulled myself now from the pillows without any effort and was bending towards her.

And she muttered, 'I could have had, I wanted to, but ... but I had an abortion.' Her eyelids lifted and she stared at me for a moment. 'He wanted it that way. An' ... an' Mum an' all, 'cos as she said, he'd never be able to work to keep it, an' what a life it would have had. Of course we didn't know then that he could have worked and was already workin' sort of. Anyway, it had to go. And ... and I was bad after. I couldn't stop cryin'. I was sent away for three weeks so I could pull meself together. He was nice about it.'

Gran's retort was in my mind. 'Bloody hell!' she would have said. 'He would be nice about it.'

'I ... I think if I'd had the baby I wouldn't have minded so much, I mean about now, being left. May's been a brick. She's taken me in an' looked after me 'cos I started that cryin' bout again. But I'm over it now.

199

Well, I mean, I've got to face up to it like, haven't I?'

She had forced a smile to her face, but at this moment it was I who wanted to cry.

'May was for me comin' to you about him, but Mum nearly went round the bend. She swore what she'd do to me if I did. But' – her smile widened a bit – 'here I am, and I know I'll get it in the neck but I had to try. Do you understand, Mrs Leviston?'

'Yes, Hilda, I understand. And you know something? And I mean this: I think you are too good for him, far too good for him.'

'Oh, no, no, Mrs Leviston; he's educated an' . . .'

'Damn education!' The jerk I gave made me take my hand from her arm and hold my neck, and she said, 'Oh dear! there I am upsettin' you.'

'Oh, no, of course you're not; it's just when I jerk my head I think it's coming off. But to get back to what I said, or to say something further. I could only wish that you'd get over your feeling for him and find a nice young man who'd make a home for you and you for him. How old are you?'

'I'm on twenty-five.'

I was again surprised for I had thought she was nearer the Mohican's age . . . The Mohican. How could I ever have thought . . . ? What had I thought? Again the pain went down my back as the movement of my head denied my thoughts. He was a snob, an upstart. Who did he think he was, anyway? After all, he was just a policeman.

'Will you speak to him if you see him, Mrs Leviston?'

I had to force myself to say, 'Yes, yes, I'll speak to him, Hilda.' I had not said in which way I would speak to him.

'I'd better be goin' now.'

'You aren't at work?' I asked.

'I've been off these last two or three days. I wasn't feelin' up to the mark. The doctor gave me a note. Nervous debility, he said. Well, goodbye, Mrs Leviston, you've been so nice. Mum says you're always nice. She thinks the world of you, does Mum. She says it was a lucky day for her when you married Mr Nardy. She's meanin' about you takin' Harold. None of us can get over how you handle him, because he's a holy terror.'

'Is he not behaving himself?'

'Oh. Oh, he's all right now, because' – she laughed now – 'he knows he's got to be, else Mum'll tell you. An' you know, he's terrified of not comin' back to you. An' you know somethin' else?' She bent over me now. 'It had the lads in stitches at first until Mum said, the next one that laughed she would kick his ar ... smack his face for him, 'cos you see Harold says his prayers at night.'

'He says his prayers?' My smile was soft, my voice was soft.

'Yes. Yes, he does, Mrs Leviston.'

Harold saying his prayers. I had never made him kneel down and say his prayers ... That must be the school. Bless them. Of a sudden I longed to be home with Harold and Tommy. Oh yes, with Tommy. My mind had strayed from Tommy ... Damn that Mohican.

'Goodbye, Hilda. And just a moment.' She was turning away, but I caught her hand again and said, 'You won't believe this, but you'll get over him. I know you will. And you'll meet a nice fellow one of these days. You're too warm and kind to be passed over. He's a fool. Oh yes, he's a fool and he'll find it out one day.'

She was unable to speak, her lips were moving in and out as she attempted to swallow, and hastily she turned from me.

She'd had a baby. He had made her have an abortion. And she had wanted a baby, especially his baby. Some men were cruel and cruelty didn't only come through ignorance, it came through education and the feeling that because of it you were different, superior, and of a class that wouldn't deign to marry beneath it. Make use of it. Oh yes, make use of it, as he had done of Hilda to help him complete the picture of the drop-out. I hoped I never set eyes on him again.

And I didn't for a week; and then I was sitting up and had more strength with which to speak my mind.

In the meantime I had another visit from a member of Janet's family, and this one not only surprised me but amazed me after I'd got over the fright of seeing her walking into the ward with her son ... my son.

The only name for Maggie Stoddart was blowzy: she was big-busted, big-hipped, and with a wide face and mouth to match; her hair was dyed inky black, and her eyes were deeply mascaraed. What age was she? She could have been thirty or fifty. She had a bouncy air about her, and in the following half-hour I came to know that it would always defy whatever age she reached.

When Harold had tugged his hand from hers and run to the bed I put my arms about him but said nothing. Nor did he speak, he just looked up at me as I now turned my gaze towards his natural mother, who said, 'S'prised to see me, Mrs Leviston? I'm ... I'm his mum.' And she thumbed towards Harold.

'How do you do?'

'Well, take a look.' She patted her stomach none too gently. 'I do seven and a half months.'

What could one say to that except, 'Do sit down.'

She sat down, then said, 'Don't look so worried; I've not come to try an' get him back. Oh, no, not me. Anyway, he wouldn't come. Would you?' She leant across the bed as she demanded an answer to this question from her son ... our son. And he replied simply, 'No, Mum.'

'There you are, isn't that a dutiful son for you? Well brought up, speakin' the truth.' She opened her mouth wide, to show a surprisingly fine set of teeth; then

202

turning her attention to me again, she said, 'You're still lookin' surprised. Wonderin' why I'm here, aren't you?'

'Yes; yes, I am a bit.'

'Well, it's not that I want to put a spoke in your wheel with regards him' – she again nodded towards Harold – 'not that I could because it's all been signed and sealed, but I thought I'd put your mind at rest about somethin' else that I know you haven't taken to, and that's his nibs comin' to claim his rights every other week or so. Gawd! that sounds funny, doesn't it?' Her large stomach and big breasts seemed to wobble in unison. 'Claim his rights. But you know what I mean?' She broke off here to open her handbag from which she took out a fifty pence piece which she handed across the bed to Harold, saying, 'Go on to the 'ospital shop an' get yourself a bar.'

Harold looked at the money, then looked at me, and when I said, 'Yes, go on,' he went, but with evident reluctance.

The door closed, I looked at my visitor. Yes, I knew what she'd meant the first time. And now she went on. 'Mum says she hasn't told you the full story.'

'No; Janet hasn't told me anything, I mean with regards to yourself.'

'Better comin' from me, I suppose she thought. Well, it's like this, Mrs Leviston. You know I was in for a divorce 'cos I was goin' to marry this bloke . . . I'm a bad lass you know.' She leaned towards me and grinned widely as she made this statement. 'He was the third bloke I'd made a mistake about since walkin' out on Jimmy. But anyway, when I found I'd one in the pot' – she patted her stomach again – 'I thought it was about time I stayed in one place, so Ralph, this fellow, said we'd get married. So all I wanted was a divorce. And of course I'd given enough grounds, you could say, to let a battalion off the hook.' Again she laughed. 'Then, I

203

ask you, what did Ralph do? The bloody swine . . . Well, he was, an' I'll say it again, he was, he takes a pattern from me an' he scarpers. But James Stoddart wasn't to know that, was he, when down he comes to see me. My! I nearly fell off me perch when I opened the door to him. Well, the long and short of it was, his piece had done the dirty on him an' he was left with Doris and Gloria. By the way, I don't suppose you know that the kids aren't mine, they were his by his first wife. Anyway, we got to talkin' . . . Am I borin' you, Mrs Leviston?'

'Boring me, Maggie? No, I've never felt so entertained for a long, long time.'

We laughed together now, and her hand coming on the shoulder of my still-plastered arm in no light slap definitely quelled my laughter and almost made me cry out. But I said, 'Go on. Go on.'

'Well, there we were sittin' tête-à-tête, as they say, 'aving a cup of tea, an' what 'e says to me is, "You intent on goin' through with this an' marryin' him?" And I, like the good liar I am, says, "Well, of course; what else can I do, Jimmy? You can see me condition." And you know what? *Do . . . you . . . know . . . what, Mrs Leviston?* He said to me, "I don't mind your condition, I've had it once afore if you remember, all I want is you come back." Well, I 'ummed and 'aaed and 'ummed and 'aaed; then finally thankin' God on the side, I said, "All right."'

Again her head was back; again she was laughing. Then of a sudden her laughter stopped and her face lengthened as she said, 'I slipped up there, didn't I?'

'What do you mean you slipped up?'

'Well, what I said about 'im takin' me before in the same condition.'

'Oh.'

'Anyway' – she shrugged her big shoulders – 'I think you've got a right to know; you see, Harold isn't his.'

'No? He's *not his father*?'

'That's what I'm sayin', Mrs Leviston, Harold isn't his. Mind, he tells himself that he is, but at bottom he knows what he knows. That's why he's never been able to stand the kid, and 'Arold sensed this from the beginnin'. That's why he became such a little terror, I think. No, his father was the only decent bloke I've ever known. But I wasn't up to his standard, you know like, so he scarpered.'

I was singing inside. Of course the boy had nothing of Jimmy Stoddart about him; but he had his mother's humour and impishness. Oh, yes, yes, I could see that. But Maggie was going on.

'You know, when I walked into the kitchen the other day I thought me mum would pi ... kill herself laughin'. An' the lads, all they could say was, "Oh! Maggie." Like our Max said, I could take on a brigade of guards an' they'd all be worn out by the mornin'. Well, you know what I mean, Mrs Leviston.'

She was flapping her hand at me now. And yes; yes, I certainly knew what she meant.

'Anyway,' she went on, 'when things had quietened down in the kitchen I had a talk with Mum and she told me about the rumpus there'd been between him and Mr Tommy. Well, I said, I'll put a stop to that. It isn't as if he cares anything for the lad, it's just that he wants to be bloody contrary ... Excuse me swearin', Mrs Leviston.' I excused her swearing. 'Anyway, I said I'd take the girls back, 'cos, you see, they weren't mine no more than young 'Arold was his. So that's what I said, "I'll take the girls back if you let go altogether on 'Arold. He's got the chance of a lifetime, something that I could never give him nor you. No, never you." That's what I said. Oh, yes, that's what I said. I don't pull me punches.' Again her mouth was wide. 'So that's why I thought I'd come an' tell you meself. You've got no need to worry about any more visits from him. If 'e starts shoutin' about his rights, 'e'll get his rights all right, but I'll see they're curtailed.' Again her breasts and stomach were wobbling. 'Mind, not that I'd like to cut off from him, the kid, altogether, you know what I mean; now and again I'd like to see 'im. That's if you don't mind.'

I put my hand out and laid it across her fat fingers, saying, 'Of course, Maggie, of course. And I can assure you he'll be a credit to you.'

For the first time I saw her show some genuine emotion. She turned her head away for a moment, sniffed, then said, 'No credit due to me. I've ... I've always pleased me bloody self. Made like that you see, where the other thing is concerned: can't 'elp it, sort of. I don't know who I take after. Likely our old man. 'Cos Mum always said he was determined to have a baker's dozen but she put the cork in at eight.'

She turned to me now. Her eyes were blinking, her mouth was tight. 'People don't understand; we're all made different, aren't we? Aren't we?'

'Yes, of course we are, Maggie.'

'There's you, so nice'n kind an' normal like, who would think you have spent years talkin' to a horse that wasn't there and gettin' it to kick people's arses? I read your book. I did, an' I laughed till I cried, because, oh! God, the people that I've wanted to kick in the back of the front.'

'Maggie! Maggie!' It was a groan now. 'Please!'

'What is it?'

I was choking: 'Please, don't make me laugh like this, it hurts all over.'

'Oh! Mrs Leviston, does it?' She was laughing more loudly herself now.

The door opened and in came Harold. He looked from one to the other, then said, 'You're laughin'.'

'Yes. What d'you think we're doin', big head?'

He looked at his mother but didn't answer her; then

he looked at me and said, 'For a minute I thought you was cryin'.'

'Were!'

'Oh, you!' He glanced at his mother again, then grinned and said, 'That's what she does,' before turning to me and asking, 'What d'you want, a Smartie or a piece of Mars bar?'

'Ask your mother first.'

He stretched across the bed, and I watched her take a Smartie, say ta, then pop it in her mouth.

When he offered me the packet I also took a Smartie and, laying it on the bedside table, I said, 'I'll keep it for after; they'll be bringing the tea round in a moment.'

And when presently the nurse entered with a tea-tray on which there were three cups and saucers, a teapot and water jug, and a plate of small cakes, Maggie exclaimed, 'My! My! Isn't this nice now. This is the life. What I wouldn't give to have a fortnight in 'ere.' And when her son replied quickly, 'Don't be daft, Mum, you'd have to be knocked about to be in 'ere,' she looked at him and said, 'You're right. You're right, boy; you would have to be knocked about to be in 'ere, and I 'aven't been knocked about enough yet.'

She turned her gaze on me, and the look in her eyes made me want to reach out to her and say, Oh, Maggie, Maggie, but she was laughing again, saying, 'Will I play mother?' And so I said quietly, 'Yes. Yes, Maggie, you play mother.'

4

Later, when Tommy came in laden down as if it was Christmas with a great bouquet of flowers, three books, and a bottle of perfume, that's what I said to him, 'Is it Christmas?' And his answer was, 'Yes, every day I'm with you.'

Tommy was nice.

While describing to him the reason for Maggie's visit I had him laughing so loudly he had to put his hand over his mouth to still the sound.

'That family,' he said. 'You know, you should write a book about them, starting with the day Harold was made legal.'

'That's the idea,' I said.

'But you'll have to be careful how you introduce the Mohican: you'll have to be truthful and say he put me off from the start, yet you recognized something in him that neither I nor anyone else did . . . clever clouts!' He had picked up Gran's phrase, clever clouts.

I wasn't clever or even perceptive in this case: as a silly woman I had responded to the emotional appeal of a young man with a very attractive voice who had presumably opted out of the system. I felt ashamed that, after living with a man like Nardy and knowing a man like Tommy here, I could allow my emotions to be so affected by such an unprincipled individual. And there was another thing: he had a nerve, hadn't he, to imagine that I . . . Oh, shut up!

'What did you say?'

I hadn't realized that I had lain back and closed my eyes while facing up to the fact that yet once again I was a very ordinary individual, and in more ways than one.

'I was thinking.'

'I thought you had gone to sleep. I've got a confession to make,' he said.

'What have you done now?'

'I bought *Spring Fever*.'

'The ... the boat?'

'The ... the boat.'

'Oh, Tommy.' I shook my head; then asked, 'How much did you finally pay for it?'

'Thirty-one thousand.'

'Oh my!'

'She's a beauty. I can't wait to get you on to her, and I promise you that she'll move no further than the Thames if you feel at all afraid; and I wouldn't mind that because she's just lovely to be in. I can't explain it. Captain Lee feels the same way about her. He's been with her as he puts it, since she was born, seven years ago. He saw her being finished off in the yard a week after he was made redundant because his company was cutting down on their line. You'll like him ... Ned. He's a fine fellow. He's dying to meet you.'

'Oh, be quiet!'

'Yes, he is, because he knows as well as I do that it depends upon you whether he keeps his job or not. It's down to practicalities now. I can manage her on the river, but I should need some practice before I could cross the Channel and go up the French rivers. Just think of it, Maisie.' He hitched himself further towards me and took my face between his big hands, saying quietly, 'We could have our honeymoon in France. Come on, how say you?'

I looked into his dear kind face and knew that I must stop stalling. Nardy had wanted it this way, and I did too. Yes, I did now more than ever. And just as I had felt grateful to Nardy for taking on this commonplace woman, as I knew myself to be, so I again felt grateful to Nardy's friend. But such were my emotions at the moment that I couldn't answer like a sensible individual with a simple 'Yes,' but had to say facetiously, 'That seems quite in order, Mr Balfour.'

'Oh, Maisie, darling.' His arms were about me, his long lean face was close to mine, and his words came thick and muffled as he said, 'I love you so much, Maisie.'

That was the odd thing about it, the weird thing, the intensity with which I created love and hate in people ... in men. Look at Stickle. At this thought I metaphorically shook myself, my mind crying at me, I'm not looking back on Stickle or my mother; I'm going to look ahead and count my blessings and realize that the love I've inspired is much stronger than the hate.

'Don't cry, darling.'

'I'm not crying.'

'No, of course you're not.' He wiped my eyes; then softly he asked, 'Do you think you'll ever be able to say you love me, really love me?'

He did not add, 'as you did Nardy,' because he knew that would be impossible, and I knew I could never love again as I had loved Nardy. But there were so many different kinds of love and so many levels of love, and I knew in this moment that on one of the levels I loved this man, and so I replied simply, 'I love you now, Tommy, and I thank you for loving me.'

He didn't kiss me, he just laid his head on my shoulder and said softly, 'We'll make it soon, straight after the court case is over.'

The court case.

The following day they took the plaster off my leg and arm and what followed was almost as painful as when I

210

returned to consciousness. Yet, I forced myself to laugh with the therapist, the nurses and the doctor as they made jokes about the 'two sticks' they had to get moving.

Three days later I was wheeled from the room to the therapy ward; and my efforts there to move 'the sticks' were even more excruciating. But at last I was out of bed, which was wonderful.

And it was towards the end of the week that while I was sitting by the window the Mohican came in. He was carrying a bunch of flowers. They were roses, red ones, and as in such cases I guessed there would be the conventional dozen.

'Back to life?' He looked down on me.

'Yes. Yes, back to life.'

'How do you feel?'

'Very well, fine in fact.'

He continued to look at me; then holding out the roses at arm's length as a child might and in the same manner, he said, 'Brought these for you.'

I looked at them, then said quietly, 'They're very nice, but you're offering them to the wrong person.'

His arm dropped: he turned and laid the roses on a side table; then going to the bedside he lifted up a chair and brought it towards the window and, sitting slowly down on it, he said, 'I thought we'd discussed that at the last board meeting.'

'Not quite.'

I looked at him. He was staring me full in the face and again I felt sorry that I'd found him to be other than the nice Mohican, and also I knew that I couldn't flail him with words as I would have done had he appeared shortly after Hilda's visit. So my voice was quiet as I said, 'Your roses might have been of some solace to Hilda in place of the baby that she wanted and could have had.'

I watched the expression on his face change: his

colour deepened, the muscles under his cheekbones moved in and out; and his voice came from between tight lips as he said, 'She was no more fit to have a child than I as the Indian was fit to provide for it.'

Now my voice was angry as I said, 'If you didn't consider her fit to have a child why did you give her one?'

'Well, if you want to know the truth, *Mrs Leviston*, it was because she pestered me. I never took up with her in the first place; she became my shadow. She got rigged out as she did because she thought it would draw me to her. You could say that I didn't give her the child, she took it from me.'

'Then why did you keep on with her?'

'Because in that particular job I recognized she could be good cover. A loner is always under suspicion, but squatting with someone like her you were accepted. It's a dangerous business, which has been proved to you, I hope.'

I looked back at him and heard myself say, 'I'm sorry.'

'And I'm sorry too.' His expression altered.

'She loves you so much.'

He tossed his head impatiently to the side, saying, 'Only because she saw I was a little different from her usual acquaintances. Maisie' – he was gripping both my hands now – 'don't you see it's impossible? What kind of a life would we have?'

'Perhaps better in lots of ways than with a girl you consider of your own class. And she would learn. Why, she came in here the other day and she looked so ...'

He screwed up his face. 'She came?' He had pulled back from me. 'I thought it might be her mother or May, but *she came*?'

'Yes, yes, she came.'

'Good God!' He got to his feet, put his hand to his head and turned towards the window and stared down onto the forecourt.

I said softly, 'You would make something of her, make her what you want, she would learn. As I said, she would learn.'

He swung round on me. 'She would learn nothing. She is of a type. All she wants is bed; she's as over-sexed as a bloody rabbit.'

On other occasions I would have laughed, and when he said, 'I'm sorry,' I muttered, 'Oh, you needn't apologize.' He came now and stood close by my side. 'You see me as a louse, don't you?'

'No, I don't, John.' The fact that I'd spoken his name changed the light in his eyes, and I turned my gaze from his and looked out of the window as I continued, 'But I'm sorry for Hilda, for I know that she sincerely loves you. Whichever way it is, she loves you, and it's a pity you can't see it that way. But I understand.' I looked at him again and watched him slowly smile, and then he said, 'You know, you have a funny face, an appealing funny face.'

There it was again, my heart knocking against my ribs. I brought my defences up and heard myself lying, 'Huh! It's odd you should think that, that's what Tommy says. By the way, we're going to be married shortly.'

His smile slowly seeped away and after a moment he said, 'Yes?' And I replied, 'Yes.'

'Well, well! So life moves on. I hope you'll be very happy.'

'Thank you.'

Getting away from this touchy topic, I said quickly, 'Have you any idea when the case will come up?'

'Oh' – he pursed his lips – 'about three weeks' time I should say.'

'How ... how long will it last?'

'Who knows? We've picked up eight of them altogether, including your three and the woman. There'll be the drug charges first; I should imagine

213

abduction and attempted murder – that'll be your case – will be on the last day or so. You'll be the main witness in that, naturally, you and the man on the cliff top. And me of course. So we'll meet again.' He buttoned the middle button of his light coat, then said, 'Well, I'll say goodbye.'

'Goodbye, John.' Then I added, 'In a way, I should say I'm sorry we ever met because of what has transpired.'

'I can endorse that wholeheartedly, *Mrs Leviston*.' He stressed my name. 'Oh yes, wholeheartedly.' Then, pointing to the roses, he said, 'Give those to one of the nurses; they may recognize their significance.'

When the door closed on him I seemed to slump in the chair and I asked myself a question: If Tommy hadn't been on the scene, would I?

Yes, yes, I would.

5

On the day I left hospital I felt a little like royalty. I had said goodbye to the night staff earlier on and they had paid me the compliment of saying I was the only patient on that floor who had never rung the night bell; and the day staff had said they were sorry to see me go. The doctor who happened to be doing his rounds when I was leaving jokingly cried at me, 'I'm going to see you off the premises and make sure you don't break anything more of that gigantic frame of yours.' And so, supported at one side with a walking-stick and by Tommy's arm on the other and flanked by the sister and doctor, I departed from the hospital and made for home.

And there was Janet waiting outside the lift, and there were tears in her eyes as she exclaimed, 'I never thought to see you walk out of there again. Welcome home, Mrs Leviston, ma'am.'

Her voice was almost drowned by the sound of Sandy's barking coming from the kitchen and she said, 'He sensed you were coming, he's gone mad since Mrs Brown brought him up, but I won't let him loose till you're settled, else he'll have you over.'

The flat looked strange, very large and sort of empty. The yellow drawing-room was still beautiful but aloof somehow. There was something missing. I said, 'Where's Harold, Janet? I thought ...'

'Well, ma'am, that's another thing: I left him at home; I just thought he would run wild an' all, an' you would want to get settled in. He's been like a cat on hot bricks this last couple of days, in fact, for weeks now. You're goin' to have a job gettin' him back into form. Anyway, I told them I'd give him a ring as soon as you wanted him here, and Hilda would bring him. She's back, you know, ma'am. She's been stayin' home for a time, but she's goin' to room with May as soon as May gets rid of the girls. They're goin' back to Maggie's. Oh, what a mix up there. I've got things to tell you you wouldn't believe. Maggie's settled in with him again like, but she said she wanted space to move around before gettin' down to housekeepin' again. And so the lasses are still at May's. Oh!' She looked at Tommy now, saying, 'I can never believe she's one of mine ... Maggie. I've bred some queer 'uns, but she takes the cake.' She turned away, saying, 'Everything's ready in the dining-room when you are. Oh, it's lovely to have you back, ma'am ... lovely.'

Tommy sat himself down beside me on the couch and, putting his arm about me, said, 'I endorse that. You've been a very missed woman, if you follow my meaning ... ma'am ... How do you feel, darling?'

'Do you know, Tommy, I couldn't tell you, I really couldn't. I suppose I feel tired, but I had expected to feel elated just to be back here.' I looked around this beautiful room, then said, 'But strangely I feel flat.'

'That means you want a holiday. Tomorrow, if you feel up to it, or the next day, we're going down to the boat. If that doesn't cheer you up nothing will.'

'Tommy.'

'Yes, my dear?'

'I know what's worrying me, it's the case. I'm ... I'm terrified of courts.'

'It'll be all right. Everything's been arranged, and you won't have to appear until the last day.'

'How do you know?'

'Oh, I haven't been idle. I've had a talk with the

216

barrister, and he said the Indian's bodily harm business will come up first, then the attempted murder charge against those three fellows; all you've got to do is to identify them. I don't think the woman will be charged with them except as an accessory or some such. Don't worry, all you'll have to do is just walk in and then walk out again. It'll be over in no time.'

I remained silent whilst thinking, I hope so. Oh, dear God, I hope so . . .

Two hours later I was sitting on the couch with Sandy curled up at my side when Harold came bouncing into the room. I say he bounced, but that was as far as half-way up the room, for there he suddenly stopped, stared towards me, then did a little run and came and stood by my knee and looked at me.

'Hello,' I said. 'Haven't you anything to say to me?'

He didn't answer immediately; then he asked, 'You better?'

'Yes; yes, I'm quite better.'

'You'll not go away again?'

'No.'

'Ever?'

'Not ever.'

At this he knelt up on the couch, put his arms around my neck, then whispered something, and I said, 'What did you say?' And now I heard his voice very small say, 'I was frightened.'

'What were you frightened of?'

'You wouldn't come back, an' I'd be stuck at Gag's.'

I pushed him from me. 'Oh, that's all you were frightened about, because you would be stuck at Gag's?'

'No, no.' He made an impatient movement with his head, and when I laughed and pulled him towards me he said, 'Oh! you. You're funny.' He then added, 'An' he missed you an' all.' He put his hand on Sandy's head. 'He 'owled and 'owled, had fits of it.'

217

'He never 'owled and 'owled, he *howled* and *howled*.'

He slanted his gaze at me and his response was, 'Nuts.'

'What did you say?'

He grinned, then demanded, 'Where's Mr Tommy?'

'He's gone out for a while.'

'To the boat?'

'No; not to the boat, to his flat; he wanted something. What do you know about the boat?'

'Oh' – he preened himself – 'I've been on it. It's smashin', lovely. Oh boy! Uncle Max and Uncle Billy were bloody dumbfound.'

We looked at each other. His head was bowed for a second before it jerked up and he said, 'Well, that's nothin'. They were.'

'Harold!'

'Oh ... well, they all say it. Oh, I'm sorry, I am, Mrs Nardy, I'm sorry.'

'All right. All right. But tell me, how did your uncles and you see the boat? And where?'

'Mr Tommy, he ... he took us one day in the car. Oh, that car! Uncle Billy nearly cried over it. He loves cars. His is four wheels an' a biscuit tin. He made Uncle Max and Mr Tommy laugh when he said he'd exchange any pair of boobs for Mr Tommy's headlights.'

'Harold!'

'What?'

'You musn't repeat things like that.'

'Like what?' He was definitely puzzled and amazed. 'I never swored.'

'Swore.'

'Well, I never did.'

'No; but you repeated something rude.'

He looked to the side as if his words were imprinted there and he was sorting them out. Then his head jerked towards me and he said, quietly, 'Boobs?'

'Yes.' I made a deep obeisance with my head.

'Well, huh!' There was now a grin on his face. 'That's nothin'. They're in the papers an' magazines; women 'ave 'em. And—' I drew in a deep breath as I turned my gaze from him, and he went on, 'Uncle Max says some of 'em haven't even got their bootlaces on.'

My gaze returned to him sharply.

'Bootlaces! What do you mean bootlaces?'

'Well.' He demonstrated now with a finger pointing across each side of his chest. 'Those bits they wear. He calls them bootlaces. An' down on their bell . . .'

'All right, all right, we won't go into that any more. But tell me' – my speech was rapid now – 'what was the boat like? I mean, what did you think of the boat, besides it being smashing, lovely? What are the rooms like, the cabins?'

'Oh.' He turned from me now, linked his arms about his knees, brought his feet up onto the couch and rocked himself as he attempted to describe what he had seen: 'Well, it's green . . . and well, it's big like a house inside, and it's got rooms. Oh' – he turned quickly towards me – 'you'd have to see it. As Uncle Max says, even on the outside it made all the other boats round about look like a heap of old odds and sods.'

We said nothing: our thoughts were exchanged by our eyes which stared into each other. When I spoke I said, 'Your Aunt Hilda's in the kitchen. Go and ask her if she wouldn't mind coming and having a word with me?'

He slipped off the couch, stood looking at me for a moment, then said, 'Well, it's . . .' but didn't finish; instead he slumped away out of the room.

Uncle Max, Uncle Bill, all those uncles, it looked as if I had to start from the beginning again. One thing I should be pleased about, he had taken to Tommy. But Tommy was no fool: the boat was an asset on his side in

219

the cause of future relationships . . .

Hilda came quietly into the room, and I said, 'Hello, Hilda.'

'Hello, Mrs Leviston.'

'Do sit down.'

'How are you feelin'?'

'Still a bit shaky, I'm afraid, Hilda.'

'You look much better than when I last saw you.'

'Yes; yes, I am. But I'm afraid I'm worrying about the court case.'

I hadn't been very diplomatic there, had I? But it seemed that I need not have worried because she said, 'Well, that's natural; it will be quite a big affair.'

I narrowed my eyes at her. She seemed different; she was dressed very nicely. And after a short silence she said, 'I'm sorry for upsettin' you that day I called at the hospital. I should never 'ave done it. I upset you and you were so concerned for me. But anyway, I've got over it.'

'Oh. Oh, I'm so glad, Hilda.'

''Tisn't nice to be chucked aside . . . thrown off, you feel like dirt, but as our May said, the only thing to do is to show him that he's made a mistake, and that's what I'm gonna do.'

'Good for you, Hilda. Good for you.'

'I've . . . I've left the factory.'

'You have?'

'Yes. I'm workin' in the same hotel as May, chambermaid. But that's only a start. May says I can rise an' I will. Yes I will. An' you meet different kinds of people. As she said, you pick up their lingo . . . how they talk. And anyway, as she says, I can pay for lessons an' be learned to speak properly.'

'Oh, don't do that.'

'No?'

'No; don't alter yourself, Hilda. You'll speak properly all right, mixing with other people. Don't lose your identity, I mean don't change your character, because you're such a warm person.'

The head drooped now and I saw the old Hilda, and her voice was low as she said, 'I went through a bad time. I think I would have done meself in if it hadn't been for May. May's good; she'll get on. She's got a fellow now. He's in a very good position, he's an assistant chef in one of the big 'otels. He's goin' to have a place of 'is own, a restaurant. Oh, May'll get on. An' she says I will an' all.' She was looking at me again. 'You know, Mrs Leviston, there's supposed to be no class distinction, everybody's the same, that's what they say, but as May says, it's a lot of codswallop. And the lads say it an' all. Max says you can't get into the Conservative Party unless you have a twang. John Drake had a twang, or James Bainbridge as he is. That's what got me in the first place, the way he spoke. Well, it's over. But I'll let 'em see in the end. That's all I want to do, let 'em see.'

'You'll come out on top, Hilda,' I said softly; and she looked at me and, her own voice now low and her eyes blinking, she said, 'I still love him though, Mrs Leviston. I haven't seen him since, but I was goin' to go to the court on the day, but May says that would be a mad thing to do. What do you think, Mrs Leviston?'

'I think with May, Hilda. Give yourself a year, perhaps longer. By that time you will have ... well sort of acquired a veneer and if you were then to meet him again it would be on his own ground. You know what I mean.'

'Funny; that's what May said: aim to be somebody; that'll make him sorry he turned his nose up.'

'She's right, Hilda. Yes, she's right.'

She stood up now, saying, 'You'll be glad to 'ave him back.' She jerked her head kitchenwards.

'Harold? Oh yes, yes.'

'You won't 'ave to expect too much of him at first.

The lads 'ave had a field day with him, went out of their way they did, not meanin' it badly, you know. Max is a caution, but he's very fond of him, in fact, he thinks it's a shame he's goin' to be spoilt, I mean, altered.'

'Well, you can tell Max he won't be spoilt. And also tell him the only thing I'll aim to alter is his language, most of it having been learned from him.'

She laughed now. 'I'll tell him, Mrs Leviston, I'll tell him. Well, goodbye, and thank you ... well, for listenin' to me.'

I held out my hand, and when she took it I pressed hers tightly, saying, 'Now I mean this, Hilda, I'm not just being polite, but I want you to pop in and see me every now and again when you have time, and we can have a talk.'

'*You do?*'

'Yes, I do. I'll want to know how you're progressing.'

She turned from me now and went quickly from the room, and I lay back and willed that she would come out on top and one day in the future meet the Mohican again when by the sound and sight of her he would have to eat his words.

Then I asked myself, if Tommy hadn't been in the way, what would I have done about her and her feelings for the Mohican, and her being Janet's daughter and Harold's aunt? For answer, I thanked God I had Tommy.

It was almost a week later when I saw the boat. Tommy first took us to meet the captain, who shared a house with his sister and brother-in-law overlooking the canal.

Captain Edward Lee, who asked to be addressed as Ned, was a stubby man in his late fifties. He was of Welsh extraction and had apparently sailed the seas since he was a boy. His brother-in-law had served as first officer under him in the merchant navy.

Tommy was retaining Captain Lee's services on a full-time basis, for two reasons he said: the house overlooked the canal and in the winter months he could keep an eye on the boat; the second reason was it would be one less on the dole and would help a man such as Ned Lee to keep his self-respect which was something that many men were losing. He was thoughtful, was Tommy. I had found that out in more ways than one.

At my first glimpse of *Spring Fever* I exclaimed, 'Oh, my goodness!' she looked so long and high. And when the Captain jumped aboard and pushed a gangplank down onto the canal bank, Harold dived up it like a squirrel up a tree; but I looked at Tommy and said, 'Oh, no.' Whereupon and without any further words, he stooped and picked me up, and at the top of the gangplank he put me into the arms of the captain and for the first time I was hoisted aboard.

Well, I looked from one to the other of the three faces looking at me; then I looked about me. This, I saw, was the wheelhouse. It was shining. The wood was gleaming; there were leather-cushioned seats at one side, and a high seat fronting the wheel and a panel of instruments. I said nothing. Then Tommy, walking quickly from me, went down a short flight of steps, turned and held up his arms, and with their aid I slowly descended the stairway.

'The saloon.' He spread his hand wide.

I couldn't believe it; it looked so beautiful. It had the same impression on me as had my drawing-room when I first saw it, the day when Nardy took me there to cry and to tell him the truth about my life.

'Isn't it smashin'?' Harold was jumping up and down.

Still I said nothing.

Now I was being led through a door and Tommy was saying, 'This is the dining quarter.'

And it was a dining quarter, it was a dining-room.

Through another door, 'Here's the galley,' he said. 'What do you think of it?'

What did I think of it? I couldn't believe my eyes. It was much better and more modern than the kitchen back at the flat and I thought that was good. As he described it to me, it had everything, and what I noticed, too, was that there were no portholes so far but windows, as one would get on the first-class deck of a cruise ship.

When I stood in the main bedroom I spoke for the first time. Looking from Tommy to the captain, then down to Harold, I said, 'I can't believe it. It seems impossible to get so much into ... well, this space.'

'There's a bath,' Harold had pushed open a door; and indeed yes, there was a bath with a shower and toilet.

'Come and see my cabin.' He darted out, and we followed him along what I termed a short passage and so into another cabin, smaller but also beautifully fitted. And Harold, pointing, said, 'That's my bed. And there's a space underneath it for Sandy's basket.'

'Bunk.'

Harold now grinned up at the captain and repeated, 'Bunk.' And we all laughed.

'Who said you were coming to sleep on this boat?' Tommy was looking sternly down on Harold now. And Harold turned his gaze on me enquiringly; then looking back at Tommy he stammered, 'We ... ll, I ... I th ... thought ... well the captain said –' And the captain, shrugging his shoulders expressively and holding out his hands, said, 'Oh , it's got nothing to do with me, has it, sir?'

'No, nothing whatever, Captain.'

And now I put in my say: 'It all depends on how you behave yourself.' And we stood looking down on the crestfallen face, and Tommy ruffled his head, saying, 'Of course, you're coming. We couldn't manage to get out of the canal without his help, could we, Captain?'

'No, no, sir. He guided us pretty well the other day.'

'Of course with the help of his uncles.'

Now Tommy and the captain exchanged laughter and a relieved Harold became himself and cried, 'There's still some more.'

And there was some more.

When later the captain served us tea in the saloon with thin bread and butter and home-made scones, I looked at him and said in amazement, 'Don't tell me you cooked these?' I pointed to the scones. And for answer he said, 'I've had to learn a lot of things during the last eight to ten years, madam; and I've never believed in living rough.'

'They're lovely. I ... I think this is the biggest surprise of all, this beautiful tea.'

'Tut! tut!' The captain tossed his head from side to side but was definitely very pleased at the compliment; then he said, 'You like her?'

'How could I help it? But I must tell you, I'm no sailor, I'm terrified of the water ... I mean, being so close to it.'

'You needn't be afraid of sailing in her, madam; I've guided her through some pretty stormy waters. At least, I say I did it, but no, she did it. She's got a mind of her own, like all women.'

I smiled at Captain Lee. I liked him.

'Would you like a run into the river?'

'I thought we were on the river.'

'This is the canal, madam. It's a fine day; she'll be as steady as a rock. What about it?'

'Well, I suppose' – I looked at Tommy – 'it's got to happen sometime.'

Tommy took my hand and squeezed it, and when Harold jumped up, crying, 'Good-oh! I can take her again?' the Captain said, 'Yes, yes, of course, she'll need your help. I wouldn't dream of attempting to take her out myself.'

Harold looked at me slant-wise: he knew he was being kidded and he couldn't find words to answer the captain in this vein, but he did it in his own way, and what he said was, 'Baloney!'

And so we went up the river. And I sat in the wheelhouse and looked at the bows cleaving through the water, and of a sudden I felt happy and knew that I would come to love this boat and that it would show me yet another way of life. And Tommy sat quietly looking at me while Harold stood within the arms of the captain and presumably took the wheel. And when at one point Tommy leant towards me and whispered into my ear, 'I love you,' I felt that life ahead was going to be good.

I'd forgotten about the trial.

6

I had been sick in the night; in fact, I had been sick for
the past two weeks, the dragged-out time of the court
proceedings of The Indian Drug Case, so termed by the
newspapers because the Mohican had, of course, been
the main witness in the trial which covered a sea
captain, a yacht owner, a well-known business man,
besides two pushers and the three men accused of
attempted murder, and a woman who ran a boutique.
The sentences on the captain and the yacht owner had
been similar, five years each, but the business man, to
most people's surprise, had been given eight years, for
this particular man had used his connections abroad
to bring the stuff into the country using various young
people who found themselves stranded abroad or down
on their luck. The other men were given two and four
years respectively. But when the judge had come to
sentencing the three men who were to stand trial for
attempted murder his remarks were that he would
reserve judgement on these men and their woman
associate after the charge had been heard. And then he
had praised the detective sergeant who had for two
years risked his life in his endeavour to bring the
convicted men to justice. And it had been a dangerous
task, as had been demonstrated in the end when he had
been attacked and left for dead by a drug addict. The
sergeant could quite easily have taken to drugs
himself; in fact, in order to suggest that he was one of
them, he had deliberately punctured his arm with a

needle. The whole community and all decent people, the judge went on to say, owed this man a debt of gratitude.

I had been in such a state before I left the house this morning that Tommy had insisted I swallow a glass of milk in which he had put a stiff measure of brandy. But this hadn't prevented my shaking inside and I was shaking now as I stood in the witness-box, after being brought into court by the usher as the first witness in the case. I had taken in the fact of the judge being arrayed in a long red robe with a white stole, and wearing a grey wig. He was sitting high up as if on a throne. Below him was a large table with a clerk sitting at the head of it and beyond this rows of seats occupied by the solicitors and counsel; those, as I had previously been told, for the prosecution on the right and those for the defence on the left. And above these was the dock. My mind seemed to blur to my present surroundings for I was remembering when I was last in court, before the judge had passed sentence on Howard Stickle and he had screamed at me that he would get me in the end. And he nearly had with his power of thought.

I was staring towards the dock; I could see his face. Yet there were four faces there, all blurred, but as the mist cleared from my eyes I saw the woman called Liz, the man called Bunty and then the one called Trucker, and then that dreadful one, Danny, and I started to whine to myself: I shouldn't be asked to do this, I'm not well enough. I'll pass out again.

I was once more walking along the top of the cliff with two of these men, one on each side of me holding my arms; I seemed to be lifting my feet up high ...

The prosecuting counsel was now asking me to tell the court, in my own words, what had happened.

Haltingly I brought out the words that gave the

picture of my meeting the Mohican ... I actually said the name before changing it quickly to Mr John Drake, as I knew him to be named then. The judge looked at me kindly. I think there was a smile on his lips as he said, 'Is that the name you gave to Detective Sergeant Bainbridge?' And I said, 'Yes, my Lord.'

When he turned his eyes from mine I saw him looking slightly to the left, and there for the first time I saw the Mohican himself sitting. He was looking at me and he smiled.

'Why were you meeting the ... Mohican or as you knew him then, Mr John Drake?' the prosecuting counsel now asked.

I then hesitantly told him that I'd had some articles stolen from the house and Mr Drake had discovered some of them in an antique shop, and he had told me he would show me where the shop was, but he didn't want me to meet up with him.

'What happened when you did meet up with him?'

Haltingly again I described the fight and the car drawing up and the men getting out.

'Mrs Leviston,' said counsel for the prosecution, 'can you identify the men who got out of the car?'

I looked towards the dock and met the three pairs of eyes riveted on me. Again they merged into Stickle's face. I nodded before I said, 'Yes. They are the men in the dock.'

At this point the counsel for the defence stood up saying that his clients had already admitted all that had been said; the main issue now was their presence on the cliff-top at Fairlight on the night in question.

The prosecuting counsel said calmly, 'We are coming to that.' Then turning to me he said, 'Describe what followed, Mrs Leviston, after you had been thrown into the car.'

I told him.

'Can you remember anything that was said before?'

My mind became blank for a moment; then I seemed to be back on that couch and I heard the woman speaking and I told them what little I remembered and added how she had said that she didn't want anything to be done to me in her house. I recalled she mentioned the name of Benson and said she didn't want that to happen again in her house.

At the mention of his name, the judge now said, 'You are sure, Mrs Leviston, that you heard the woman mention that name with regard to something in the past?'

When I answered, 'Yes, my Lord,' the judge wrote something down. Then once again he returned his attention to me, saying, 'Kindly proceed, Mrs Leviston.'

I now said, 'Well, they talked a lot about how' – I lowered my head as I muttered – 'to get rid of me. And it was the man called Danny who suggested the cliffs.'

'What happened then?'

'I . . . I cannot remember very much except that after they stuck a needle in my arm I . . . I sort of became resigned: I knew what was happening yet could do nothing about it. The last thing I remember is being pushed in the back and the air rushing into me. That is all.' . . .

'And that is all that is required of you, Mrs Leviston.' At this stage counsel for the defence indicated that he did not wish to cross-examine me.

As I was helped down from the box there swept over me a wave of relief, yet at the same time I thought I was going to faint. I sat on the front seat, and someone took my hand and patted it.

Someone else called a name out and a man stepped into the witness box. I didn't know him. He took the oath, then the prosecuting counsel said, 'Are you Mr Peter Dyke?' and the man answered, 'Yes.'

'Where do you live?'

'In Fairlight, outside Hastings.'

'Where were you on the night of August 10th, 1984?'

'I was taking my dog for a walk, as I do every night.'

'Can you describe to us anyone in this court you saw whilst out walking on that particular night?'

All eyes were on the man now as he turned to the dock, and he pointed, saying, 'Two of the men there, the big one and the thin one.'

'What in particular did you notice about these men?'

'I noticed that one looked like a boxer and the other didn't seem to be half the size, in fact not much taller than the young woman that was walking between them.'

'What were they doing?'

'They were each holding one of the young woman's arms.'

'What else did you notice about the men?'

'They were laughing; but the young lady looked solemn. I thought she must have just told them a joke. I remember the small man took her hand and wagged it.'

'How was it that you recall such a small action as that? They were, in fact, only passers-by.'

'Because sometime later I saw the same two men return to a car. I had passed the car earlier and the third man' – he pointed now – 'was standing outside leaning on the bonnet. But the other two men hadn't the young lady with them now, and I was a little puzzled at this until I thought they might have been seeing her home; there's a path leading to cottages and houses further along the cliff top.'

'What time of the evening was this?'

'I cannot say exactly but it was almost dark.'

There followed some more questions, but I found I wasn't listening. My sickness had increased, I longed for fresh air. Someone said, take a deep breath. I did just that.

There seemed to be a lapse of time; then my head

cleared and I listened to a man's cultured tones. It was the defence counsel speaking and he was saying, 'Neither William Smith, nor Thomas Robberton, nor yet Daniel Foxbrown, deny they bundled Mrs Maisie Leviston into their car, and they admit they took her to Fairlight, which they reached about one o'clock, and that there they pushed her out of the car and this is the last they saw of the lady in question. However, they admit that she might have been in a dazed condition as they had given her a sedative prior to bringing her from London.

'Therefore I suggest she wandered and later fell over the cliff. In the meantime, the accused men went to Hastings, a few miles away, parked the car, had several plates of cockles and wilks . . .'

'I think they are called whelks.'

'Yes, my Lord, yes whelks.'

There was a titter of laughter in the court; I looked towards the public seats and saw Tommy and he gave me a smile, which did nothing to help me.

The defence counsel was now repeating, 'Whelks, they had several plates of these, and later they visited two or three public houses.'

'How many public houses?'

'Two or three, my Lord.'

'They either visited two or they visited three.'

'Yes, my Lord, but I'm only repeating what they remembered, because to relate my clients' words, they became rather full.'

There was another titter.

Now the judge's voice rang out clear across the court; 'I can see nothing to cause amusement in this case. Proceed.'

He proceeded, saying flatly now, 'My clients can prove that they had returned to London and had had a meal in the flat above their friend's shop well before dusk.'

232

'You are referring to the boutique?'

'Yes, my Lord.'

'You have a witness?'

'Yes, my Lord, the accused, Elizabeth Myter.'

'Call Elizabeth Myter.'

It seemed from where I was sitting that the woman had to be lifted into the witness-box. I couldn't hear her swearing the oath nor could I hear her giving her name but the judge said, 'Ask your witness to speak up.'

When I looked up again the woman was muttering now. Half her words were unintelligible. But the gist of them was she had lived with the man known as Bunty for the past three years and her premises had been used to store drugs which he distributed, and yes, they had taken the woman with the intention of doing her in.

This last statement caused a commotion in the dock: it was the big fellow yelling, 'She's a liar, a bloody liar. Just wait.'

Two policemen were restraining the man, a voice was shouting, 'Order in court!'

The woman was now almost gibbering as she said that she knew about the drug racket all right, but that she would never have anything to do with polishing anyone off. And the man Bunty knew that. She was then asked if any one of them had threatened her. And after hesitation, she replied, no, not really, but that she was frightened of one of them. And to the surprise of the court she named the man called Danny.

Why was she frightened of him? she was asked.

Because he was weird, wrong in the head, twisted.

The man Danny made no response to this, he just stared at her . . .

There followed more procedure. The prosecuting counsel spoke to the jury. The defence counsel spoke to the jury. Then the judge was summing up and when he had finished the jury retired to consider their verdict and the judge also left the court.

There was a stir in the court, then a movement of people. I had moved too. I was now standing in an outer hall. Tommy was by my side, and in front of me stood the Mohican. His look was kindly as he said, 'It'll soon be over.'

'What do you think they'll get?' Tommy was addressing him now.

'Hard to say. The old boy's against them, which is good, but it's amazing, you never know with juries, there's always one or two who like to sit back and show they're different.'

'It must have been pretty rough for you all this.'

The Mohican now looked at Tommy and smiled saying, 'No; quite a holiday compared to the other business.'

'Yes, I suppose so, but it's certainly put a spoke in the drug racket.'

The Mohican made a strange sound in his throat as he said, 'You said the word, a spoke, and that's all it is. They'll still get in somehow.'

'After all you've done?'

'Oh, yes. What I've done had been done before. It'll be quiet for a time, but then they'll find other ways or means. Once you're hooked, it's either drugs or death. They won't recognize that the death comes through the drugs, they just think they'll die if they don't get them; and they'll get them.'

I looked at the Mohican. I was searching for a word to fit his mood, and the only one my mind presented me with was, disconsolate.

His voice was kindly now when, looking at me, he said, 'You want to take a long holiday when this is over.'

I nodded at him, saying, 'Yes, I mean to.'

'She's going on a honeymoon.' Tommy had bent towards him.

'Oh. Congratulations.'

'I've acquired a boat; we're going to do the rivers, if not the channel.'

'Very nice. I hope you'll be very happy.' He was looking at me now, and I said simply, 'Thank you.'

Why did I feel sorry for him? Why did I wish ...? What did I wish?

I looked to the side now and there, standing at the end of the room, were three of Janet's family, Max, Greg, and Rodney. They were looking towards us but they made no move to come forward, and the Mohican, turning his glance towards them before looking at me again, said, 'They would like to have a word with you but I'm in the way.' Then on a note of ironic humour he added, 'We don't want a punch-up in court, do we?' And with this he nodded at me and turned away, and Tommy, bending down, asked quietly, 'What did he mean by that?' And I replied as quietly, 'Well, you know he's dropped Hilda and the boys are not very pleased. He ... he was made very welcome in the house.'

'Oh, yes. Yes, I see the point. Let's go and have a word with them.'

They all said in their different ways, 'Hello, Mrs Leviston. How are you?' And I said frankly, 'Feeling dreadful.'

It was Greg who stated bluntly, 'I hope that old boy gives the buggers what they deserve, life, and not just for ten years or so. If I could get me hands on one of them there wouldn't be any need to sentence him.'

The other two nodded in agreement; then Max, touching on a lighter subject, said, 'Glad to have the nipper back, Mrs Leviston?' There was a grin on his face.

'Very glad, Max.'

'Has he been behavin' himself?'

'Well –' I slanted my gaze at him now and pointedly

said, 'It all depends, Max, on what you mean by behaving himself.'

He took my point and said, 'Like that is it, Mrs Leviston?'

'Like that, Max,' I said.

And at this the three men laughed and Tommy said, 'For my part, I always think the English language is very dull; it needs a bit of colour.'

'You're right there.' Rodney was nodding at him now. 'And I think the youngster'll always bring a little colour in his chatter. Trust him.'

And now I put in quickly, 'And if I may say so, Rodney, I trust you not to help him, or any of you.'

'Oh, Mrs Leviston.' The heads were wagging, the grins were wide, and Max's widened still further when I said, 'As for you, Max, we'll have to have a talk.'

'Yes, ma'am. Yes, ma'am.' He took on the attitude of a child to a teacher, and the laughter from the three of them caused heads to turn ...

Two hours later we were back in the court again; the jury filed in; the foreman was standing; you could have heard the proverbial pin drop. The judge's clerk asked the foreman of the jury, 'Do you find the accused guilty or not guilty?'

'Guilty on all charges, my Lord.'

'And is that the verdict of you all?'

'It is, my Lord.'

The three men in the dock remained still for a moment; then the boxer and the thin man bent their heads deeply, only the one who acted as chauffeur remained straight, there was even a smile round the corners of his lips. I could understand that woman being afraid of him.

The judge was speaking again, first to the jury.

'Ladies and gentlemen of the jury I want to thank you for the care and attention which you have given to this case. Lest any of you may have any lingering doubts as to the correctness of your verdict let me say that it is overwhelmingly supported by the evidence. The accused have already been found guilty by another jury of serious offences involving drug running which has had dire repercussions on thousands of lives. They were distributors of heroin and LSD, and when they were finally apprehended they had in their possession drugs with a street value in the region of two million pounds. I have had some despicable creatures stand before me in the dock in my time but never have I faced any as low as the three before me now. On their own admission they drugged this young woman and although she was unable to resist them they knew that she was quite conscious and would be in a state of terror when they cold-bloodedly tossed her over a high cliff trusting that the turn of the tide would take her body out with it and so cover up their dreadful deed. Fortunately the tide did not do as they had planned but the injuries which she sustained in the fall almost succeeded in ending her life.'

The judge now turned his attention to the three men in the dock addressing each of them by name: 'William Smith, Thomas Robberton, and Daniel Foxbrown, on the charge of abduction and attempted murder I sentence each of you to life imprisonment to run not less than twenty years, and on the charge of drug trafficking, I sentence each of you to ten years imprisonment to run concurrently.'

There was no word or movement now from the dock, and the warders led the men down to the cells.

The woman remained in the dock. There were two women warders, one on each side of her seemingly to support her, and the judge, looking at her, said, 'Elizabeth Myter, on the charge of harbouring drugs and assisting in their distribution, I sentence you to five years imprisonment. And on the charge of being associated with the three male accused and having

237

knowledge of their intention to commit murder and in no way endeavouring to stop them, which you could have done by an anonymous phone call to the police, I sentence you to five years, the sentences to run concurrently.'

Did I feel pity as I watched the woman being helped from the dock? No, I didn't, for she hadn't really been concerned with what would happen to me, only that it didn't happen on her premises ...

It was over. Or was it? In the hall I came under a barrage of cameras and reporters, and when I found the Mohican pushed to my side and a camera lined up to snap us, the Mohican swiftly turned his back and stood in front of me; and there we were, close, and our faces almost touching. The next minute he had gone, pushing his way through reporters, and Tommy was shielding me with the help of Janet's three boys as we made our way to the car.

Once inside, I lay back and thought for a moment that this was the time when I was actually going to pass out; and then I told myself not to be silly, it was all over.

'You'll soon be home,' Tommy's voice was soothing, calm, reassuring. It wiped the Mohican's face from my vision.

Janet, Harold, and Sandy, were waiting for me. Harold grabbed my hand, Sandy jumped all over me, and Janet said, 'Well?' and Tommy answered for me, saying, 'Life for the three of them, the woman five years.'

'Good. Good.'

A few minutes later, seated in the drawing-room, a drink in my hand, I looked up at Janet and said, 'The lads were there.'

'Yes, I know; they said they were goin'. Max has got a job an' all at last. I said he was riskin' things to take a day off but he said he wasn't going to miss it. Did ... did you see John?'

'Yes. Yes, he was there.'

'Did the lads see him?'

'Yes, I think they did, but they didn't speak.'

'No, I told them to keep clear of him 'cos I wouldn't put it past them to have a go at him 'cos of our Hilda. Well, I'll get you somethin' to eat; I bet you're starvin'.'

I did not say food was the last thought in my mind; and when she left the room and Harold, standing before Tommy and me where we sat on the couch, said flatly, 'I liked the Indian,' I almost burst into tears.

And it was Tommy who said, 'So did we; we were very fond of him;' and he took my hand and looked hard at me and said, 'Isn't that so?'

'Yes, yes,' I answered; 'we were very fond of him.'

Tommy was no fool.

7

It was a Friday towards the end of March, the twenty-ninth to be exact. Tomorrow I was to be married to Tommy, and, as on the day I married Nardy, Gran and George were with me. They had arrived late last night. George had definitely intended to be present, but, apparently, Gran had deliberated, her excuse being, there were so many things to see to, with Kitty once more in hospital having another grafting, and Mary needing company at this time. And then there was the club: she was running an outing due to take place next week, the first one of the season. Oh, there were so many things she had to see to. Nevertheless, here she was; but keeping clear of the kitchen, for, as she had plainly stated, she couldn't stand that Janet: uppish she was, and her only a servant.

It was the word uppish applied to Janet that gave me the idea. And when I thought of Janet's family, the word caused me to gurgle inside. And I had been gurgling a lot inside of late. I was feeling so much better: I could walk without the aid of a stick; I had no more pains, either in my stomach, leg, arm, or head. Oh, my head was very clear now; and I had turned to my writing again.

But now I was determined to do something about Gran and her animosity towards Janet and Londoners in general. She was now sitting in the drawing-room turning up the hem of her coat which she considered too long. Tommy, had last week started a month's holiday, and had spent his time between dashing in to see me, getting rid of his flat, and visiting the boat on which we were to spend the first three days of our honeymoon, the idea being that Captain Lee would take it to a mooring somewhere down the Thames, leave us on our own for three days, then bring Harold to join us before we set off to cross the channel – fearful thought to me – and, as he said, meander around the French countryside just as the boat's previous owners had been wont to do every year.

So now I went into the kitchen and Janet greeted me with, 'I've cleared the two shelves in the pantry and the top half of the fridge for them caterers to put the iced things in. Now I'll clear the dresser ...'

'Janet.'

'Yes, ma'am?'

'Will you do something for me?'

'Well now' – she turned fully towards me – 'I don't think you've got to ask that, ever, unless it's somethin' that nobody else in my position could do, such as drive a bus, or pilot a plane.' She was laughing heartily now.

'I think it's going to be harder than either of those things.'

'Yes?' She poked her head forward in enquiry.

'Sit down.'

She sat down, and I sat down, and after looking at her for a moment I said, 'Will you take Gran along to your house tonight and introduce her to your family?'

'Wh ... at!'

It was so like my wh ... at that I laughed and said, 'You heard.'

'Gran? Me! She ... she can't stand the sight of me, that woman, she's ...'

'She thinks you're stuck-up.'

'Wh ... at! me?' She was digging her finger into her chest now while her face spread wide in laughter and amazement. 'Me stuck-up, with our lot? How could

241

anybody be stuck-up with our lot? Now I ask you, ma'am?'

'Well, I know that, but she doesn't; she's never met any of your family. She's got this thing about southerners, and I think she's only got to meet Max, and Billy, and Joe, and the rest, and she'll change her mind. Quite candidly I think she'll call them her cup of tea.'

'And what about me? She'll still think the same about me.'

'No she'll not. I'm sure she won't when she sees you among your family.'

'Oh ma'am, I couldn't do it. How could I go up to her and ask her?'

'You could.' I pulled a face at her. 'You can be very diplomatic when you like.'

'Huh! Diplomatic. I don't even know the meanin' of the word. As for being it, how could anybody be diplomatic with our crew? Everything comes straight out.' She covered her eyes with her hand and her shoulders shook as she said, 'Oh! but you know, ma'am, I'd like to see her in our kitchen, yes I would, and Georgie an' all. But Georgie's different.' She was looking at me again. Her eyes were moist and mine were too as I replied, 'Yes, Georgie's different. He's been about a bit, has Georgie. He's always the same, no matter whom he's with, king or commoner.'

'Yes, I like him. Our lads and 'im would get on all right together, but . . .'

'Yes,' I put in, 'like a house on fire. Well, what about it?'

'Well, give me time; I'll have to think about it. Well, how will I say it? how will I approach 'er?'

'As you say, think about it.'

I got up and left her still seated, her face cupped in her hands now but twisted up with laughter . . .

Gran finished her coat; we had lunch. I said I was

242

going to rest for an hour and she should do the same. I went into my room, not only to give Janet a chance to speak to her alone, but I really did want to rest or rather to think of tomorrow and the step I was taking. I wasn't afraid of it; I knew I'd be happy with Tommy, safe, secure, and I didn't mean money-wise.

I'd always considered that I knew myself: I'd had plenty of time years ago to get to know the person inside my plain frame, to probe into her mind and understand the reason why she said this or did that. When I'd fallen in love with Nardy it had been the first time I had experienced love, and during the comparatively short time we spent together I had seen myself as a very sensible and matter-of-fact individual; my emotions ran on straight paths: I loved, I disliked, and I hated. Oh, yes, I hated. I hated Stickle, although he was in prison and could not possibly do me any more harm, for twelve years that is. That was my first mistake. The second was when I imagined that my emotions could not be drawn away from their central point: I was too sensible to be affected by an attractive voice, two deep brown eyes, and a personality that at first was a mystery and then became attached to somebody who was very brave; only to respond finally to this like any young girl without the experience of life, of good men or bad. The Mohican had become Sir Percy Blakeney, the modern Scarlet Pimpernel.

I had thought about him a great deal after the court case when, for a moment, our faces almost touched. But Tommy's love had gradually pushed him into the background. And now I rarely thought of him except when I saw Hilda. Hilda was doing what she said she would do, making something of herself. Janet often gave me a progress report on her and always ended up by saying, 'Oh! I never thought to see the day when Hilda would become sensible.' And with the last report she said, 'She beats May now. She'll go some place yet, our Hilda. Funny how things turn out: if it hadn't been for that fellow she would have still been the dimwit I always thought her.'

So much for a mother's opinion of her offspring.

I lay thinking about tomorrow, not about the wedding, or Tommy, but about how the company would mix, because the whole of Janet's family would be at the reception. And then nearly all of Tommy's friends from the office, some of them, no doubt, who had attended my marriage to Nardy. And, of course, Mike and Jane.

There were sixty people all told invited. The flat would take them, but would they take each other? Well, that was up to them; we wouldn't be here after the first hour or so.

I closed my eyes and softly I said, 'I'm doing right, Nardy, aren't I?' And his reply seemed to come to me, 'Of course you are, dear. As Tommy said, I wanted it this way.'

I had lulled myself almost into sleep when Gran's voice came at the door, saying, 'Can I come in, lass?'

'Yes. Yes; Gran.'

As I pulled myself up on the bed she almost skipped towards me, her wrinkled face stretched wide. She sat down with a plop on the side of the bed and she flapped her hand at me as she said, 'You'll never believe it, not in a month of Sundays.'

'Believe what in a month of Sundays?'

'Her! Her in the kitchen, Janet.'

'Oh, my goodness!' I pretended to be upset and I closed my eyes and put my hand to my brow; and this brought quickly from her, 'Now, now, it's all right. Don't get yourself in a tizzy; I'm not goin' to blow me top about anything. But listen, just listen, will you?'

I took my hand away and said, 'Yes, all right, I'm listening.'

She laughed now and her body began to shake. And

then she said, 'She's asked me and Georgie along to her place the night.'

'Wh ... at?' It was my old wh ... at.

'Aye, you might say what? her askin' me along. I tell you, I couldn't answer her until she said, "Oh, I'm sorry. You mightn't like it, you see we're rather rough and ready." Then I thought to meself: What! her lot rough and ready?'

I put in here, as I shook my head at her. 'I've told you before, Gran, that ...'

'Yes, I know you've told me afore, but there's rough and ready and rough and ready, and I imagine very rough an' ready comin' out of that one.'

'Well' – I shrugged my shoulders – 'you've seen Harold.'

'Yes, but he's a bairn and he's been knocked from dog to devil and so that's understandable. And it isn't only workin' men that swear, the nobs can do their share, my God! don't I know it. There's the Tweddles that live two doors down from our Georgie. He's supposed to vote Conservative but you should hear him. As our Georgie said, he's worse on a Sunday, in the pub, 'cos then his talk comes out under blasphemy.'

I again put my hand to my brow, and as I did so I said, 'Well, are you going?'

She drew in her lips and wagged her head from side to side, saying, 'Well, as I said to her, if you didn't need me an' our Georgie, we could slip in for an hour. Anyway' – she now poked her face close to mine – 'I want to see what the set-up is. She's always so damn particular here: everything in its place an' a place for everything.'

'Well, that's how I want it.'

'Oh, she'd be like that if you didn't want it.'

'Don't forget, as I've told you, Gran, she worked for Nardy's mother from she was a young girl. She nursed Nardy from a ba ...'

245

'Aye, aye, aye, I've heard all that afore. Anyway, I'll know more the night, won't I?' Her eyebrows moved up to her dyed hair, then she asked quietly, 'I won't have to get dressed up, will I?'

'Oh, no!' My voice was emphatic. 'Good gracious! no.'

'Well, what I meant was, put on me suit that I've got for the morrow.'

'No, of course not. You're keeping that, surely. Just your ordinary frock and coat.'

'Yes. Well' – she rose from the bed – 'I wonder what our Georgie'll say.'

What Georgie said was, 'Never! Maisie. She's accepted a booking to go round to Janet's. Can you believe it?'

'Not quite, Georgie.'

'I'm expected to go with her. Mind, I thought old Tommy would be havin' a bachelor do, but he tells me, no. He said he's had experience of them and he wants a clear head for the morrow, else you could walk out on him at the last minute.' He now chucked me under the chin, saying, 'You wouldn't do that, would you? He's a nice lad. You've been lucky, you know, in a way, lass: two good fellas like that; they don't often come in pairs, good fellas.'

'No, they don't, Georgie. I've known three good fellows, four in fact. The first one was called Georgie.'

'Aw! go away with you.' He pushed me from him, then pulled me back to him with his arm around my shoulder.

'Then there was Mike.'

'Oh aye, Mike.'

Musingly now, he said, 'She's like a cat with nine tails, would you believe it? 'cos she's hated the sight of that woman, you know, never stopped talkin' about her back home. Eeh! she's a marler. By! altogether, women are queer cattle. All except you, hinny.' Then he changed the subject abruptly by exclaiming, 'Eeh! that boat. God above! I've never seen owt like it. An' you're goin' on your honeymoon on her. You know, lass, when I look back on your life, it's like something you'd see on the pictures, so much has happened to you. As Mam says, you're hardly ever out of the papers. But here's one that doesn't mind. They say back at the depot: "Your lass is in the papers again I see." Do you know that? You're known as ... my lass.'

I put my arms up and pulled his big grey head down to mine, and as I kissed him I said, 'I'll always remain your lass, Georgie, because you were the first good man in my life.'

Patting my cheek gently, he said, 'Well, if that's the case I know now why I was born, 'cos, you know, at times I've asked meself why I was put on this earth. I'm not all mouth you know, Maisie, I do use me napper sometimes. But anyway, now I know.'

On this he smiled, then turned slowly about and left me, and as the door closed on him again it came to me how lucky I had been: weighed against the disasters there had been four wonderful men in my life and of these three were still with me. Not every woman could say that.

Tommy had driven Gran and Georgie to Janet's. They were to get a taxi back. He had then spent the evening with me; at least, he had spent it with Harold and me until, at nine o'clock, I had bundled that gentleman off to bed, after persuasion I might say, lined with threats that I could easily change our plans and not have the captain collect him in four days' time and bring him to the boat. He had laughed at me and said, 'But you wouldn't do that, Mrs Nardy, would you?'

And I had replied sternly, 'Oh, yes, but I would.'

He had appealed to Tommy, and Tommy had

strugged his shoulders and said, 'I can't help you here, laddie. If she makes up her mind . . . well, you know her better than I do.' This piece of diplomacy worked and Harold went to bed, and after I'd tucked him in I left him with his books and comics and a promise to come back in fifteen minutes to see him.

When I was once again sitting beside Tommy he did not look at me but towards the fire as he said, 'What are we going to do about this . . . Mrs Nardy?'

'Do you mind so much?'

'No, no; not really, but every time I hear him say "Mrs Nardy" I've got a feeling somehow . . . well, that you still belong to Nardy, that you'll never really be mine.'

'Tommy' – I had taken his hand – 'we've been through this in different ways. Nardy was a part of my life, a wonderful part, but that is past now. I won't say it's forgotten, I could never forget Nardy, but now there is you, and I love you, in a different way from how I did Nardy. Now don't ask me to explain which way, I can't, only I beg of you, be content to know that I do love you. I want to be near you; I want you to be near me; the house is empty when you are not here. I want to do things for you. Aren't these all facets of love?'

He made no answer but kissed me long and hard, and then I said, 'I shall try to get him out of it. How would Mrs Tommy sound?'

'Not bad.' . . .

It was around half-past ten when I said, 'I'm going to throw you out.' And to this he answered, 'Oh, I'll wait till Georgie and Gran come back.'

'No, you'll not. I'm going to get ready for bed; I want a good night's rest. Anyway, Georgie's got a key.'

Taking me in his arms, he said, 'This is the last night we'll be separated. What do you say?'

I looked up at him and solemnly I said, 'I wish you were a little shorter or I was a little taller. Don't you think we look ridiculous together?'

'Terribly ridiculous.'

'And you don't mind?'

For answer he put his hands under my oxters and lifted me off my feet. Now I cried at him, 'Don't do that! It always makes me feel so small.'

'Well, you are small.'

'Well, you needn't rub it in.'

And so it went on, our silly chatter, until I almost pushed him into the lift. And when I entered the hall again I stood for a moment and looked round it. The house was empty except for Harold, Sandy, and myself; it would be the last night we should be alone together.

I now went into Harold's room. He was lying on his back, his arms above his head, the bedclothes were around his waist. I lifted them gently up to his chin and resisted bending to kiss him in case I should wake him; then I went into my own room, got into a dressing-gown, and went back into the drawing-room to await the return of Gran and Georgie because, as I told myself, I couldn't put off until the morning to hear Gran's reaction to the Flood family.

It was when the clock in the hall again struck the half-hour that I rose to my feet, thinking to myself, They're leaving it late. And it was as I made my way down the room towards the hall that I heard the distant sound of high laughter. When I opened the hall door into the outer hall and the lift stopped there almost tumbled out three figures, Gran, George, and Max Flood, and to use Gran's own expression, they were all as drunk as noodles.

As I backed into the hall they joined arms and came staggering towards me, singing now a favourite of Gran's:

'Keep your feet still, Geordie hinny,
Let's be happy through the neet,

249

For we may not be se happy through the day,
Oh gie us that bit comfort,
Keep your feet still, Geordie lad,
And divvent drive me bonny dreams away.'

Definitely Max had been tutored because he was singing as loudly as they; and now, flapping both my hands at them, I cried, 'Soften it! The child's asleep, and there are people now downstairs.'

'Sorry, Mrs Nardy.' Max was supporting himself with one hand against the stanchion of the door and he spluttered, 'Had to fetch 'em home. Gran' night, Mrs Nardy, gran' night. Taxi waitin'.' He thumbed. 'Good-night, pal.' He reached out and slapped Georgie on the shoulder, then looking at Gran, he said, 'Good-night, old girl,' and to this she answered, 'Good-night, lad. Good-night, lad. See ya the morrow.'

'Aye, see ya the morrow. Good-night. Good-night. Good-night, Mrs Nardy.' Max was stumbling now towards the lift, and I rushed forward and pulled the door back and foolishly said, 'Will you be all right?'

''Sright as rain. 'Sright as rain. Good-night, Mrs Nardy. Good-night.'

I did not wish him good-night but, pointing, said, 'Press that button,' then slammed the door into place and watched his grinning face disappear from view.

When I returned to the hall, Gran was divesting herself of her hat and coat, and with one sleeve still in her coat she rounded on me, saying, 'Why didn't you tell me, eh?'

'Tell you what?'

'They were a decent lot. Best night I've had in me life. Eh, Georgie?'

'Splendid fellas.'

'Stuck up you said they were.'

'*What?*' I poked my head towards her swaying figure.

'Janet's lot, stuck up, that's what you said, Fine lot of lads, Janet's lot. Speak as ya find. Speak as ya find.'

'*Go to bed.*'

'Oh! Oh! Gettin' on your high 'orse, are you? D'you hear her Georgie? Go to bed, she says. Go to bed. Where d'you think I'm goin', Buckingham Palace?'

She now fell against Georgie, and he, being able to hold his drink better than his mother and sensing my indignation, said, 'Come on, Mam. Come on. Talk 'bout it in the mornin'.' He led her now towards the passage, but looking over his shoulder, he said, 'Grand night, lass. Grand night. As good a pub as any I've been in. Good-night, lass. Night, lass.'

Why wasn't I laughing? Why was I full of indignation? How dare Gran turn the tables on me like that? Well, I'd wanted her to get to know Janet's family, hadn't I? And she had definitely done that. But to come back in that state.

All the years I'd known them I'd never seen them drunk. I knew Gran liked her drop, and definitely Georgie could put it away, but they were now both paralatic. That was a northern term and the only one that really described their condition . . .

When I heard the bedroom doors close I thought, I should go and help her to get into bed. But why should I? No, no; I wouldn't. I turned round and went towards the hall door and locked it, and I was making for the corridor again when Harold appeared rubbing his eyes. Going hastily towards him, I said, 'Now what's the matter?'

'The noise, somebody yellin'.'

'Oh, it was only Uncle George and Gran coming back from your Gag's; they'd been having a party. Come on, back to bed with you.'

When I tucked him up again and said, 'Go to sleep now,' he answered, 'I don't want to go to sleep, I'm not tired any more. What time is it?'

'Nearly midnight.'

He gazed up at me, then said slowly, 'We're nearly in tomorrow.'

I pursed my lips, raised my eyebrows as I said slowly, 'Yes, we're nearly in tomorrow.'

'When you're goin' to be married?'

My face sank into its usual pattern as I replied, 'Yes, you know I'm going to be married tomorrow.'

'Why?'

'Well.' Candidly I was stumped for an answer that I thought he could cope with: I couldn't say, because I love Mr Tommy, that would have likely caused him to think that I didn't love *him*. I fluffed as I said, 'Well, so that Mr Tommy can stay here all the time.'

'He stays here all the time now.'

'Not at night-time.'

'If you get married he'll stay here at night-times an' you can't push him out.'

'Well, I won't want to put him out. Now go to sleep.'

I attempted to tuck him in again and he pushed my hand away, saying, 'I don't want to go to sleep.' Then he added, 'You'll want to put him out if you get divorced.'

'I have no intention of getting divorced.'

'Well, you can't until you're married an' then you might.'

There was logic in that. But why was this conversation taking place? I thought he had accepted the situation.

I said now, 'I thought you liked Mr Tommy?'

He turned his head away, then bit on his thumb nail which I hadn't seen him do before and I repeated, 'I thought you liked Mr Tommy.'

'Sometimes.'

'When are the times you don't like him?'

'When you like him . . . a lot . . . over much.'

I had to remind myself that this child wasn't yet eight. His reasoning could have stamped him as being fourteen, or more. There had been a lot going on in his head that I hadn't been aware of; I'd been concentrating so much on his language and his manners that I'd skipped the fact of more important issues that must have been troubling him.

I sat down on the side of the bed now and, pulling him round towards me, I said, 'Listen to me, Harold. I love you. I love you very much. You came into my life when I was very sad. Yes, I know, you lived here before that when Mr Nardy was alive, but when Mr Nardy died I was very, very alone and if I hadn't had your company then I might have become very ill in my mind. You understand?'

He said nothing, but his eyes were wide. 'The fact is your companionship kept me sane. You meant more to me then than anyone else in the world, and you still do. I ... I love Mr Tommy, but ... but in a different way, a quite different way. The love I have for you is very special, nobody can take it away.'

'Not Mr Tommy?' His voice was small.

'No, no. And he wouldn't want to, he too loves you. And he knows how I feel about you; we have talked about it. You are my son now and you will be his too. He will be a father to you. I know you have a real father.' As I spoke I wasn't thinking now of Jimmy Stoddart, but I went on, 'Who would you rather stay with?'

For answer he did not say Mr Tommy, but, 'Not my dad. I don't like my dad.' He turned his head away and as he did so I thought, someday I will tell him why he doesn't like his dad.

He hitched himself round now and asked softly, 'Can I come and lie in your bed?'

He had never made this request before, and I hesitated a while before I answered; and then it was by evasion: 'No, you're not going to get up again. I'll tell you what. Look, I'll lie beside you until you go to

253

sleep.' And at this I pulled the eiderdown to one side and got under it, and when I put my head on the pillow beside his, he put his arms around my neck and, bringing his head under my chin, he lay perfectly still. And I didn't speak, not until I felt something wet on my skin, and then I murmured, 'Oh, my dear, don't ... don't cry. Anyway, what are you crying for? There's nothing to cry about.'

When I tried to press him away from me to dry his face he held on all the tighter, and when I heard him mutter something, I said, 'What did you say?' and then more plainly his words came to me: 'I thought you'd be like my mum when she got another man an' you'd go off. Although she said she wouldn't, she did. She said she'd come back for me but she didn't. An' you had Mr Nardy an' now you've got Mr Tommy, an'...'

'Oh, Harold.' I pushed him from me and, my voice full of indignation, I said, 'You didn't really think that I would ever leave you or let you go or be like your mam?'

'Well' – he choked on his words – 'People do go off. Johnny Rankin's mum's gone off. He told me she had. His dad's on night shift, so he comes an' fetches 'im. People do.'

'I'm not people, Harold. I'll never go off and leave you. You'll be the one to go off and leave me someday.'

'No, I won't.' He sounded like his old self. 'I'll never leave you.' His arms were once more tight round my neck, and as I stroked his hair I thought, here was I thinking I had an insight into people, imagining I knew what they were thinking. Clever clouts, as Tommy had called me, yet I didn't know what this child, this beloved child who was under my nose every spare minute of the day, was thinking, nor had I detected beneath his brashness the feelings that must have been troubling him for some time, the insecurity that lay deep within him and which he had explained by the fact that a woman could somehow disappear after taking a second man into her life.

We held each other tightly for a long time. When his head sank into the pillow mine did too, and we both slept.

8

I was aroused by someone shaking me gently by the shoulder, saying, 'Come on, wake up! I brought you a cuppa tea. It's eight o'clock. Come on.'

I twisted round and groaned. There was a kink in my arm. I opened my eyes and looked at the bright face hovering over mine.

'Harold!'

He was laughing. 'You went to sleep in my bed.'

Last night's scene flashed back into my mind and, pulling myself up onto the pillow, I said, 'Oh, I'm sorry.'

'Oh, that's all right.' He wagged his head widely. 'You were under the eiderdown an' I couldn't pull the clothes round me this mornin', so I got up.'

'And you made me a cup of tea. Oh, that is kind of you. Oh, dear me, fancy falling asleep in your bed.'

'Come on,' he said now, 'an' drink your tea. You've got to get up, you know; you've got to get dressed an' all that.'

'Oh, yes,' I sighed; 'I suppose so. But I could just sit here.'

'Don't be silly; Mr Tommy'll be around any time.'

'Yes, yes of course he will. By the way, is Gran up?'

'No, Mr Georgie is, but Gran's moanin', she's got a thick head. I took her some tea in an' all.'

'That was nice. I'm sure she'll be glad of it.'

He stood and watched me while I drank the tea; then I said, 'Well, I'd better get away to my room, hadn't I?'

'Will I put some toast on?'

'Yes, that would be nice, dear.'

'Are you gona have a fry?'

'Not for me.'

'Mr Georgie will want one, an' so will I. An' Gag's comin' early, she said she would, so I'll set the table, will I?'

'Yes, dear. Yes, you could do that.'

He was near the door when he turned and said, 'Funny thing.'

'What's a funny thing?'

'Sandy. He went into your room and sniffed round and he couldn't find you so he's lyin' on your bed.'

'Poor Sandy. I must go and see him; he's felt neglected of late.'

The door closed on him and I lay back for a moment. Either my boy was completely reassured or he was putting on a good act, and I didn't think he was that clever yet.

I felt very happy.

When I entered the bedroom, yes, there was Sandy lying on the bed. On the sight of me he jumped into my arms, and as he snuggled his head under my chin I had the warm feeling that I had a family, and this morning I was to have a man to be at the head of it.

I heard Janet arrive, and I heard Gran leave the room next door, but I didn't go out to speak to one or the other; I should hear all about it later.

I had a bath, made up my face, then put on my clothes, except the costume in which I was to be married, donned a housecoat, then went out and into the kitchen to find Janet clearing away the breakfast things. She was on her own and when she turned towards me I could see that it wasn't only Gran who was suffering from a thick head; but she grinned at me and I at her. Then I said, 'No need to tell me how it went.'

257

'Oh! ma'am. I've never known a night like it.' She put her hand to her head. 'An' you know, it's the first time in my life I've known what it is to have a thick head. A drop of sherry's my limit, as you know, ma'am, but I couldn't tell you, if I tried, what I had last night. And Gran' – she now gave a short laugh – 'you talk about "Knees Up Mother Brown" you should have seen her with the lads. Oh! she's a star turn. She had the whole pub roaring; they think she's the cat's pyjamas. They couldn't knock her down; she had them all singing Geordie songs. I couldn't believe it, at least what I remember of it. And when we got home it started again. If Georgie hadn't reminded her that there was a wedding today she would have stayed there all night. I'll say this much, ma'am, your ruse worked all right.'

'Yes, it worked all right for you, Janet, but she blamed me in no small voice when she got in last night because she said I had given her the wrong impression of you and your whole family.'

She shook her head. 'You know something? I think she'll be payin' London a visit pretty often after this, if you ask me.'

'After last night, I've no doubt about it. Well, I'd better go and see her.'

As I was crossing the hall I met Georgie who said, 'Mornin', lass.'

'Morning, Georgie. Have a nice time last night?' My voice was prim.

'Never better. Bugger me eyes! You should have seen her. I can only remember bits. Eeh! she was at the height of her form. I can tell you that, lass. And aren't they a nice crowd, Janet's folk?'

'Where is she?' I asked.

He thumbed towards the dining-room: 'Hidin' her head, I think. Go canny on her.'

I slanted my eyes at him, then went into the dining-room. She was sitting looking out of the window. She had her back to me, but she knew it was me, as her words proved when she said, 'Now don't you start.'

'Who's going to start?'

She remained still until I was by her side, and then, turning towards me, she said, 'Oh, you might as well say your piece; if you don't say it now you'll say it sometime.'

'I'm not going to say any piece, only with a face like that you'd think you were going to a funeral and not a wedding this morning.'

'Aw, lass.' She put her hand to her head. 'I must have gone really over the top. A drop an' me aren't strangers as you know, but I feel I must have got attached to a hogshead last night.'

'You enjoyed yourself though?'

She focused her eyes now on the outside scene of first-floor roofs and patches of garden, and after a moment she said, 'Well, we can all make mistakes, can't we? But you've got to admit, from the look of her' – now her gaze flashed at me – 'you'd never think she bred that lot.'

'But I've told you before, haven't I?'

'Aye, you have; but you have to see them to believe them. All I can think of is that some of Nardy's mother must have rubbed off on her, her manners like.' Then a twisted smile coming onto her face, she said, 'Plainly it didn't rub off onto her family.'

I pushed her.

She narrowed her eyes now as she looked at me, saying, 'I see you're all made up. You nearly ready?'

'Yes; just my suit to slip on.'

'Well, here you go for a third time. Eeh! who would believe it? And you're the one who imagined that nobody would ever want you. Do you remember?'

'Yes, yes, I remember.'

'An' went an' married that maniac. You know' – she leant towards me – 'there's strange rumours goin' round about him: what he was up to afore he did himself in or somebody did him in, one or t'other, 'cos from all accounts he was hated in there as bad as bairn abusers. But they were sayin' in the club he was dealin' in black magic. Now that's so far-fetched I told them they wanted to get their heads looked. How could he deal with black magic in there? He'd have no chance of startin' a convent in there, now would he?'

I stopped a loud explosion coming from my lips and said quietly, 'You're thinking of coven.'

'What?'

'What you're thinking of is called a coven. It's usually applied to witches, a coven of witches.'

She stretched her nose, pushed out her lips, then said, 'Well, I suppose you should know. Whatever it was, they said he started it. But some people'll say anything ... How you feelin'?'

'All right.'

She nodded, then said, 'In a way you've had a bellyful, but in another way you've been lucky, you've had two men that are the salt of the earth.'

She now bent towards me and her head emphasized each word as she added, 'One thing I'll ask of you, for the future that is, keep out of the papers. It got that way I couldn't open the *Journal* or the *Evening Chronicle* 'cos there you were, headlines, an' I had to stand the racket at the club. So I'm tellin' you.'

'I'll do my best, Gran.' My tone was polite. Then changing it, I barked at her, 'And now, you old misery, go and get yourself ready, and quick! We're due out in a half-hour's time.'

She got to her feet, a tight smile on her face now as she said, 'You don't change, do you?' And I answered in the same vein, 'And I'm not the only one, am I?'

'Aw, lass.' She suddenly bent towards me and kissed me, saying now, 'Things haven't been right atween us for some time. That's all over. It's me, I know. You see,

I ... I thought I had lost you altogether, but now I know I haven't, you're still my lass.'

We held each other tightly; then, pushing me away, she walked smartly down the room. But at the door she turned and said, 'That bit was only soft soap 'cos I want a trip on that boat of yours.'

When the door closed on her I stood blinking and smiling to myself. That boat of mine. In her eyes it was already mine. And there was no doubt, too, as Janet had suggested, that she would be making the journey from Newcastle to London more often in the future.

I went to my room, and there I got into my suit and four inch heeled shoes to give me just a little added height. Next I placed an apology for a hat on the top of my head and, looking in the mirror, I saw a woman in her middle thirties who, although still plain, did not look her age. Next, I picked up my handbag and matching gloves and went out and into the corridor, and across it towards the far end I could glimpse Harold's door was open and I could hear his voice talking rapidly to someone. I looked into his room, and there he was with Sandy. The dog had its forepaws on his chest and was licking his face and my adopted son was admonishing it in his most natural form: 'Stop it; you soapy sod,' he was saying. 'If you spoil me tie I'll pull up your guts an' strangle your tonsils with 'em.'

I did not rush into the room and upbraid him, this wasn't the time, but I stepped back and leant against the wall for a moment, repeating, 'I'll pull up your guts and strangle your tonsils with them.' That was certainly a new one.

As I made to walk away, there he was coming out of the room, half bent over, keeping Sandy down with one hand. He stopped, straightened up, looked up at me for a long moment, then said, 'I ... I wasn't swearin', not really. Well ...'

261

This was no time for a confrontation, so I said, 'Who said you were?'

'Your face.'

'My face?'

'You always look like that when I'm swearin'.'

'Oh. Well, if that wasn't swearing, what was it?'

'You ... you mean about pullin' up the guts and ...'

'Yes, yes, that's what I mean.' I noticed we had by-passed soapy sod.

'John Rankin learned me it.'

'Taught me.'

'What?'

'Taught me?'

'Oh, well, yes, well I only said it 'cos of him.' He stabbed his finger towards Sandy. 'You see, he was jumpin' up an' upsettin' me tie.'

He was wearing a white frilled shirt, topped by a bow tie.

I bent forward and straightened it, and as I did so he looked to the side, gave a yell and said, 'There's Mr Tommy!' and darted from me.

I stayed where I was looking down the corridor into the hall, and there was this tall attractive man. He was always well dressed, but this morning he looked different, not younger, older, if anything and very, very handsome.

As that unnerving, irritating, and questioning thing called my mind opened a door yet again to ask, What did he see in me? I kicked it closed and turned swiftly and went back into my bedroom, and a minute later he knocked on the door, and when I said, 'Come in,' he came in, saying, 'What made you disappear like that?'

'Oh' – I made a small face – 'I wanted to bang a door.'

'Bang a door?'

'Yes. I'll tell you about it later.'

'Have you had trouble with his nibs?'

'No. Why do you ask?'

He smiled before he said, 'He's just said to me: "She thinks I swored."'

'Well, he did, and brought out a new one.'

At this point it struck me to ask myself why we should be standing here talking about my charge and not about ourselves? But I went on to explain how I overheard Harold's reprimand to the dog: 'Soapy sod, I've heard before,' I said, 'but never, I'll pull your guts up and strangle your tonsils with them.'

'What?' He was shaking with laughter.

'Just that: pull your guts up and strangle your tonsils with them.' I too was shaking now, saying, 'Did you ever?'

I fell against him. His arms were about me and his voice came over my head: 'Well, there's one thing, my dear,' he said, 'we'll never be dull where he is. But then' – he pressed me from him and looked down into my face – 'I'll never be dull where you are. That's your charm, you know.' He looked me up and down. 'You look lovely.'

'I don't look lovely. Smart, yes, but not lovely.'

'Why do you ...? Oh, shut up! and come along, I want a wife.'

We clung together again; then we went out and there in the hall was Gran, and George, and Harold, and Janet. But Janet wasn't dressed for outside.

Tommy now said, 'Hello there, Georgie. Hello Gran. How did it go last night? Enjoy yourselves?'

Her face perky, Gran said, 'Oh, she hasn't told you then?' She now turned and smiled at Janet, saying, 'It's a wonder she didn't get that in, isn't it?' And then she added, 'You should be comin', you know.'

What a changed Gran. And Janet, smiling at her, said on a laugh, 'I could never stand weddings. They recall the mistake I made many years ago. And anyway, somebody's got to see to the caterers.' She now cast her glance towards me. 'Everything'll be in order when you get back. So get yourselves away.'

We were going into the outer hall when I stopped, and turning to Janet and for the first time in our acquaintance, I kissed her and said softly, 'Thank you, Janet, for everything right down the years, and especially for Harold.' Then we held each other tightly for a moment until she said, 'Oh, go on with you.' Her nose wrinkled and she chewed on her bottom lip, then pushed me through the door into the outer hall.

Gran and Georgie were now in the lift, Harold was standing at one side of it and Tommy at the other, their faces bright and smiling, and they both said almost in unison, 'Come on, if you're coming.'

And I went towards them and into another world.

THE END

TILLY TROTTER
TILLY TROTTER WED
TILLY TROTTER WIDOWED

Beginning in the reign of the young Queen Victoria, the three Tilly Trotter novels tell the story of a beautiful girl growing to womanhood amid hardship and despair. Pitting her wits against the local Tyneside villagers, who hate her and accuse her of witchcraft, Tilly's strong instinct for survival leads her to become, in turn, the loving mistress of a wealthy man, and then the wife of his son, travelling to the strange and perilous land of America.

When her husband is killed, Tilly returns to take possession of his estate. The villagers prove ever hostile and suspicious, but Tilly is supported by faithful friends and warm memories. Life still has much in store for Tilly Trotter, old loves and enmities providing fresh challenges to a woman as spirited as ever.

Tilly Trotter	0 552 11737 4	£2.50
Tilly Trotter Wed	0 552 11960 1	£2.50
Tilly Trotter Widowed	0 552 12200 9	£1.95

CORGI BOOKS

Catherine Cookson

THE MALLEN STREAK
THE MALLEN GIRL
THE MALLEN LITTER

Thomas Mallen of High Banks Hall had many sons, most of them bastards. But to all of them he passed on his mark – a distinctive flash of white hair running to the left temple, and known as the Mallen Streak. It was said in the Northumberland countryside that those who bore the streak seldom reached old age or died in bed, and that nothing good ever came of a Mallen.

Starting in 1851, this compulsively readable sequence of novels follows the stormy lives of the Mallens through succeeding generations, linking the England of Victoria with the dark days of the First World War.

The Mallen Streak	0 552 09720 9	£2.50
The Mallen Girl	0 552 09896 5	£2.50
The Mallen Litter	0 552 10151 6	£2.50

CORGI BOOKS

THE WHIP

Emma Molinero's dying father, a circus performer, had sent his beloved daughter to live with an unknown grandmother, not realizing that he had sentenced her to a life of misery.

But the graceful Emma, mistrusted by the local people for her beauty and her "foreign blood", nevertheless became a woman who mystified and fascinated men because of her fiery independence and her skill at performing with the whip – her father's only legacies.

The Whip is an affecting and irresistible novel – Catherine Cookson at the height of her powers.

0 552 12368 4 £2.50

CORGI BOOKS

THE BLACK VELVET GOWN
by CATHERINE COOKSON

There would be times when Riah Millican came to regret that her miner husband had learned to read and write, and then shared that knowledge with her and their children. For this was Durham in the 1830s, when employers tended to regard the spread of education with suspicion. But now Seth Millican was dead and she a widow with the pressing need to find a home and a living for herself and her children.

The chance of becoming a housekeeper didn't work out, but it led to Moor House and a scholarly recluse obsessed with that very book learning that could open so many doors and yet create so many problems: especially with her daughter Biddy, who was not only bright, but wilful . . .

THE BLACK VELVET GOWN is the story of a mother and a daughter often at odds with each other, facing the need to challenge and fight the prejudice of an age – a narrative of great power and diversity that is one of Catherine Cooksons major achievements.

0 552 12473 7   CORGI BOOKS   £2.95

GOODBYE HAMILTON
by CATHERINE COOKSON

It seemed the clouds that had darkened so much of Maisie's early life had really cleared away. Freed at last from a disastrous marriage, she had also become a best-selling author with her very first book: all about Hamilton, the remarkable horse who existed only in her imagination, but had nonetheless proved to be a real guide, philosopher and friend over many years.

Now she was to be married again, and Hamilton marked the occasion by taking a wife himself – a mare called Begonia.

So the outlook was fair; but perhaps Maisie was destined never to know happiness untouched by sorrow; and certainly the next few years would bring their share of fresh troubles. Luckily Hamilton and Begonia would be there to provide support in winning through . . .

Catherine Cookson's HAMILTON has already taken its place among the most widely enjoyed of her novels. In this delightful sequel, she again peoples her story with characters so vividly alive, they leap off the page to meet you.

0 552 12608 X   **CORGI BOOKS**   £1.95

A DINNER OF HERBS
by CATHERINE COOKSON

A legacy of hatred can be a terrible force in life, over which not even an enduring love and all the fruits of material success may prevail. Catherine Cookson explores this theme in a major novel that will absorb and enthrall her readers as irresistibly as any she has written.

Roddy Greenbank was brought by his father to the remote Northumberland community of Langley in the autumn of 1807. Within hours of their arrival, however, the father had met a violent death, and the boy left with all memory gone of his past life.

Adopted and raised by old Kate Makepeace, Roddy found his closest companions in Hal Roystan and Mary Ellen Lee. These three stand at the heart of a richly eventful narrative that spans the first half of the nineteenth century, their lives lastingly intertwined by the inexorable demands of a strange and somewhat cruel destiny.

A DINNER OF HERBS is Catherine Cookson's most stunning achievement to date – a work that displays outstandingly the true storyteller's gift.

0 552 12551 2   **CORGI BOOKS**   £3.50

A SELECTION OF CATHERINE COOKSON NOVELS IN CORGI

THE PRICES SHOWN BELOW WERE CORRECT AT THE TIME OF GOING TO PRESS. HOWEVER TRANSWORLD PUBLISHERS RESERVE THE RIGHT TO SHOW NEW RETAIL PRICES ON COVERS WHICH MAY DIFFER FROM THOSE PREVIOUSLY ADVERTISED IN THE TEXT OR ELSEWHERE.

☐	12551 2	A DINNER OF HERBS	£3.50
☐	12473 7	THE BLACK VELVET GOWN	£2.95
☐	08700 9	THE BLIND MILLER	£1.95
☐	11160 0	THE CINDER PATH	£1.95
☐	08601 0	COLOUR BLIND	£1.95
☐	09217 7	THE DWELLING PLACE	£1.95
☐	08774 2	FANNY McBRIDE	£1.95
☐	09318 1	FEATHERS IN THE FIRE	£1.95
☐	08353 4	FENWICK HOUSES	£1.95
☐	08419 0	THE FIFTEEN STREETS	£1.95
☐	10450 7	THE GAMBLING MAN	£1.95
☐	10916 9	THE GIRL	£2.50
☐	08849 8	THE GLASS VIRGIN	£2.50
☐	12608 X	GOODBYE HAMILTON	£1.95
☐	12451 6	HAMILTON	£1.95
☐	10267 9	THE INVISIBLE CORD	£2.50
☐	09035 2	THE INVITATION	£1.95
☐	08251 1	KATE HANNIGAN	£1.95
☐	08056 X	KATIE MULHOLLAND	£2.95
☐	08493 X	THE LONG CORRIDOR	£1.95
☐	08444 1	MAGGIE ROWAN	£2.50
☐	09720 9	THE MALLEN STREAK	£2.50
☐	09896 5	THE MALLEN GIRL	£2.50
☐	10151 6	THE MALLEN LITTER	£2.50
☐	11350 6	THE MAN WHO CRIED	£2.50
☐	08653 3	THE MENAGERIE	£1.75
☐	08980 X	THE NICE BLOKE	£1.95
☐	09373 4	OUR KATE	£1.95
☐	09596 6	PURE AS THE LILY	£2.50
☐	08913 3	ROONEY	£1.95
☐	08296 1	THE ROUND TOWER	£2.50
☐	10630 5	THE TIDE OF LIFE	£2.95
☐	11737 4	TILLY TROTTER	£2.50
☐	11960 1	TILLY TROTTER WED	£2.50
☐	12200 9	TILLY TROTTER WIDOWED	£1.95
☐	08561 8	THE UNBAITED TRAP	£1.95
☐	12368 4	THE WHIP	£2.50

All these books are available at your book shop or newsagent, or can be ordered direct from the publisher. Just tick the titles you want and fill in the form below.

TRANSWORLD READERS' SERVICE, 61–63 Uxbridge Road, Ealing, London, W5 5SA.

Please send cheque or postal order, not cash. All cheques and postal orders must be in £ sterling and made payable to Transworld Publishers Ltd.

Please allow cost of book(s) plus the following for postage and packing:

U.K./Republic of Ireland Customers:
Orders in excess of £5; no charge
Orders under £5; add 50p

Overseas Customers:
All orders; add £1.50

NAME (Block Letters) ....

ADDRESS ....

....